S0-ADU-274

She came to him dressed in rags, wretched, and begging him not to turn her out of his bed for fear of what her master—who had promised her to him —would do if Abdee rejected her.

Within hours, Richard Abdee discovered that the quaking black girl was the most proficient lover he had ever known—and the most clever, vicious and deceitful.

Of all the women in his life, only the strange and sensual Naomi could match Abdee's lust and greed. She alone—a freed slave, mistress of a brothel in which the darkest sexual fantasies were fulfilled, priestess to the dread Leopardmen of the Fanti tribe —understood the man behind the mask of Dragonard . . .

DRAGONARD

One of the most lusty and savage sagas of slavery ever written!

GOLDEN APPLE BOOKS by Rupert Gilchrist

Dragonard

RUPERT GILCHRIST

GOLDEN APPLE PUBLISHERS

*This low-priced Golden Apple Book
has been completely reset in a type face
designed for easy reading, and was printed
from new plates. It contains the complete
text of the original hard-cover edition.*
NOT ONE WORD HAS BEEN OMITTED.

DRAGONARD

*A Golden Apple Publication / published by arrangement with
Souvenir Press, Ltd.*

Golden Apple edition / December 1984

Golden Apple is a trademark of Golden Apple Publishers

*All rights reserved.
Copyright © 1975 by Rupert Gilchrist.
Cover copyright © 1984 by Golden Apple Publishers.
This book may not be reproduced in whole or in part, by
mimeograph or any other means, without permission.
For information address: Golden Apple Publishers,
666 Fifth Avenue, New York, N.Y. 10103.*

ISBN 0-553-19818-1

PRINTED IN CANADA

COVER PRINTED IN U.S.A.

U   0 9 8 7 6 5 4 3 2 1

CONTENTS

NOTE

By the 18th century, England was the leading colonial power in the West Indies. Behind her came France, Spain, Holland, and Denmark. But as England began to lose her grip on the colonies to the north—America— she realized the necessity of tightening her hold in the Caribbean. Often this action took the form of increased taxation or a stronger militia. In one particular circumstance, though, on the Leeward Island which the English had dubbed "St Kitts," an additional method to thwart insurrection came into existence. But England directed this new form of domination not toward the white colonials who grew rich from the sugar plantations. Instead, the inflictions fell upon the slaves brought in shackles from Africa to work those fertile fields. And the Crown also sought its mercenaries, the men paid to execute the latest rigours of obedience, from non-English ranks. Or, that had been England's original intent: to keep both motherland and subjects as untainted as possible from the brutal, albeit brief, institution known on St Kitts as the *Dragonard*.

R.G.

Book I
A SPARK

1

Master and Lord

Richard Abdee waited impatiently in the main hall of
Government House, half-listening to a final briefing
which the petty official was dragging into a sermon. But
the thought slowly began to cross his suspicious mind
that this lengthy audience might be just one last attempt to find out more about his personal life—why
had he come to the West Indies? But, more important,
why would he want a job like this?

Apart from his name, Government House knew very
little about Richard Abdee. He was not what men
tagged a "big-talker." And neither would bigness be
quickly attributed to his size. Not by a casual glance.

Richard Abdee stood over six feet tall. His shoulders
were capped with hard but unostentatious muscle. His
chest tapered to a medium waist. His arms, paired in
power. But he was not a *big* man. He was not strik-
ingly large.

The fine features of his slim face, the blonde hair
tossed back from his forehead, the small and well-
shaped ears all contributed to Abdee's air of leanness.
He possessed the agility usually developed only by the
well-born. Fencing. Light wrestling. The gentleman's
pastime of stalking. Yes, Richard Abdee certainly
looked like a stalker. But his cornflower blue eyes—set
hard under his brow—separated him from the brain-
less, thump-happy louts: the hooligans who had pre-
ceded him as master in these public spectacles.

So why then did this mysterious young Englishman
want to become a Dragonard?

One of the Government's suppositions was that Abdee owed gambling debts back home. That explanation would cover both his quick flight here and the lack of money.

Another theory held by Government House was that he was a wife-deserter. Or even had to support two households. Was a bigamist.

Also, there was the possibility that Richard Abdee had only recently been released from one of His Majesty's gaols. He had not been able to find better work anywhere and had arrived here before the posting of ex-convicts. Could even be an escapee.

But the answers to all those questions were negative. And they had all been specifically asked when Abdee first signed on for this post last week, three days after he stepped ashore from the German frigate, *Klaus Heinrich*. But the local representatives of the Crown were still puzzled why an Englishman such as Richard Abdee would want to exert himself whipping Negro slaves.

In desperate need of a recruit, though, the Government cursed the French fleets for luring away all the roustabouts they had previously hired and agreed to try this sullen Richard Abdee. And, today, here in Government House, Abdee was receiving his final briefing before he entered into His Majesty's service. Actively.

The Lord Governor's Assistant-to-the-Secretary-of-Justice, Lionel Cranwell—who resembled a tall, wet turkey in his rumpled white frockcoat, mop of ginger hair, and a large Adam's apple protruding from his skinny neck—had been pontificating to Abdee for fifteen minutes since giving him a parchment scroll. On that scroll were listed the names to which the Negroes answered and the description of their crimes. And returning to the subject of that scroll, Lionel Cranwell said airily, "You must realize, Mister Abdee, that it is out of respect for the plantation owners that we even bother to compile this cattle sheet. If it were not for the esteem we have for His Majesty's colonials, we would go ahead and deal with the niggers in the most simple way. The most elementary method."

Apart from disliking this pompous flunkey, Abdee cared little about custom—local or otherwise—and he answered him simply, in a voice which was deep and dry. "It is not up to me to ask questions, Secretary Cranwell. I have been hired for one purpose and it's out there." He nodded toward a fan-topped window.

Pulling back his head at the curt reply, Cranwell said, "Don't be so single-minded, Mister Abdee." Then, dropping his beady eyes to Abdee's gleaming black boots, he slowly raised his gaze over the snug-fitting breeches and the white shirt which tugged across Abdee's firm chest, saying, "But while we're on the subject of the action itself, you might find the job more demanding than even you suspect . . . Mister Abdee."

Abdee stood tall and impervious to Cranwell's inquisitive stares. He was accustomed to being mauled by people's eyes, especially people who were trying to impress him—or themselves—with their own importance. He answered matter-of-factly, "If I put myself into the first ten, fifteen strokes, I think I can lighten up toward the end."

Walking around Abdee now, inspecting him as if he might be some fine animal being offered for sale—or even a Negro buck in a *vendue*—Cranwell loftily conceded, "Frankly, Mister Abdee, no matter how you 'put' yourself, I think you will evoke a certain delight from your audience today—regardless of all these opinions which have been circulating in our society about an Englishman accepting such, such," Cranwell paused to choose his words, "a barbaric position!"

Abdee laughed, letting his weight rest on one leg again. "The people in your society keep slaves. They want them whipped. They even come into town to see it. Yet they turn around and call the practice barbaric."

Cranwell said coolly, "Certainly, Mister Abdee, most certainly some people here think that way. But they are mostly the ladies, the weaker sex. But I have no doubts whatsoever that you will convince the *ladies* of your place in our society."

Abdee said, "I had no idea I was hired to impress women."

"Well, let us hope for your sake, Mister Abdee, that you make an impression on one or two of the men, too. I am speaking of your professional merit, you realize. And it is the men—the masters of our fine estates—who subsidize your fee. Their wives might well be titillated by the spectacle of a young English *gentleman* gallantly flailing a whip on the platform, but we can only gauge your worth as a Dragonard by the approval you receive from their husbands. Our patrons."

Cranwell's sarcasm did not annoy Abdee as much as his point of social position. He said, "If I am a gentleman, Secretary Cranwell—and I do not remember saying that I was—then I am obviously the first who has ever been without money here on St. Christopher."

Flicking his handkerchief in the air, Cranwell said impatiently, "Oh, not 'St. Christopher.' No, no, no, *no!* We are St. Kitts now. St. Kitts. The island is ours again. It belongs totally to King George and we familiarize it now as we English are so fond of doing with all our names. No, it is not St. Christopher. Not *Sant Christophe*. Not even *Santo Cristofo*. But St. Kitts! St. Kitts!"

Abdee said, "If there is such anglicizing going on, then why do you still keep a name like 'Dragonard'?"

Cranwell gaped at such impudence. "But what about the whip? We cannot change the name of the whip just because the French have been put to sea!"

"But you told me yourself that the whip is called 'the Dragon's Tongue.' "

Abdee's argument, however true, was only turned into further fuel for Lionel Cranwell's bureaucratic polemics.

"Ah, yes. But the Dragonard is more than his whip. The Dragonard is the force behind that whip. The might behind the sting. But, if it consoles your sense of neatness, Mister Abdee, try to think of the word 'Dragonard' as a polite token of English generosity. A considerate semantic combination of both English and French.

We two nations shared this island. We still do. But the English, being in governmental control once again— and being very generous—can allow that wicked, wicked catchphrase, Dragonard, to have the guise of a French *mot* while still keeping it familiar to our own tongues."

"What you are saying, then, Secretary Cranwell, is that the English are too lazy to learn a second language. Or to assign new equivalents to out-dated expressions."

Cranwell eyed Abdee. "You are English. Why be so critical?"

Abdee answered, "I was born English. It stops there."

"So why did you bother to stop *here* if you're so unsympathetic towards the English, Mister Abdee? Why disembark at St. Kitts? Why did you not continue to Guadeloupe? That is French. Or Martinique? Or why did you not choose a Spanish colony? You could have gone to Puerto Rico. Santo Domingo. Cuba. Or even a Dutch or a Danish territory. No, you did not have to stop on St. Kitts, Mister Abdee. We were not standing out on our sandy shores and beckoning you in with our palm trees." He held his hooked nose high in victory as Christopher Columbus might have hoisted the flag of Isabella when he landed here three hundred years earlier.

"My passage was booked to the first stop and our German captain was anxious to sell his cargo here in Basseterre."

"So you allowed a load of osnaburgh and iron skullery ware to determine your fate? How sad," Cranwell said, shaking his head.

"I needed the passage to go on from here," Abdee answered, beginning to wonder how long his temper was going to allow him to withstand this acrimony.

"So you settled for this? Of all the positions available in Basseterre—clerk, chandler, assistant in a public house—you choose *that*?" Cranwell asked, flicking his handkerchief toward the raised platform beyond the fan-topped window.

"I needed the money."

Cranwell said softly, "Young men like you certainly can get money in many, many ways, Mister Abdee."

"Exactly what kind of young man do you think I am, Secretary Cranwell?" Abdee asked, his fists clenching at his sides.

And, for the first time, Cranwell was at a loss for words. He could see anger rising in Abdee's cool, blue eyes. He realized that he had goaded him quite enough. He knew, too, that he must not say any more because it was one thing to think that a young man might look like a hard-shelled cavalier. It was another matter, though, to say so to his face. Especially if he had a hint, even the slightest hint, of good breeding to him. Unlike louts—or Negroes—one did not insult a gentleman on St. Kitts. So, quickly deliberating with one long finger against his cheek, Cranwell returned the subject to Abdee's origin. "Perhaps I am beginning to see why you left England, Mister Abdee. The majority of young men we see arriving here are looking for a new start. Or in quest of some great and noble adventure. But, perhaps you are merely fleeing from the disciplined world."

"I am not a criminal on the run, if that's what you're trying to say. But I thought we went through all this before."

"Yes, yes, we did. But I still have not come to any satisfactory conclusions why you should agree to perform a task which, up to now, has only been chosen by Frenchmen. And not very desirable Frenchmen at that."

"And you will not allow that the English can be footloose and shiftless, too?"

"If I may be frank, Mister Abdee, you are a contradiction to me. You are certainly no ordinary Englishman. And, in short, well, you do not make sense to me. You are an anachronism."

"Only time makes sense of people, Secretary

Cranwell. But if it will console you, let me tell you that I do expect a little more out of life than beating the tar out of people."

"But Mister Abdee," he began slowly, "niggers are not people! Niggers are slaves. *Animals*! I thought we went through that before, *too*!"

"My gratitude for your patience with me, Secretary Cranwell. I apologize. But if you don't mind, I do think that I will continue regarding the Africans as human-beings. You see, I've never liked being cruel to animals."

"Ah, so you're a misanthrope! At least we're making some headway."

"No. I don't hate people. Nor do I necessarily like to inflict pain."

"I see. You are just terribly fond of insuring order," Cranwell said.

"I do not see myself as a soldier, either, if that's what you mean," Abdee said, even amazed at his own patience.

Stepping closer to Abdee, Cranwell said, "But surely, becoming a Dragonard is to be a soldier of sorts, Mister Abdee. Yours is a mercenary position because you accept pay. You maintain rule by executing punishment."

"I must confess, Secretary Cranwell, that I will not be concentrating on King nor country when I step outside."

"So what will you be thinking about, Mister Abdee?" Cranwell asked, cocking a thin, ginger-coloured eyebrow. His grin had changed, too, became less of a sneer.

"How did my predecessors answer that?" Abdee asked, wondering what this slight change of tactics meant. Cranwell seemed to be suddenly warming to him.

"That's just the point, Mister Abdee. Your predecessors have all been French. And I speak only a smattering of French. Certainly not enough to follow the reminiscences of a Dragonard," he confessed, letting his eyes quick dart again to Abdee's breeches. Then, point-

ing one finger at Abdee, he said, "So, I will have to depend on *you* to fill that gap in my education. Yes, Mister Abdee, you are hereby appointed to inform me
what a man thinks when he finds, say, a nubile, young
Negress manacled helplessly in front of him. Or what
runs through your head when a great, hulking black
male—say a buck twice the size of even *you*—is
spread-eagled naked on the posts." Cranwell paused,
adding quickly in his more official voice, "That will be
the normal procedure, you realize—the Negroes
spread-eagled in front of you ..." Then, having Abdee's eye, he began to trickle his words, "... Rippling,
hot arms. Strong legs. A back swelling with fibrous
muscles. Sweating ..."

But Abdee stopped Cranwell's inexplicable and alto-
gether uncharacteristic outburst of fantasies. And, beginning to realize that there was another side to this offi-
cious secretary, a facet which could prove to be more
repulsive than his pomposity, Abdee said for good
measure, "When I finish today, I am going back to my
room. Do not forget that some of your esteemed landowners aren't as prosperous as others. Some must pay
in kind. And Mister Branwell of Lark's Song has
promised to have me a black wench waiting at the
inn."

"A wench?" Cranwell blurted.

Abdee nodded pleasantly. He had been right.

"But ... but immediately after? Will you be capable? I mean, are you so energetic? To go from one display? To another? So soon?"

It was Abdee's turn now to laugh. "I assure you that
my second execution will be no display, Secretary
Cranwell. It will be only myself and the wench."

Cranwell's eyes quickly dropped to Abdee's breeches
again. He was trying to control himself—return to the
decorum of his office—but he was not being very suc-
cessful. "You know what they expect, don't you? Those
sluts from their niggers? What those black men have?"

"I have heard stories about the blacks, yes. But I

didn't think you called them 'men.' I thought they were all animals to you?"

But Cranwell's retaliations were gone. His fight. His haughty attitude. Almost like an innocent child now, he asked, "And you are undaunted by what satisfies the black women? What they are constructed to ... accommodate?"

Holding out his hand, Abdee said, "The only thing I have ever been daunted by, Secretary Cranwell, is asking for my wages."

Cranwell sniffed, looking down at Abdee's surprisingly long, thick fingers.

"My wages, Sir," Abdee said, holding his hand steady as he watched Cranwell begin to dig nervously into the pockets of his frock coat. And seeing him finally produce a small pouch of coins, he added, "I said I needed the money."

So, dropping the pouch into the palm of Abdee's hand, and very reluctantly, as if this act of payment symbolized the end of their relationship, Cranwell admitted, "I would like to know the true story of you, Richard Abdee. The whole, true story."

"Hopefully, there is much more to play out."

"But every young man has a past."

"I am not young. I am on the doorstep of thirty."

Cranwell managed a smirk. "That is not exactly death's porch."

"From the moment we are born, Secretary Cranwell, we are reaching death."

Staring him straight in the eye, Cranwell asked, "And that intrigues you, too? Death?"

Shaking his head, Abdee said, "No, Secretary Cranwell. Only the punishments of life."

Cranwell lowered his eyes and held out his chin. He looked as if he was defeated, about to retreat. But, fixing a passive gaze on Abdee again, he said, "You do confuse me. And, if you don't mind me saying so, you are not instantly likeable. But," he said, turning his head away from Abdee now and adding, "perhaps I will grow to understand you, though."

"Let's hope you don't get the chance."

Cranwell jerked. "What do you mean?"

Abdee then clearly saw this man, a government official who had been so grand, so certain of himself at the beginning of this meeting. And now here he was virtually ready to eat out of Abdee's hand. The breakthrough had been, not surprisingly, sex. Sexual fantasies. Physical capabilities. Endowments. Superiorities. And that had been the moment when Abdee had seized command of the situation, when Cranwell had forfeited his so-called authority. Yes, there were words for men like Lionel Cranwell. And there were women, too, who fell into the same category of desires. Males and Females who spend their lives searching for a stronger force. Human-beings who surround themselves with achievement, even luxuries, but are willing to be stripped of everything—even self-respect—if the right dominant power ambled into their life.

But repelled by that human phenomenon on this level, Abdee answered, "I merely meant, Secretary Cranwell, that I hope to find a better job."

Toying with his handkerchief, Cranwell answered quietly, "And I hope you do, Mister Abdee. I sincerely hope you do."

Abdee thanked him with a nod.

Reluctantly, Cranwell headed toward the carved door of his office. His hand paused on the handle as he turned to call, "Good luck, Mister Abdee."

But Abdee did not answer. By now, Lionel Cranwell was merely one more bug who had just crawled through his life. And Abdee had had many of them, too. Those maggots.

The door closed with a timid click.

And standing alone now in the cavernous white room of Government House, Abdee glanced down at the pouch in his hand.

Yes, he had money.

Then he looked at the room itself.

What am I doing here, he quickly asked himself. Why this tropical pot?

The only movement in the tall, white room came from a small black boy—a piccaninny—standing against a wall with a rope in his hands. As if he were tolling a bell, the piccaninny slowly pulled the rope up and down, up and down. Overhead, a palm fan gently circulated the humid air. The boy stood staring dumbly at a patch on the polished floor in front of him, a join in the parquet about three yards beyond his bare toes.

Abdee looked at the boy and then back to the parchment scroll in his other hand. Criminals, he thought. Hell, a spaniel wetting a carpet would be more of a criminal than some of these Africans on this list.

But, next, Abdee thought: Why should I worry about it? What affair is it of mine? I am getting my money. And that is what I'm doing here, by God. Getting money. My own start.

So, quickly rolling up the parchment and stuffing the pouch into his waistband, Abdee turned toward the front doors.

Passing the boy, Abdee patted his cleanly shaven head.

The island of St. Christopher—or St. Kitts—was a small speck of green in the shape of a fish. When charted on a map of the Caribbean, St. Kitts was positioned to swim from its snug place in the Leeward Islands, up past the Greater Antilles, through the Bahamas, to the tip of East Florida.

But St. Kitts was not going anywhere. It was stuck in the tropical cacophony of chattering parrots, the swarms of monkeys swinging down the hills in screeching forays, the mournful wails of the freed negroes who roamed the sixty-five square mile island as they beat on their begging gourds.

The capital of St. Kitts was Basseterre, a town with a population of nine hundred Europeans. The nine thousand Africans—roughly ten slaves to every white person—were not counted in the official concensus.

Basseterre's vanilla, French-styled buildings rose in a low semi-circle on a mauve hillside which faced the brilliant blue sea. For nearly fifty years now—since 1717—this outwardly lazy town had been dominated by the English. From the Treaty of Utrecht, an Anglo supremacy was established in this part of the West Indies. Before that, the English hub of St. Kitts had been Old Town, a settlement farther up the island. But now the English were lords and they kept away the military might of King Louis with the protection of battlements on Brimstone Hill. And, in the meantime, commerce continued between the people of those two nations while warships were momentarily silent.

Richard Abdee was thinking about England and its people's unique knack of colonizing as he walked away from Government House. This area in front of him was a prime example of that phenomenon. The English had renamed this lush meeting place "The Circus." Its spreading Banyan trees, the fancy fretwork on the surrounding buildings, and the flagstone street which dipped in the centre were meant to comprise a far-flung token of London's Piccadilly Circus. But Abdee could not understand such sentiments at all. Around him, the brightly painted jalousies were pulled shut against a hot, morning sun. There was that general feeling of malaise which Abdee was to find unique to Caribbean towns. But even now, he recognized the mood of this spot as being totally foreign and he wondered why the colonials—French, Spanish, but especially the English—had to drag home everywhere they went. Why not choose a name from the language of the Caribbe Indians who had first inhabited this volcanic island? The natives whom the early settlers had killed from overwork, the forerunners of the African slaves.

Abdee wondered, too, if he himself was really English when he looked to the far side of The Circus and saw his fellow countrymen. They were not unfamiliar to him.

A large collection of polished barouches and encrested landaus had gathered under the leafy banyan. The brass and silver studding of their horses glistened in the sun. In the back of the smart carriages a light babble rose from the ladies who leaned toward one another, twirling their white or pink or lavender parasols over their feathered bonnets. Or fluttered their silk fans around their ivory complexions. Sitting next to them in the open conveyances, or perched above them on great stallions, were their husbands, their brothers, or their beaux. But, to Abdee, all a sad, foppish sight of manhood. Their meticulous clothing hid soft, pale bodies which sagged from luxurious living. Too much wine had lessened their virile powers, and Abdee realistically conceived how only the careful lies and flattery from the mouth of a black woman—forced into sex with these white men by the mere definition of a role, the slave—could rescue these ludicrous heroes from encroaching impotency.

And seeing these landowners turned out to watch a flogging of their slaves, Abdee asked himself if the English were really that blood-thirsty? Or was life so boring here on St. Kitts that all they had to do was to watch their chattel being slowly destroyed? And gossip about the man who did it? Perhaps even prolong their sexual abilities.

As Abdee moved toward the platform in the middle of The Circus, voices began to call to him:

"Viva la English!" the first rake shouted, standing in his stirrups and waving a silver flask. He reminded Abdee of the typical second son: little money, great pretensions, his stomach bigger than his mind.

"The Dragonard is a blimey," goaded the second, a dubious buck wearing a pale blue frock coat and a floppy white hat banded with pink camellias.

"But is our friend planning on blood? That's what we want to know," called the third, a lanky youth who lounged in the back of his carriage with a fair-haired girl on each arm. But from Abdee's experience, he knew that young ladies such as those were nothing but alabaster dolls. They wanted no role other than being decorative; for them, their sex meant being spoiled and sported. They blinded themselves to the more rudimentary pleasures, the enjoyments to be had at the base of the pedestal on which they allowed themselves to be placed.

Abdee continued toward the platform, smiling to himself as he thought about how angry this gentry would really be if they knew exactly how much he was a part of them. Perhaps they would even forgive him for being a Dragonard, make some excuse, call the occupation a quirk of his personality. Abdee hated the English, too, for that permissiveness. If you make a rule, hold to it.

Taking deep breaths as he moved, Abdee filled his chest with this new, sea-swept air: a thick bouquet of over-ripe fruit, fresh manure heated by the sun, and the sweetness of the oleander. And, as new and incongruous as that combination of ingredients was to Abdee's nose, so did the second faction of people he now saw—when mixed with the English—make an odd stew for his eyes.

Abdee was looking now at the crude wagons, the rustic work carts which had carried or led the Negro slaves along the palm-lined roads from the plantations to Basseterre. The white overseers in straw hats now shouted at the Negroes, pushing them into positions on the ground. There the Negroes would squat—feet firmly planted, knees bent, their buttocks hanging free—and wait until it was their turn to be punished.

As Abdee studied the blacks already crouched across the flagstone like some strange stock at a county fair, he saw how their skin ranged from a deep indigo to the creamiest of yellows. Their foreheads varied greatly in height. Their faces were either very flat or most accentuated. But their eyes were all large and anxious, white spheres glowing from a bank of black faces. The men's heads were all shaved. But, noticing one or two females, Abdee saw how their hair had been intricately plaited, patterned like linear tattoos on their scalps. He also saw that neither male nor female wore clothes. Their fulsome bodies were not even protected by the slightest rag or string. Perhaps such nudity, he thought, also adds to the thrill of the English.

But, putting these thoughts of the white-black society out of his mind, and how he would deal with a West Indian plantation of his own, Abdee slowly mounted the wooden steps of the platform. For the moment, Abdee had to concentrate on making money to live. Like his fellow Englishmen, his survival also included a certain exploitation of the Africans.

Abdee now handed the rolled scroll to a soldier in an embroidered mitre cap who would perform the role of The Crier, the person who would announce the name of the slave, make public the offence, list the details of punishments, and then count the strokes of the lash. Not exactly the job for the Regiment of the Foot Guard, Abdee thought, but we must keep it official.

From the soldier, Abdee turned to the structure built on this raised wooden floor. He saw an arch composed of two posts supporting a third. Four pairs of iron rings hung in set levels on the two side posts. Abdee knew that those were the manacles. He saw that the leg fetters were attached to the plank flooring itself and would accommodate either man or woman. Buck or wench.

As that arch, though, only concerned Abdee by the function it served in holding the slave in a powerless position, he shifted his attention to the table which held the true equipment. And, of course, the whips. At his disposal, he had two bull whips. Three whips called "cats." And, then, there was the Dragon's Tongue: a six foot length of oily black leather with an extra deep splay at its tip—the tongue of the dragon.

Reaching immediately for the fabled Dragon's Tongue, Abdee heard voices rise again from the carriages. Ignoring the calls, though, he lifted the six feet of coiled leather from the table and, first, felt the handle like a man in a shop trying a walking-stick.

Next, as Abdee suddenly threw the whip over his back, the jibes grew louder from the carriages. Abdee now could quite clearly hear that they were truly insulted—or pretended to be—that an Englishman would take on this job.

But Abdee let the tip of the Dragon's Tongue sing through the air, landing with a sharp crack against the plank floor. As the jeers continued, Abdee neatly recoiled the whip and set it back on the table. No, he would not begin with the Dragon's Tongue. He would save that beauty until later. He wished that it would be on some of those white people, though.

The first applause which greeted him all morning came when he stripped off his shirt. But that reaction, too, was derisive and continued only until two more Foot Guards led the first Negro up the wooden steps, toward the pillars.

As they were manacling the black, Abdee slipped on a pair of leather gauntlets. Then, standing with his hands firmly planted on the railing, he bent his head and waited to hear the manacles snap, the pins being hammered into the fetters.

The Crier began:

Male Negro—Answers to the name of Tacky—Property of Mister Winslow Granger—Frigate Bay Park—Frigate Bay—Guilty of stealing one tortoise shell comb—First offence—Punishment of public flogging—Not more than TWO HUNDRED STROKES—And amputation of BOTH EARS.

Having stepped toward the table, Abdee chose the bull.

The crowd was silent, even to the point when the first strip cracked across the rippling back of the Negro.

But, before the second lash fell, voices began to call out from the carriages:

"Can't you get a better job?"

"Don't you have any pride?"

"What about England?"

Abdee, though, was deaf to the calls and jeers. He was as silent now as the bulky Negro spread out by irons in front of him.

And neither did the second African squirm in the shackles. The muscles of his inky body rose tight and hard as Abdee's whip streaked across his back. His skin was tough, not breaking to spout blood until The

18

Crier reached the forty count, and then the redness mixed with the shiny flood of perspiration, forming an iridescent coating across the Negro's shoulders.

The third African was also a male—a stocky man with short, thickset legs, and strong shoulders which even strained toward the lowest notch of the manacles. The English lost no time in drawing attention to the length and thickness of his maleness, calling to Abdee, "Don't get yourself tangled up with him, Blimey!"

But Abdee still ignored their jibes. The steady cracking of his whip was the only sound he heard. And when Abdee's audience called to him to spare the breasts on the fifth victim—a woman whose corpulent body sagged with both bosom and spreading-buttocks—Abdee resumed to work on her, too, with a stony, solemn dedication. But he frequently let the tip of the cat crack before it touched the woman's dark, soft-looking skin. He knew that if every stroke made contact with her flesh, she would most certainly die. Also, Abdee stopped short at thirty-five. He was no henchman.

Beneath the raised platform now, screams were beginning to rise. The soldiers had begun severing the ears on the first Negroes, the ones who had already been whipped. The soldiers were slicing the ears from the Negroes' heads with swords heated in a brazier. But the painful wails of the Africans—and the smell of burning flesh and hair—also eluded Abdee. He was concentrating on his aim, that black expanse from shoulders to upper buttocks, and he threw his body into each toss of the leather.

Between slaves—while the soldiers unshackled one black, dragged him down the steps and under the platform for his ears to be severed, and brought up the next—Abdee stood with his arms placed on the railing, his head drooped, his chest heaving to catch his breath. He was in a world of his own.

Buggy wheels were now clattering away from under the Banyans, a beginning of the mass exodus from The Circus. They were leaving in disgust. "Barbarian,"

voices shouted to Abdee. "Where's your pride?"
"Scum." "Maverick."

But it was also time now for Abdee to use the
Dragon's Tongue for the first time. So, reaching toward
the black nest which it made on the table, Abdee un-
furled it through the air with a quick, neat snap. Then,
turning toward the pillars, he saw . . .

The Crier announced, "Number Nine."

But, before The Crier could continue with this tall
male's name, offence, and punishment, Abdee had already let the first bite fly toward the pinioned black.

And, more like two sharp teeth of a rodent—instead
of a Dragon's Tongue—the tip of the fabled weapon
streaked across the spine of the Negro. Blood instantly
gushed from his sweaty, black skin.

A loud protest arose from the few remaining carriages, rebuking Abdee for not allowing The Crier to
complete the announcement.

But Abdee did not halt. By now he had registered
the touch of this whip. He had quickly gauged that he
must lighten his force. And pleased with this whip's
balance, the way in which it sped through the air, he
smiled as he fell into his new rhythm.

His white body twisted again with each new pitch.
And drops of perspiration rolled from the hot recesses
of the black leather gauntlets, streaming into the downy
bed of blonde hairs which covered his forearms.

If it had not been for the stinging sensation on his
back, Abdee would have sworn that only one hour at
the most had passed. But with his shoulders aching
from sunburn, he realized that it had taken much longer than that to flog twenty-six Africans. He wished
that he had been sensible enough to have worn his
shirt.

The exhaustion which Abdee felt, though, was no
more than the fatigue following a pleasant swim. The
same muscles had been exercised. The difference between flogging and swimming, though, was that water

contracted the proportions of his masculinity and this second activity only made him larger, undeniably erect.

So, readjusting himself in his breeches, and checking to see that the money pouch was still in his waistband, Abdee grabbed his shirt from the railing and slowly sauntered down the narrow steps.

In the darkness under the platform, the soldiers were still severing ears. Abdee now smelled the hot iron against flesh. He heard the singes, the screams. He did not approve of punishment like that. It was overt mutilation.

Reaching the foot of the steps, Abdee looked up and was surprised to see that all the carriages had gone. The rough work carts were still there but the English had completely disappeared. And Abdee had not even heard them leave.

Again, though, he was distracted by a woman's piercing scream. Abdee heard the sizzle of hot iron again and smelled the bittersweet odour of burning flesh and hair. The woman's screams suddenly stopped.

She has fainted, Abdee thought, and then let his mind quickly pass to another Negress, a woman he himself would soon enjoy make scream, that black wench waiting for him back at the Lucky Seven. Yes, he was in the mood for something consummating.

He began to make his way across the cobbled square, looking at the wrought-iron railings on the surrounding buildings. He saw that some of the ironwork had been painted shades complimentary to the mansard-roofed buildings—rich blues, vermillion, luxuriant greens—and that other ironwork had been left black, forming stark but florid curlicules against white-washed walls.

Suddenly a voice called behind him. "Master La Dragonard! Master La Dragonard!"

Throwing back a shank of perspiration-soaked hair, Abdee stopped at the far edge of The Circus. He saw an old man, wearing a tattered green frock coat and a tricorn hat. He was rushing toward Abdee with a portmanteau in one hand. He called, "Master Dragonard! *S'il vous plaît!*"

Stopping, Abdee asked, "What can I do for you?"

Quickly removing his felt-worn hat, the old man breathlessly answered in a heavy French accent. "Excuse, Master La Dragonard, I am Monsieur Delon and I have the honour of bringing you the latest instruments from Paris!" Then, with that brief introduction, he quickly placed one buckled shoe a few inches in front of the other and brought the portmanteau up to his knee. He began to unsnap its lid.

"No, no, no, old fellow!" Abdee objected quickly when he saw the contents of the leather case. "I have had enough whips for one day. Go. Do your business with Secretary Cranwell. He is the man in charge of buying." Abdee motioned toward Government House.

But Monsieur Delon implored, "These are for *you* to see! These are new! The latest! Look," he said, balancing the case with one hand and removing a short crop from the case with the other. "The newest invention which has both leather and hemp in its plaiting. Feel. Lift it. See how light it is."

Slipping on his shirt—but gently, to ease its contact against his burnt skin—Abdee said, "If these whips and crops are as good as you say they are, then go make an appointment for yourself at Government House."

"That is impossible, Monsieur! You can hear I am French. And if I am French, they will not let me through the front door of their house of government."

"I thought that the English and French were such good neighbours now. What about your freedom of trade?"

"Freedom of trade? Do you think the English offer their free trade to a man who once dealt in munitions for the other side?" he asked, also motioning toward the forboding whiteness of the official building behind him, its neat row of fan-topped windows. "No, Monsieur, such trade as free as that does not exist on *Sant Christophe.*"

"*Sant Christophe?*" Abdee said, smiling. "No, no. It's St. Kitts now."

The Frenchman caught Abdee's tone of ridicule. He spat.

Suddenly, they were friends. Two renegades.

"A munitions man?" Abdee asked, smiling. "But one who is reduced to selling whips?"

Delon objected. "Ah, not just whips, Monsieur. I sell the finest pistols in all the islands. I fill orders for the whole Caribbean. If anyone offends your honour, Monsieur, remember that you have someone. Remember Gerrard Delon. I come to your assistance at any time. I have only the best. Even I serve as your accomplice. Your second."

"That all sounds good and fine, my friend, but what I need now is not a duelling iron."

With the instantaneous intuition granted only to a Frenchman, Delon lowered his voice. "Ah, a lady."

Abdee cocked his head. "It is not exactly a lady."

Winking, the old Frenchman said, "You English, of course! I understand now. *Le vice anglais!*" Then, moving closer to Abdee, surveying The Circus for possible eavesdroppers, he whispered, "I have just the thing for you, Monsieur. It is not the ordinary cane. No, this little jewel will not put the slightest welt on the bottom of your tiny fellow. He can run back to Mama as if nothing had happened!"

"No, no, no, *no!*"

"*Helas!*" Delon exclaimed, his eyes widening. "You DO want to welt the little pink bottom? Then, it is not a cane you want but one of my Spanish straps! Hand-treated in Seville."

"No. You do not understand, old man. It is not a boy I want to welt. I don't even want to welt. I am going to my first black wench!"

But Delon was still not hindered by this information. To him, little had changed. So lowering his voice even more than before, he said cautiously, looking quickly around him again, "Please do not misunderstand, Monsieur. You look like the fine specimen of a man. You look, well, most *bon*. But these black wenches, ah, they are used to the black stallion, you understand. It is like you taking the place of a horse when you go with one of those savages from Africa. But your demand is not the first I have had," he said, opening a hidden compartment on the lid of his portmanteau. "I have been asked before for this device which extends across continents. Oh yes, some of the most noble English gentlemen on this very island use this when they go into the fields at night."

But they were suddenly interrupted. A voice called from the direction of a large, dome-roofed warehouse. The voice thundered, "Delon! What are you selling now?"

The old Frenchman quickly moved to insert the black rubber apparatus back into the secret compartment.

But Abdee turned and saw a second stranger. This new intruder was near the same age as the Frenchman. And, apart from being taller and more stout, his clothing was equally as shabby, with the exception that this man's frock coat had once been more ornate, piped and fronted with dove-coloured satin. And, although stained, a jabot fluffed under the many folds of his chin.

Stepping alongside Abdee, the newcomer removed his tricorn hat with a flourish and bowed. He said, "Franklin Topper, Esquire."

To Abdee he looked like an impressario who had stepped out of a pantomime into this lush, tropical surrounding.

And before the over-dressed Mister Topper had risen from his deep bow, Abdee quickly said, "If it's whips or canes or leather straps that you too are selling, Mister Topper, I am not interested."

"Whips or canes?" Topper asked with the affectation of a high-born person. "I offer nothing so banal as that ... Your Lordship."

Abdee knitted his brow. *"Lordship?"*

Monsieur Delon suddenly tugged at Abdee's sleeve,

whispering, "Do not listen to him, Monsieur. This man is cunning. I know this man. I would warn you the same if the devil himself would be approaching you. Watch out!"

Shrugging off Delon's arm, Abdee said, "I would like to meet the devil. But as far as wasting my time on a confidence trickster, a petty horse-trader—no, I am in too much of a hurry."

Untouched by either Abdee's or Delon's remarks, Franklin Topper stepped even more forward and asked, "Are you also in too much of hurry to listen about money?"

"What would you know about money?"

"I would know how you could make yourself a fortune—your *own* fortune."

"Thank you, Mister Topper, but I will go about that in my own way. And only when the right time comes." Abdee moved toward the curbing.

Topper, though, held up his hand. "But would not a small inventory get you started in the right direction until such a time arrives? An inventory which would include, say, three hundred kegs of rum. One hundred and seventy-five casks of brandy. Eighty-five hogshead of sack. And land! Do you so readily reject the idea of having your own land on this lush, fertile island ... Your Lordship?" Now, Topper was holding up both hands, gesturing to the leafy branches tenting them in The Circus.

Abdee frowned. Then, he began slowly, "Mister Topper, I am always willing to stop and exchange stories with strangers. To hear about their deeds or misdeeds. Preferably misdeeds. But when they start calling me names such as 'Lord,' then, naturally, I begin to suspect them as being—shall I say—obsequious? Now, if you will please step aside, I will get on my way."

"To spend that paltry sum of money you earned today?" Topper asked, motioning to the pouch bulging under Abdee's waistband. "Or is it because you want to go back to your room to collect further payment? Oh, yes, I know the ways of our lesser landowners. If they can not pay the Dragonard in cash, often the fee is arranged by an hour or two spent with one of the wenches from the endebted plantation. And that is right, isn't it? You have a black wench waiting for you at your rooms?"

Abdee answered blandly, "Your knowledge does not impress me."

Holding out his great stomach, Topper said, "I have not come out into this heat to impress you with my knowledge. I came hoping to make you listen to some sense . . . Your Lordship."

"I told you to stop calling me that!"

Studying Abdee's lean face, Topper asked, "But are you not the eldest and only son of Jonathan Abdee, the eighth Earl of Wycliffe?"

Abdee froze. Even old Delon could see the sudden effect which Topper's words had on Abdee.

Bowing again, Topper said, "I must confess that I was a bit surprised to hear that the Earl of Wycliffe arrived with so little fanfare on our lovely isle."

Abdee asked slowly, "And you are the only person who knows of this particular arrival?"

"I would say so," Topper answered smugly. "But even I, who am so understanding of men's ways, was a bit surprised to discover further that the Earl of Wycliffe stepped ashore without a farthing in his purse. That, indeed, he had to take a job as . . ." Topper turned to look in derision at the platform standing behind him, the white-overseers now dragging the last Negroes back to the work carts.

Straightening himself, Abdee said, "Perhaps if you knew as much about finances as you do about lineage, Mister Topper, you would know that the House of Wycliffe went bankrupt after the Battle of Minden."

Topper shook his head woefully. "No, fortune has not been kind to your family. First, your father died. Then, your mother could not exist alone. Your sister followed one year later. And only you are left."

Narrowing his eyes, Abdee asked, "Who are you? What do you want?"

"The question is, Your Lordship, what do *you* want?"

"AND STOP CALLING ME THAT NAME!"

Smiling, Topper said softly, "If that truly is your wish, then why not join me in the public rooms at your inn? Say, seven o'clock?"

Delon spoke now. "Do not listen to him, Master La Dragonard. He is a trickster."

But smiling at Abdee—watching him trying to decipher what he had said—Topper added, "On second thought, if you are going to have your first taste of the black mysteries this afternoon, we had better make our appointment for one hour later. Not seven. But eight. It will take you that long to recover. And I do want you to be very rested when you listen to my proposal . . . Your Lordship?"

Then, turning on his heels, Franklin Topper walked away from them, stepping carefully over the octopuslike roots of the Banyan trees.

Tugging at Abdee's sleeve, Delon begged, "Master La Dragonard. Do not listen to that man."

Abdee was silent. More maggots, he was thinking.

So, trying harder to get a reaction from Abdee, Delon tried ". . . Lord Wycliffe?"

Turning to him, Abdee said soberly, "Stick to 'master'."

Then he proceeded toward a sidestreet—its narrow whiteness reflecting the sunlight like an oven—and he was relieved that he had money. It wasn't much but it represented freedom. It would bury His Lordship.

2

"Lucretia Borgia"

Abdee's room was in the attic of the Lucky Seven, one
of the inn's dark and humid cubbyholes reserved for
the compulsory billeting of sailors.

The room contained one small wooden table, a ba-
sin-and-cistern, both of which were equally cracked,
one rickety stool, and a straw-mattressed bed so narrow
. . . with legs so tall . . . that it stood high and wobbly
like one more mosquito waiting to pounce upon the
first thin-skinned white person to stoop through the
door. Now that Abdee had money once more, though,
he could move downstairs to larger quarters, where the
beds were wider, the air circulated more freely through
the larger windows, and insect netting was provided for
the guests. He preferred that rather than becoming a
lodger with some family, a widow and her children who
had lost her husband at sea. He would choose mosqui-
toes over a family surrounding any day. Or night.

But Abdee had decided to stay in this room for a
few more hours, thinking that it would be senseless to
putrify the air immediately in his new place with the
mustiness of a Negress.

That careful plan, though, had been made before he
had actually seen the ebony female, "Lucretia Borgia,"
when he had so innocently anticipated his first adventure with an African.

But when he saw the skinny, wild-haired girl sitting
on the Slave's Bench in front of the Lucky Seven, Abdee
wondered if he really wanted one all that badly. Anyway, this one. Instead of wearing her hair intricately

plaited, a thick black bush covered the pinhead sticking out from the rough, shapeless slave's dress. Her arms and legs were splinters. Then, listening to her whine and moan as she trailed up the narrow staircase behind him, Abdee felt his entire desire for blackness completely disappear. Niggers obviously aren't for me, he thought. Anyway, not these plantation blacks so accustomed to fetters. The stories I've heard must have been about black women on their home continent.

Now, standing in his room, Abdee studied the poor specimen as she grovelled on the floor in front of him like some sick mongrel. It was that overt prostration which annoyed him the most. He had enjoyed slim women before but how could he become excited over a female like *that*? How could any white man satisfy himself with such a sad wreck of life as her?

He said sternly, "Go back to Branwell and tell him that he still owes me a debt."

The girl looked mournfully up at Abdee with huge, watery eyes. Abdee saw that she could not have been more than eighteen or nineteen years old. She was shaking with terror. He doubted if she would reach twenty.

Abdee demanded, "Doesn't Branwell teach you to answer when you're spoken to?"

Lowering her head, the large-lipped girl whispered, ". . . *Master.*"

Abdee grunted, "I should have guessed you would know that much!"

Suddenly grasping his boots, she implored, "You *must* like Lucretia Borgia, Master Sir."

"Get on your feet, you broken slut," Abdee said, jerking one leg free from her grasp. The flogging had made him randy but, not relishing her, he was already thinking how he could send downstairs for that redhaired Irish pudding who had been eyeing him in the public room. The blacks would have to wait.

But in a thin and feeble voice, the young Negress pleaded, "Don't send me away. Master Branwell, he flog the life right out of Lucretia Borgia he hears she

29

don't pleasure you, Master Sir. Master Branwell lock Lucretia Borgia in root cellar for twenty nights he hears you not take her."

Abdee's stomach turned at her "nigger-talk." He had heard about it taking hold in the American colonies but he had not expected it down here. He said, "If Master Branwell wants you stuffed, then let him do it himself."

"What's matter with Lucretia Borgia, Master Sir? What she do wrong?", she asked, kneeling upright now. Then, waiting for an answer—but receiving none—she reached down to the hem of the shapeless dress. Pulling the rough, oatmeal-coloured garment over her head, she threw it to the board flooring. Brushing back her thick hair in a quick sweep, she crouched in full nudity in front of Abdee and said, "Mayhap, Master Sir not see enough of Lucretia Borgia?" She knelt now, tilting her head on one side. Her teeth were surprisingly all intact. An even line of gleaming white.

Abdee stood, staring down at the naked girl. He saw, too, that the indigo skin on her body was smoother than that on her face and arms. And her arms did not appear to be so skinny now that they were positioned across her flat stomach. Yes, Abdee thought, it was probably the bulk of that dress which made her limbs look so feeble. Her prune-coloured body was actually very shapely, and her breasts, even on the frame of a much larger woman, would be generous.

Then, the transformation in Lucretia Borgia became *more* than visual. As Abdee stood staring down at her, the Negress—who had suddenly become statuesque— slowly rose to her knees and began to undulate her bare shoulders against the thighs of Abdee's breeches, murmuring, "You likes Lucretia Borgia better this way, Master Sir?"

Yes. Even her voice had changed. The whines, the mewling, the moans had been cast off with her shift. Her voice had lowered two octaves.

Feeling her shoulders and arms twist and rub against his legs, Abdee asked, "Where did a nigger girl like you learn to act like a Liverpool whore? Do they teach you that on Lark's Song, too?"

"White masters always like niggers better shucked down," she said, adeptly working her long fingers against the front of Abdee's breeches. And sensing a response within, she opened her large mouth and moved her red tongue forward to moisten the fabric.

Pulling back, Abdee said, "You stink worse than a pig!"

Suddenly, throwing back her head, Lucretia Borgia laughed. It was a loud, abandoned laugh and her white teeth glistened with saliva.

"Shhhhhhhh," Abdee said, quickly clamping his hand over her mouth. "You crazy bitch. Do you want to bring down the roof on us?"

Stifling her laugh, Lucretia Borgia's eyes danced with mischief over the top of Abdee's hand on her mouth. She shook her head.

Then, grabbing her by the chin, Abdee said, "Tell me, nigger girl, are you *all* like this? First, you whine and cry like some kind of demented child. Then, snap, do you all change into a slithering, laughing jungle animal? Are you all like this? Or are these tricks just more of the lessons you learn from your white masters?"

But Lucretia Borgia did not answer now. She was working her nimble fingers around Abdee's waistband. And, grabbing the fabric in a wad from his waist, she dropped it to the floor by her dress. Next, she turned to concentrate on the lowering of his breeches.

Abdee protested: "If this is how Branwell and your other masters like it, it doesn't mean I do, too!"

But she did not answer. She was busily tugging at his breeches and, once she had lowered them to his thighs, she suddenly stopped and stared, her eyes widening.

"What's the matter? Haven't you seen a white man before?" he asked. Despite his first displeasure, the girl had managed to arouse him.

In more of her Louisiana jargon, she marvelled, "Master Sir, you the first white nigger I ever sees!" Then, giggling, she lunged for Abdee with her mouth.

He struggled with her, dragging her up to the bed. Although her legs quickly spread, pumping for attention, she would not let go of him with her mouth. But a hearty slap across her buttocks remedied that. Then, as she sprawled across the narrow bed on her back, holding out her arms and legs for Abdee to come toward her, she again broke into peals of laughter.

Quickly clamping one hand over her mouth—turning the clasp into slaps—he guided himself into her. The movement was smooth at first, easy, but as soon as he began to attain his rhythm, Lucretia Borgia began to move faster. She held up well under his further attacks—even taunted his roughness—and then with a sudden clamp, Abdee began realizing the truth inside those African rumours. Still wearing his boots, and his breeches down to his knees, he plowed his way through the dark heat of the jungle.

After his third voyage, as he lay with his head on the pillow, the smell of musk suddenly began to overwhelm him again.

Drowsily, he said, "Get dressed. Go downstairs to wait for the wagon."

But Lucretia Borgia was silent now. Appearing to be more exhausted than Abdee, she lay with her arms around his thighs and the pink soles of her feet cradling his black boots.

Abdee said, "Branwell will be sending a wagon for you soon."

Snuggling in closer to Abdee, she whispered, "You my Master now." She added, "Sir."

"Get out!"

"Lucretia Borgia stay with you, Master Sir."

"Like hell she is. Now put on that rag of yours and get out of here." He irritably shoved her off the bed to the floor.

Clamouring to her knees, the girl knelt by the bed, pleading, "What Lucretia Borgia do now, Master Sir? What Lucretia Borgia do wrong now?" Her register was rising again.

"Stop whining! I thought you got over that."

"Lucretia Borgia shut her big mouth, Master Sir. Master Sir just lay there and let Lucretia Borgia gets Master Sir jug of water and Lucretia Borgia wash Master Sir."

"Like hell you will," Abdee said, bolting forward, pulling up his breeches.

"Lucretia Borgia belong to you, Master Sir."

"You lying little slut. Even if that were true, what makes you think I would want a stinking black sow like you around me. You whine one minute and you turn into some kind of a laughing lunatic the next. Now, get out!"

"Didn't you enjoy Lucretia Borgia, Master Sir?"

"I enjoyed myself."

"Lucretia Borgia gives Master Sir babies!"

"Babies?" Abdee shouted.

Nodding, she said, "Suckers! Lucretia Borgia has this many suckers so far!" She proudly held up seven fingers. "Master Sir can sell half-human babies for lots of money. People come down from New Orleans and pay lots of money for half-human suckers. They a novelty. Likes to have half-human niggers waiting on table. Fetch errands."

"Get dressed before I give you the thrashing of your life."

Collapsing to the board flooring, she begged, "Don't send Lucretia Borgia away, Master Sir."

The situation was becoming too ludicrous for Abdee. True, she had been the most abandoned and animated wench he had ever experienced, but now it was over. She was back to acting like a European parlour charade of a Negress.

Walking to the door, Abdee opened it and turned to her lying on the floor.

"Get out," he ordered.

Lucretia Borgia lay curled, clutching the lump of her dress, sobbing.

So, moving behind her, Abdee gave her a quick kick to the door. Then, he gave her another kick. And a third. Then, the fourth.

Lucretia Borgia crawled now on her hands and knees, crying for Abdee not to send her away. She was pledging her loyalty. She was promising suckers. Clinging to her dress as if it were her sole possession, she offered Abdee her life.

He gave her one last kick.

Then, slamming the door, he threw the bolt and faced the room.

He thought, Now that I'm rid of that carnival nigger, all I have to do is to get rid of her smell. He was glad that she was gone.

But quickly looking around the room, he realized that she was not the only thing gone. Missing. His money had disappeared, too. His waistband. That pouch.

"Hell!" he said out loud.

Lucretia Borgia was a thief—a very clever, very sly thief, too. Lucretia Borgia had tricked *him*!

And a liar!

Abdee realized that there must have been five hundred black wenches named "Lucretia Borgia" on the island of St. Kitts alone—the white people liked calling their slaves after well-known personages in history. But the Negress with whom he had just spent the last two hours had not been the "Lucretia Borgia" meant for him.

Having thrown on his shirt, Abdee thundered down the stairs and looked quickly into the timbered, low-ceiling public rooms.

Next he charged outside.

But, apart from a fat, black lady waddling along the stone wall across the street—her head balancing a bright red bundle—the only other Negress whom Abdee saw was sitting on the slave's bench in front of the inn. Wearing a shiny pink satin dress, she happily licked away at a stick of cinnamon. Like other slaves Abdee had seen, this young girl's hair was plaited into tiny strings. At the top of her head, though, the plaits had been cleverly tied into a small, four-pronged coronet of her own hair. It somehow made sense of her overly elaborate—and expensive—gown of pink satin and white lace.

Abdee quickly asked her, "Did you see a girl just run out of here?"

Lowering the stick of cinnamon, she answered, "No, Master Sir. I ain't seen no girl. Just that black wench."

More nigger talk! He snapped, "Yes! That's who I mean. Which way did she run?"

"She run nowhere, Master Sir."

"Then where is she, you imbecile?" Abdee saw that the girl was pretty—her skin, light-brown and soft; her eyes, harmless—but he realized that the tight plaits had probably stopped the workings of her brain.

Looking up at Abdee, she answered, "Nigger wench go out of here like hungry dogs after her heels!"

"But where? What direction did she run?"

"No, Master Sir. Nigger wench not run. Nigger wench grabbed the horse standing right there and done rides away. Makes so much dust, too, she near spoils this dress she done give me." Then, sticking the cinnamon into her mouth, the girl reached down the skirt and daintily held up the soft yardage with her small, brown fingers. She wanted to show the dress to Abdee.

"You said *she* gave you that dress?"

"Yes, Master Sir. Nigger wench say she craves to have *my* dress. Says she give me money to buy me sweetie, too. And I sure do pray Master Branwell not get all angry when he comes fetching me."

"You are from Branwell?"

"Yes, Master Sir. Sits here to wait for new Master Dragonard. But new Master Dragonard not showed up. You don't reckon, Master Sir, that new Master Dragonard comes when I buys sweetie." She looked down suspiciously at the stick of cinnamon.

But Abdee still was not satisfied. He asked, "That girl who gave you that dress, is she from Lark's Song, too?"

"Oh, no, Master Sir! That nigger ain't no plantation nigger. Not that nigger. By looks of that nigger, she free. Free and one of the nigger fancies that white masters pay money to. White masters takes all they want from slave niggers. But when niggers free, then white masters pay money for pleasuring."

Freed niggers and fancy niggers and plantation niggers, Abdee thought. And he stood wondering what to do when the girl asked him, "Master Sir?"

"Yes."

"Master Sir, when you think new Master Dragonard comes to fetch me?"

"You sit there and wait for your waggon to fetch you. Go back home and tell them that he did not show up."

"Master Branwell sees my pretty new dress!"

"Then, dammit, tell Branwell that new Master Dragonard gave it to you."

"But, Master Sir! That telling a lie. If new Master Dragonard never shows up, Master Sir, how can new Master Dragonard give Lucretia Borgia a pretty new dress?"

Abdee looked sharply. "Your name is Lucretia Borgia, too?"

"Yes, Master Sir!"

"And what was the name of that wench who gave you that dress?"

"Slave niggers don't ask freed niggers questions, Master Sir. Same as slave niggers don't ask white folks no questions."

"You are a very dutiful slave nigger, then, aren't you?"

But she did ask him a question. One more small question. "Dutiful, Master Sir? Dutiful anything like being pretty?"

"To some people." His mind was on money.

So, holding the cinnamon stick in one hand and picking up a tip of her pink satin skirt with the other, Lucretia Borgia looked down and said, "I sure do think this new dress is dutiful, Master Sir."

But Abdee had turned. She could work out her own problems. He had his same old one back again. No money.

There are times when a man must not rush. There are those moments when it is best for him to listen and, only then, act.

Abdee's first reaction was to comb Basseterre immediately for his fraudulent "Lucretia Borgia" and. then, as the hours passed, he longed to find the lithesome wench for cheating him. The money itself became less important. He wanted to get her.

In his temper—which cooled as the sun eased itself down into the chalky blueness of the horizon—Abdee told himself that he had no other choice than to listen to the proposal which Franklin Topper had suggested vaguely that afternoon in The Circus.

Maggots. Money. His future.

And the Earl of Wycliffe? Wasn't he dead yet? Buried deep in the ancestral clay of Abdee's England? Evidently not.

So, later, irritated by sunburn, annoyed by the din of the public room, Abdee saw Topper sitting by himself at a plank table in the corner.

Topper flourished his ruffled sleeve for more punch to be brought to the table. But Abdee declined the red sweetness. Instead, he asked for *taffa*. It was a light-brown brew which he had seen the blacks drinking. White people, he was told, usually did not lower themselves to such poison.

But soon warmed by the coarse slave's brew, Abdee sat patiently listening to Franklin Topper.

And there seemed to be nothing about life on St. Kitts which Topper did not know. Politics. Commerce. Arrivals and Departures. Items of prurient gossip. And somehow Topper had even heard about Abdee's recent adventure with "Lucretia Borgia." But Topper used a different name for the Negress. Certain other details of the encounter, too, had also been altered.

Abdee did not disturb Topper's tale. He let him spill out his version—the story which was being passed around town—of how Abdee had supposedly ignored the slave wench which had been sent to him from Lark's Song Plantation. Instead, Abdee was said to have spent his entire afternoon pleasuring himself with the most infamous black prostitute on St. Kitts. She was a fiery Negress called Naomi.

Naomi.

Abdee patiently listened for more. The pain from his sunburn was disappearing.

Fluffing at his limp jabot, Topper said, "Suddenly you are the most talked about Englishman we have. Not necessarily the most admired but certainly the most infamous. And I can see exactly why Naomi would make a call on you, too. That is a precedent in itself. She has never been known to set foot outside her house. But, for truth, I am surprised to hear that you paid her full price. I think at least you could have bargained her down to half!"

All Abdee could say was, "Naomi."

"Yes. Naomi. A devious bitch who received her freedom from a devoted French hunchback who had enormous holdings in Antigua. Naomi was his mistress for two years, starting when she was fourteen. But before the Frenchman had time to make the black waif his legal wife—at sixteen—she murdered him in his sleep, plundered his house for all portable treasures and made flight to St. Kitts. That was how she first financed her brothel here, in Basseterre."

Abdee admitted only one thing. "She has the face of a murderess." But he was wondering what he would do when he found her. And he knew that he would find her. Soon.

"Ah, but such a face!" Topper said, closing his eyes to picture it. "It is a map of hell."

Abdee asked, "Have you been to her brothel yourself?"

Topper laughed, his chins shaking like rain clouds already damp with moisture. "I am not so inclined, young man, I listen. But that is the extent of my pleasure. There are many, many men, though, who demand such perversities these days. And Naomi is an artist of the perverse, you realize, the chatelaine of physical torture. And, now, I am quite certain that she will even double her fare, basing the increase merely on the experience she has learned from the Dragonard Anglais."

Abdee chose not to discuss lessons. He asked, "But you know how to get to ... where is her establishment?"

"Don't you know?"

"Would I be asking you?" Abdee said. But, then, looking at Topper, watching the new expression twitching into formation on his fat face, Abdee said, "You realize, Topper, that often there is more than one side to a story."

"Are there two to this one?"

"If I listen long enough, I might even hear three!"

Wiping the perspiration from his chin with the top ruffs of his jabot, visibly excited by the possibility of further intrigues, Topper said, "I confess, the stories I have heard stop short once she reached your rooms."

"And I hope that that's all you're going to hear."

So, seeing that Abdee was adamant about keeping his privacy, Topper took a sip of punch now and said, "No, we must not waste too much of our time discussing the pastimes of black whores. But what intrigues me is the rare ingenuity in that particular African brain. It's very rare indeed." Turning to Abdee, Topper smacked his wet lips and said, "Who else but an extremely clever being like that would know that many Europeans have such guilty consciences about slavery? That our religious minds often beg out for penance for what we do? That, after mistreating field niggers all day, many white gentlemen are willing to leave their homes and families to creep on their knees to *Chez Naomi*! And they lay down money for it, too. Pay to be punished by that nigger and her retinue of cruel attendants. Ah, yes, what a creature of industry is a woman like that. I maintain that Naomi must be part white. No pure-blooded African could think so clearly. She must be, at least, a quadroon."

Abdee admitted, "Yes, she is clever. If it's true." He smiled, repeating, "If it's true."

"Oh, it's true. It's the secret of her success. And that

is why she obviously broke tradition by coming to you today. She seized upon the novelty of the moment. You. The Dragonard Anglais. The master of the day."

"You make it all sound very complimentary."

"Oh, but it is . . . Your Lordship."

Abdee froze.

And, beside him on the bench, Topper remained silent. Still. Waiting.

Turning to him, Abdee asked, "Yes, what about that?"

"Have we finished discussing nigger women?" Topper asked smugly.

"No games. Just tell me how you came to know my identity."

"Shall I begin with Morgan Saunders?"

The name surprised Abdee. He asked, "The London solicitor?"

"That is the man," Topper said, nodding.

"The shyster! He's mostly to blame for my father's ruination. It was Saunders who turned against Lord Sackville, too."

Topper said, "Then that seems to be as good a place as any for us to begin, doesn't it?"

A parchment scroll, tied with a grey ribbon, began the next phase of Abdee's relationship with Franklin Topper.

Momentarily leaving Naomi, the subject now shifted to Topper's ambitions, Abdee's past, and, ultimately, that scroll tied with grey.

Producing the rolled document from the pocket of his frock coat—but not opening it, merely holding it in his corpulent hands—Topper sipped at his cup of punch and began:

"Morgan Saunders is the only man who enjoys the singular honour of owing money to me! That is a detail I will not go into now but, due to that particular situation, Saunders pleaded that, as the Battle of Minden broke his clients, he, too, was near ruin. Then, in a letter to me—a letter I still have—he informed me that the heir of Wycliffe would be arriving in Basseterre on a certain German ship embarking from Liverpool. And I should look to him for my demands."

Abdee said, "You expect me to recognize a cock-eyed suggestion like that?"

Topper replied honestly, "Not really."

"And, even if I would, do you think that I have the means to follow it through?"

"No."

"Then why start with it then? Why even bring up that bastard's name?"

"Because you have something more than money which I can use. And, as times are not being particularly kind to you, I thought you might like to shed yourself of this, ah, particular burden."

"Name it."

It was then that Topper handed him the scroll tied with grey ribbon. He said, "I have already drawn up the agreement. You can read it to see what I tender. You will also see exactly what I expect from you."

Taking the document, Abdee slid back the ribbon. Then, slowly, he saw listed the three hundred kegs of rum. One hundred and seventy-five casks of brandy. Eighty-five hogshead of sack. And, for that, he would surrender his title—Earl of Wycliffe—to one Franklin Topper, Esquire.

"But this is madness," Abdee said, looking up from the document. "Pure madness. Trading spirits for the covenant of a title."

"Look more closely, my friend, and you will see that you receive land, too. Not much. But it would make you a man of certain property and with your wits, you will certainly build. And build fast!"

Abdee laughed now. Topper with his proposal was even more insane than the incident of Naomi. He said, "No, you misunderstand me. This is madness on *your* part. What on earth would you want with a title? Especially mine? It holds no seat in Parliament. There are no estates left. Nothing. Hell, it is not even strong enough to muster a few troops to help poor old George with all his trouble with the American colonials. If anything, you are bargaining for a millstone."

Bending his head, Topper began, "One man's torture is another man's . . ."

"Joy. Yes, I know. But, if it's torture you're after, pain, then go to *Chez Naomi* with the rest of them. Don't come to me!"

"So you *do* want to keep the title? You *do* want to remain the Earl of Wycliffe?"

"Not one bit. I hate it. I believe that men should be separated into ranks, yes. But not by titles. I believe in an hierarchy of strength. Not of inherited airs and foppish graces."

Topper's chins swung in pendulous folds as he held his head high, complaining, "You're just making excuses."

Banging his fist on the table, Abdee said, "God damn it! If I wanted to keep that stinking name, do you think I would have left home?"

Quickly pulling back his face, Topper mopped his forehead, gasping, "People have travelled incognito before! Perhaps . . ."

"Perhaps nothing!" Abdee shouted. He was in a rage now. "You sit here whining on the periphery of the civilized world, slobbering at people in coronets, envying them for being lords and earls and all that crap. And you probably think that they have that world laid out on their silver plates! But do you know what that world is, Mister Topper? No, I bet you haven't a clue. Not the slightest idea. Well, allow me to let you in on a few secrets, Mister Topper. Allow me to tell you about—" Abdee paused, his blue eyes blazing with anger, "—allow me to tell you about . . . Thornhurst, for instance!"

Lowering his handkerchief, Topper said, "I happen to know about Thornhurst. That's the name of your seat. Thornhurst is your home."

"No, you're wrong, Mister Topper. Thornhurst *was* my home," Abdee said, sitting sideways on the bench now, facing Topper. "But Thornhurst still could be my home if I had chosen to stay in Norfolk, chosen to bleed the tenant farmers to pay off the wolves. You see, Mister Topper, when a son inherits, he not only inherits his father's house and name, but he also inherits the debts. And that London solicitor, Saunders, was responsible for many of those debts. But the eighth Earl of Wycliffe—my father—must not rest in heavenly peace without accepting some of the blame. His compassion for mankind—one of the virtues that undoubtedly enabled him to enter into his eternal paradise—was also the reason why he left such a mess here on earth. My father died no better than a pauper, Mr. Topper. The estates were mortgaged. The house mortgaged. The silver and gold and jewels mortgaged. Nothing escaped. I tried, of course, to redeem as much as I could after he died, but then the battle got too much. The battle to cling to mortgaged properties. But the battle to survive, to live, to exist was not what conquered me. No, I could cope with that kind of struggling. Like I know the colour of my eyes, have learned my capacity for drink, how far I can pitch a stone, I also know my own strength. I know that I am a strong man. Not only with my arms and hands, but in will-power, too. I also know that people come to depend on me. I know, too, that I can sway opinion. Even bend another's dignity. I know that I do not think twice before kicking a man if he is already down. I also know that certain people are attracted to such power, place themselves at the mercy of someone who is stronger than they are. And I am a strong man, Mister Topper. But such strength does not include me battling for another man's values. For sacrificing *my* life for something I do not feel in *my* gut. And I soon realized that I did not feel my family inside my gut. Their values were frivolous to me. Shallow and hypocritical. My mother only worried about my dead father's good name. My *dead* father. What good would that do anybody? We had debts to pay! And my sister was constantly insisting on family tradition. Her! Too ugly—and too poor—to find a husband. But still she worried about 'the family'! It was all utter nonsense. While my mother lived, though, I kept battling for the smirched values of an aristocrat. But then, when she died—"

"And your sister, as well."

Abdee nodded, turning back to the table, staring at the cup of *taffa* in front of him. He did look alone. Without ties. Family nor friends.

His hair now hung like a golden helmet around his face. His lantern jaw was set in determination. His eyes, hard. But when he breathed—came to life—he looked like a young but tired Norman crusader, a young man who had just been freed from his chain armour, his body panting in relief from the burden.

Quietly, Abdee continued, "Yes, when they finally died, too, I saw that I was left fighting for someone whom I did not even know. For me. I was the sole heir. Alone. Me. The Earl of Wycliffe. Something I did not even believe. So, I said, let them have it all. Let the bloody creditors take everything. It was more theirs than mine, anyway. At least, they wanted it. Thornhurst. The estates. The tenants. The lot. It was only myself I wanted to worry about. Only me. Richard Abdee. I also said goodbye to the pale, young lady—a pleasant but totally vacuous young woman called Thorinda Clewes—whom I had even allowed myself to be betrothed to! Phlegmatic, rich Thorinda Clewes! But, then, when I didn't need her money to salvage Thornhurst Hall, why would I need her? For a wife? To give me heirs? No! A son who expects more than the light of day from me is no son of mine. I will sire strength or I will sire nothing. And strength only comes from inside a man and not from a title in front of a name. A man fights for himself. And as I fought for what I was led to believe was my birthright—a tradition—I will continue to fight. But this time it will be for myself. I will endure the same hardships, submit myself to the same labours, fight dirty, scrap like a dog, but this time for me. I would even consider again marrying a woman I do not love, a female to whom I am not even vaguely attracted if it means giving *me* what *I* want out of *my* life. Now, the Earl of Wycliffe is dead.

Has never existed. And for once—in terms of this world and this world only—death has given a man his life. Richard Abdee!"

Franklin Topper said, "So that is what brought you to St. Kitts?"

"Here? St. Kitts? *Sant Christophe*?" Abdee laughed, shaking his head. "No, not especially to this tropical nut-house. I just left England. I left with only the money for my passage and no plans in particular. Perhaps I haven't stopped yet. Perhaps I have."

Trying to generate some enthusiasm into Abdee, Topper said, "You might be well advised to give this lovely island a chance. There are many resources here for a young man with your stamina."

Abdee held up both hands. "Slow down! Stop! You don't have to sell this place to me, Mister Topper. You don't have to convince me to stay so you'll have an opportunity to get your hands on that, that, that *tawdry* gem you're after."

Topper tried to defend himself. The proposition.

But Abdee said, "I do wish you people would understand the shackles of the high life. The so-called 'court-circles'."

Topper retaliated in studied slowness. "You scorn the aristocracy. Go ahead. That is your prerogative. But, because you have been born into it, you have seen it first-hand. And, perhaps, I was expecting too much of you when I approached you with an invitation to understand my certain predicament." Pausing then, Topper lifted his head and, looking away from Abdee, he added, "I had no idea that you felt so harmed by your background."

"I was not harmed. Just delayed."

Holding his head high, Topper insisted, "No, no. There was no way for me to know your feelings. But perhaps I was a little to blame for not considering your age."

"What does age have to do with it?"

"You are evidently too young to understand what failure does to an old man's spirit."

"Failure?"

Topper nodded. His eyes were suddenly moist. He murmured, "I, too, have a family."

"And you approached me on their behalf?"

Topper managed a shrug.

"But how is one, tired, defunct, worthless title going to help anyone?"

"I have a sister."

"So?"

Topper's ruffled chest heaved as he tried to express reconsideration, to portray that he was having second thoughts about telling Abdee the story of his sister. Finally, he said, "Perhaps I was a fool even to open myself up to you. To plan. Hope."

"To be quite honest, Mister Topper, I would suspect anything that you told me. You are a clever old fox. You are probably as devious as Mistress Naomi."

"Belittle me if you want. Compare me to nigger whores. But the brandy, the rum, it is all in a warehouse for you to inspect, to confirm my integrity. Go see it with your own eyes."

Abdee smiled.

And, then, almost at the moment that Abdee had expected, Topper began to relate his story. He began to recount to Abdee how, as an ambitious young man, he had come to the West Indies. How he had struggled to build the South Sea Trading Company. How, first, bad health had hindered him. Then, next, the Spaniards buccaneered a cargo of cotton. He mumbled much, too, about his sister and how happy she would be to have her only living relative return to England with at least a small token of worldly success. Topper swore that theirs was not a noble family but it was one of the most honest which Plymouth had to offer.

Abdee finally interrupted him, saying, "Tell me, Fat Fox, where exactly is that warehouse where you keep your inventory?"

Topper's eyes lit up. He asked excitedly, "So you will accept?"

"I'm not saying that. Nor that I swallow the shameless melodrama of your story. But I will have a look at the warehouse."

Reaching for Abdee's hand, Topper said, "Fine! We will meet in The Circus at ten o'clock tomorrow morning. You can inspect my inventory and from there we can proceed directly to . . ."

"Slow down! One step at a time!" Abdee said, pulling away from Topper. "It's a long time between now and tomorrow morning. Also, there's another little piece of information I want you to give me."

Holding up the scroll, Topper said, "Everything is set down in here."

"No, no. It is not about the trade. It's the name of a street you mentioned. Where Naomi's house is."

"Barracks Lane?"

Patting Topper on the shoulder, Abdee said, "Yes, you just point me in the direction of Barracks Lane, Old Fox, and we'll take care of tomorrow when the time comes."

Abdee rose from the bench now.

Topper followed, the scroll held firmly in his hand.

Abdee had no difficulties in finding his way to Barracks Lane once Topper had told him on which end of the *quai* to find it.

It was late night now.

And a stillness lay over this decaying neighbourhood, a lull broken only by the faraway barking of a dog and the steady pounding of the surf.

From the round glow of the moon, Abdee could see that most of the houses on Barracks Lane were wooden, flat-roofed, with small *porterres* between the porches and the cobbled streets. A few of those garden-plots had iron railings. Even less were planted with flowers and shrubs.

The narrow street was deserted. Abdee saw none of the inhabitants, nor the male clients who were supposedly flocking to *Chez Naomi*.

So, to obtain his specific directions now, he was considering knocking on the door of a house lit from within. But, suddenly, he heard a rush of loud music begin behind him. He stopped in the middle of the cobbled road, listening as someone began to strum a guitar. The music was coming from a three-storied house. And Abdee recognized the sharp, staccato rhythm as being Spanish. Then as the guitarist began to chord loudly, Abdee heard a voice rise. It was a woman's voice, coarse and throaty, and the song sounded to Abdee like the wailings of the Andalusia district of Spain.

Turning toward this bleak-looking house, shuttered, showing no light nor sign of life, Abdee opened an iron gate and walked up six wooden steps. Knocking on the weatherworn door, he listened as the music grew louder, cutting the night's stillness like a serrated blade.

Thinking that his knock had been drowned by the guitarist, Abdee reached toward the door again.

But the door slowly began to open. And Abdee soon found himself looking down at a pretty white girl dressed in a low-cut, violet gown. She looked no older than eighteen; her flaxen hair was pulled back from her cherubic face, but the girl's pallor hinted at what kind of a sheltered life she led behind this locked door.

She asked in an impatient, clipped voice, "Have you got your times right?"

Abdee explained, "I'm looking for a Naomi."

The young girl lowered her eyes to study Abdee, appraising the cost of his clothing rather than to note details of his physique. She asked, "You been here before?"

"This is Naomi's?"

Raising her empty, green eyes, the girl asked, "Who sent you?"

"This is Naomi's?" Abdee repeated, glancing for the first time past the girl, studying the hallway behind her.

Unlike the drab exterior of the three-storied house, the inside was bright and had the gloss of prosperity. The blue velvet walls shimmered with the glow from the crystal sconces. Rich, Oriental carpets covered the floor and lavish curtains hung from walnut arches on either side of the hallway. The archway to the girl's right, though, was closed. And it was from behind those gold curtains that the music and wailing exploded. But the archway to the girl's left was open and a china lamp flickered inside on a shawl-draped table. And between that room and a closed door behind the girl, a mahogany stairway led to the upper floors.

At this moment, the girl turned her head and called "Callie?"

The music continued.

So, holding her head toward the closed curtains on the archway to her right, she called louder, *"Callie?"*

A second female appeared. She was Callie, a Negress not much older than the white girl, but who held herself with much more authority. Her skin was a shiny, midnight blue and she wore a towering, yellow wig of small ringlets—a French court wig—which looked stark, even eccentric against her dark complexion. At the lower, left-corner of her mouth glistened a red beauty patch, also an incongruous colour to the rest of her deep pigmentation.

But it was Callie's large, voluptuous breasts which held Abdee's eyes. Her over-generous bosom rested high and full behind the lacy confines of the black corset which she wore. When Abdee lowered his eyes, he saw her waist pulled tight by the whalebones of the black satin corset, and her long, shapely legs covered with indigo webbed stockings which made a vague pattern against the similar blue-blackness of her thighs, knees, calves. Apart from her emerald green slippers, the only other bit of adornment which Callie wore was a tuft of black netting which billowed from the pert roundness of her buttocks.

Above the guitar playing and the singing which still poured from behind the drawn curtains, the white girl said to Callie, "He wants to see Mistress."

Coldly scrutinizing Abdee, Callie announced, "Mistress occupied!"

Abdee moved forward.

But so did Callie, to block Abdee from entering into

the house. "I said—" she paused to add the regulation
title "—Sir, that Mistress is occupied!"

"Then I'll wait."

She answered, "You be waiting a long time—Sir!"

Abdee smiled, looking down at her breasts, watching
the two unfathomable black reservoirs of skin heaving,
rising in defiance to him.

But then, the next thing that Abdee saw was Callie's
saucy swagger, her train of black net switching back
and forth as she walked toward the closed draperies.
She disappeared inside. And, then, when the music
suddenly stopped, and the singing, Abdee asked the
white girl, "Am I disturbing some kind of party?"

She ignored the question.

Abdee began wondering, then, what role this white
girl played in a Negress's bordello. Did Naomi employ
her as something for all tastes?

But, at that moment, the gold damask curtains parted
and Callie came back into the hallway. And, behind
her walked a tall and powerfully built young Negro
male.

This third person—a bull in a house ruled by females, an employee whom Abdee surmised was the
bodyguard—was not much older than the two girls.
But he was lighter skinned than Callie and his hair was
closely cropped to his head, forming a snug skull-cap
of black wool. He wore a white shirt which could not
hide the muscular width of his shoulders. And his shirt
was opened to the waist, neatly tucked into the red sash
encircling his trim proportions. Barefooted, the sturdy
youth wore clinging white trousers which stopped at the
middle of his bulging calves, fitting his legs and hips
more like a tight pair of unrestricting small-clothes than
outer breeches.

Also, he was obviously the musician whom Abdee
had heard. In his left hand, he held a shiny black guitar.

Abdee asked him, "Where did you learn to play
Spanish guitar, my friend?"

The broad-shouldered boy suddenly grinned, his

wide mouth flashing with white ivory. His black eyes narrowed, softening with merriment, as he answered, "Not Spanish, Sir. Portuguese! Mistress buys me from Portuguese Master in Brazil."

Abdee asked, "Your mistress is Naomi?"

At the mention of Naomi's name, the young buck looked quickly at Callie.

Nodding her yellow court wig, Callie said sharply, "Wants to see Mistress."

The young man wrinkled his brow. He shrugged amiably. He could see no problem.

But Callie did. She said angrily, "He ain't seeing Mistress because we don't know him from . . ." She continued in mumbles.

As the boy answered Callie—also in mumbles—Abdee realized that he was not opposed to the idea of him joining Naomi. The girls were the ones protecting their mistress. The females operated the barricade at this bordello.

The boy was motioning toward the closed draperies now, arguing louder with Callie. "But I got Master Scott in there. Josephine and Miss Juanita waiting for me, too. Master Scott pays plenty. He might take all night but he pays enough for all week. So *you* goes to Mistress and lets me do the job she tells me to do." Then, looking from Callie to the white girl, he said, "Or let Clover go see." His voice was soft even when he was impatient.

The white girl—Clover—nodded at the closed door behind her. She said, "I'm downstairs now. And you better be there pretty soon yourself."

But he insisted, "We got Mister Scott to finish first."

"Stop your arguing!" Callie said irritably, throwing up her hands. Then, turning, she walked petulantly toward the stairs. And, as she began to mount them— her round buttocks chewing under her black net tail, her yellow wig swaying with each step upwards—she called, "Sit the gentleman in the parlour, Clover."

Then, Callie disappeared.

51

And the Negro boy grinned at Abdee as he slowly backed toward the gold damask curtains.

And Clover pointed toward the room on the left, the room beyond the open arch where Abdee was supposed to wait.

Across the hallway, then, the guitar began strumming again. The only accompaniment to the music now was a light tapping, paddling, spanking of hands. Four hands? Josephine and Miss Juanita? Against bare skin? Mister Scott's naked body? Abdee did not know. He did not sit long enough to hear because Callie returned in a few minutes and coldly informed Abdee to follow her upstairs. As he quietly walked behind up the carpeted stairs, he kept his eyes on her hips, slowly undulating as she climbed toward Naomi's room.

Pausing at a door at the top of the stairs, Callie crooked a finger and rapped on the door.

Then, opening the door, she held it back for Abdee to enter.

But, inside the room, instead of seeing Naomi—as he had expected—Abdee saw a man: standing against the plum-coloured curtains across the bedroom, he saw the back of a tall, slim British officer. He was dressed in a full-collared, red and blue uniform with gold epaulets. He wore a hat.

Behind Abdee, the door closed. Callie was gone.

And, before Abdee had time to speak, the man in the uniform slowly began to turn, saying slowly, "If it wasn't for the impression you made on my recruiting officer, I wouldn't let you even lick . . ."

But then the officer stopped.

And Abdee saw that it was not an officer, a man at all.

Yes, it was Naomi.

And when she saw Abdee, her arms flew up over her head, her voice raised two octaves, and she screamed with delight, "Master, sir!"

"Lucretia Borgia," Abdee said calmly.

Naomi tore off her hat and flung it to the large, carved oak bed.

And, looking around at the gold satin walls of her bedroom, Abdee asked, "Where's all your customers? I was told there would be men lining the streets here tonight. But it's quiet as a grave down there."

"Quiet?" Naomi said, stepping toward him with long, deep stalks. "Quiet? You must be crazy, man! There's a 'motif of correction' going on in the cellar. A *musicale* on the ground floor. And when Nero's finished with that—Nero's the boy who convinced Callie to let you in."

"And I take it that Nero's also your 'recruiting officer'."

Naomi shrugged in good sport. "So what if I made a mistake? So what if you weren't a whitie coming to serve under me? That still doesn't mean we're not busy. When Nero is finished with Master Scott, he going down to the cellar, too, and start our *pièce de resistance*. Tonight we're staging 'The Rape of the Sabine Women.' Some of you white men love to see our big black boys plugging your pale, helpless little girlies!"

Abdee's vendetta was fastly disappearing. Yes, Naomi was no ordinary whore at all! He liked all this ingenuity. He said, "And so that's why you keep the white girl, Clover?"

Naomi threw back her head and laughed. It was the same, glass-shattering outburst that Abdee remembered. She said, "No, in our little theatrics, Clover isn't Clover. We sit her in a chair and call her 'Lady Alicia Busby.' Then, you see, a slave breaks in and rapes her right there on her needlepoint. Cruel and heartless, yes! But . . ." Naomi paused and began pulling off the white kidskin gloves she had been wearing with the uniform.

Turning to Abdee again—wiggling those long, slim fingers in the air—she said, "But if you still think it's quiet here tonight, let me tell you about what's happening on this floor. Next door we have a high-ranking official peeling potatoes. Under duress, you understand. And next to him, we have—"

But Abdee stopped her. "Where's the cashier? That's what I've come to see."

She looked at him.

Abdee explained. "My money."

"Ah!" she cried, throwing up her chin to unbutton the top of her jacket. "Is that the only reason you've come to see me?"

Abdee was silent. He watched her work her way down the brass buttons.

Moving toward him now, she said, "Maybe I'll pay *you* this time."

He answered, "I don't think I'll be able to put on as good a show as you did . . . '*Master Sir, I have seven suckers so far, Master Sir.*'"

Naomi threw back her head and laughed at his imitation of her.

Reaching toward her unbuttoned jacket now, feeling that she was naked and warm underneath, Abdee said, "Tell me one thing now. Why did you want to fleece me?"

"You are the Dragonard!"

"And that's your speciality here, too? At *Chez Naomi?*"

"For the whities."

"What am I?"

Pressing herself up to him, she said, "I told you once."

"You told me a lot of lies once."

"I wasn't lying when I said you're nothing but a white nigger."

"And I still think you're a black bitch."

"Have you ever stayed all night in a bitch's whore house?"

"Not a black one."

"I don't smell like a pig anymore, do I . . . Master Sir?"

"No. But what did you do with the slave's dress?"

"Keeping it for a souvenir."

"And what about my money pouch?"

"Filled it with red ants and tied it around a white man's pecker."

"I believe it."

"You kicked me, too. I still have the bruises from you kicking me out of your room."

"Show me."

"Only if I get to kick *you* this time ... Master Sir."

"I don't play that way."

"Then don't kick."

"I like to."

"I do, too. But only customers. And you're not a customer anymore. You're company. So don't go kicking your hostess. And easy on the slaps, too."

"Okay, it's a bargain. But just with you."

"The same for me. No kicking you ... dirty white man."

"Nigger."

"Hey, watch it! It's 'Mistress!' "

"And I'm master."

"Me, too."

"Both of us?"

"Together," she agreed.

And they fell onto her large, carved bed and stayed there all night. Their bodies together were like the white reefs over porous black stone—shifting, raising, settling.

3

The Pearl of Manchester

Events in the next few days moved without a hitch and Abdee knew that he was once again on the trail of his prey—a new world for himself.

This feeling of rebirth was due partially to his repeated visits to *Chez Naomi*. The two of them had much in common. But Abdee also credited Franklin Topper for helping him realize his ideals, too.

Before meeting Topper at Government House to finalize the documents of the agreement, Abdee went with him to the warehouse behind Pall Mall where Topper kept his inventory.

In one end of the cavernous freestone building rested the modest remains of what was to have been The South Sea Trading Company. But even among the cobwebs of his past, Topper's spirits were buoyant. No longer did he blubber or wail about his bad luck, misadventures, or underprivileged relatives. Instead, he walked briskly between the rows of barrels and casks, smartly tapping them with his cane. "This is yours. And this. And this." All remorse for his lost ambitions in the West Indies had vanished completely, and, once again, he was the proud, arrogant fluffed individual whom Abdee had first met on The Circus.

Abdee carefully sampled both the brandy and rum at the warehouse, but left the sack untasted. He felt that only anaemic women and fools drank sack and they did not know what they were consuming anyway. But finding the other two spirits of a satisfactory qual-

56

ity, he went next with Topper to the north end of the island on an inspection of the property.

And, still, Abdee was hopeful. Although the land was small and marshy—not exceeding fifty acres—Abdee visualized how it could be drained, planted, or leased to one of the adjoining estates, or . . .

There were many things which Abdee could do with this land. For the moment, though, he and Topper rode back to Basseterre and paid the long awaited visit to Government House. Then, alone, Abdee returned to the warehouse to mark two barrels of rum as the source of immediate revenue to trade with the landlord of the Lucky Seven for larger quarters. Next, he bought himself a roan mare which he called "Irish," not only for its reddish colour, but also because of the way it pleasantly nudged its head against your shoulder but—as soon as it snuggled in closely—would suddenly nip at you with strong white teeth.

Then, finally, outfitting himself in a new suit of clothing, boots of the same fine black leather as Irish's saddle, Abdee paid yet another call at Government House, this time to resign officially his post as the Dragonard.

Secretary Cranwell was not alone when Abdee was led into his office. A woman sat in a high-backed chair across from Cranwell's writing table. Abdee noticed that she was European, slim, about his same age, and not as attractive as she obviously imagined herself to be. Nor as genteel. He could not tell exactly what it was but something about her was common.

Cranwell was still holding Abdee's hand in his own when he said, "Let me present Mrs. Warburton. Her husband is one of Basseterre's leading attorneys-at-law."

Bowing her yellow bonnet, Mrs. Warburton held out her mitted hand and said, "Arabella Warburton, Mister Abdee."

Returning the bow—but not the familiarity—Abdee turned to Cranwell and said, "No one told me you were in conference."

Cranwell showed no signs of pomposity today. More than ever, he was Abdee's servant. Also, he wore a cleaner white coat which, Abdee suspected, was in honour of his lady visitor. Flourishing his lace handkerchief, Cranwell said, "But this is no conference, Mister Abdee. Mrs. Warburton drops in for a *tête-à-tête*, whenever she comes down from Warburton Fields."

Abdee nodded again at the English woman but she still did not strike him as being overly attractive. Her nose was too sharp; the eyes, like a bird. But she held her heavily-lidded eyes half-closed like a smouldering beauty.

"Perhaps I should come back later," Abdee said.

"Oh, Mister Abdee, you *must* do that!" Cranwell exclaimed, his Adam's apple rising in his throat. "But I know why you are here today!"

Abdee looked at him.

"Of course," Cranwell said, but signalled quickly in the direction of Arabella Warburton with his eyes, implying that matters such as the Dragonard were not to be discussed in front of a lady. "And I am most glad! But whatever you decide to do—and wherever—I wish you the best of luck."

From behind them, Arabella Warburton asked in a thin, crystal-like voice, "Are you planning to leave Basseterre, Mister Abdee?"

Abdee answered that he did not know what his plans involved at the present.

Staring at him, she said, "You must stay. We on St. Kitts welcome all the society which comes our way."

Abdee nodded the third time. He assured Arabella Warburton that he hoped to see both her *and* Mister Warburton. Then, after bidding goodbye to Secretary Cranwell, he promptly left the room, hoping never to see either of them again. His days of maggots were hopefully over.

Now, if Abdee wanted work, he had his brandy to sell, his land to develop.

If he felt lustful, there was Naomi. She was good for some conversation, too.

But if he wanted more physical veneries, there were the other girls at *Chez Naomi*. Although Abdee and Naomi had agreed on a pact of not domineering one another, she had put all her girls at his beck and call. And mercy.

But why did he like violent sex, love-making which often became a torment for the female? Naomi also asked him if he, perhaps, actually hated women?

"Do you hate men?" Abdee asked her. "You play master to them."

"I did hate every *white* man," she confessed. "But now that I know you—"

And, so, they laughed, leaving it at that: to be physically supreme in sex was maybe only a test for them to be physically supreme in all the other aspects of life.

In the meantime, though, Abdee concentrated on the island, how to stay alive and free on St. Kitts. His desire was not merely to exist here, to eke out a humble living. He wanted to put himself in one of the island's palaces.

But Abdee's childhood at Thornhurst, his struggling years as a young adult, had more than satisfied, even satiated any desire he would ever feel for a domain, a patriarchal seat. Abdee now truly believed that men must exist for themselves alone. And like their lives, men's houses must be seized like a pirate's plunder. You are as good as the glitter in your buccaneer's coffers.

Morning after morning, Abdee saddled Irish at the break of dawn, when the mist still clung to the island's conical peaks, and he rode off alone, peering through the dew-laden hedges of scarlet poinsettias at the homes of the so-called aristocracy. But they were merely men distinguished by the money which they made from this soil. Still deep in their luxurious feather-beds at these early hours, the men grew fatter—and more vulnerable—while only their house Negroes busied themselves. And the African fieldhands sluggishly trod from their wattle huts behind the main house, moving over the gentle hills like rows of half-frozen black ants.

From the Great Salt Lake in the south of the island—the tail of the fish—to Dieppe Bay in the north, Abdee and Irish roamed without care. Later, much later in his life, Abdee would remember these early, foot-loose days on St. Kitts as the most peaceful and satisfactory hours in his life. They were days full of anticipation and hope, a time when all the world was there for the taking. His financial resources were still very slim. But, cantering along the quiet roads in the soft morning light, Abdee's mind grew suddenly excited with, yes! The plan for the roadhouse he might open with his capital in bartered rum and ale. That would be his beginning! Or, slowly, as he was reaching the base of Mt. Misery, he would let his eyes slowly raise up the slope of the dormant volcano and rest on the lifeless grey barricades of the Slave Market. There stood the *vendue* where that black flesh was bought and sold. Not servants but slaves. And in auctions or by sales of scramble, people paid hundreds of pounds, dollars, and francs for living and breathing flesh. As Irish quickened his steps, Abdee rode on, still intrigued by the markets on Mt. Misery. The world was his for the beguiling. He knew that he could do it, even if he were a black man.

Past Mt. Misery, Abdee began to see the large, pristine manor houses standing proudly on the graceful slopes overlooking their cane fields. He still knew nothing of the actual work involved in sugar planting—not yet—but he stared in interest at the windmills which crushed the cane and then back to the house which profited from that wealth. He virtually itched to be a part of it.

He passed tall, mock-Greek columns standing guard like brave sentinels over the glittery Caribbean.

He saw discreet but rambling homes built in the new Georgian-style, commanding acres and acres of land, hundreds of slaves.

And, through rich walls of flamboyants and bougainvillea, Abdee caught glimpses of homes with minarets and cupolas like those on an Eastern temple. But all the property of some man probably not much different than himself. If as good.

One of the finest homes on the entire island belonged to the estate which joined Abdee's small piece of property. It was called "Petit Jour," and was owned by a Frenchman. And, so far, that was all that Abdee knew about the house—or the man and his wife—that they were French, moved in a small circle of the island elite, and the house was named "Petit Jour."

These early days on St. Kitts, Abdee also spent much time by the sea. But he avoided the long, deserted blankets of sand along the coasts, or the beaches curled into secret coral crescents within the many, hidden inlets. Instead, Abdee's fascination was directed to the harbour of Basseterre. It was there, on the *quai*, where the activity boiled.

Every day of every week, new ships arrived out of nowhere to pour a cargo before the townspeople's eyes. But the slavers, fresh from their middle voyage, standing like tall, horned insects beyond the harbour, were the most intriguing of all for him.

From those haunting slavers, messengers rowed into the harbour, seeking reports if they should stop here in Basseterre: was the market glutted with slaves? Should they sail onward to Barbados? Puerto Rico? New Orleans? Or, perhaps the messengers brought news that there was a plague aboard the slaver, that only a remnant of the original cargo was still alive. On a good day, though, the shore bell would ring and slowly, the slaver creaked townward and the frightened Africans—chained to each other in twos—were led onto this new land, carted off to Mt. Misery where their skins would be rubbed with palm oil to a bright ebony. Their teeth polished like ivory. Then, they would wait for the prying, probing fingers of the white men who came with an eye from which nothing escaped. And, more often than not, these white men came not to buy, but just to inspect, examine, study, squeeze.

But this one particular afternoon, there was no slaver in the harbour of Basseterre. The vessel which the townspeople had collected to see was a galleon preparing to sail for England. Her name was "The Pearl of Manchester" and her cargo was raw sugar and indigo. Also, a handful of her passengers were returning on her to their homeland.

Among the travellers was a stout man who had dressed himself so richly in silks and brocades that more perspiration than usual poured down his fat cheeks and dripped from his chins. In one hand, he held a silver-handled cane of malacca. From the other swung a green parrot in a wicker cage. The straw cases and hampers standing around him were all clearly marked: *The Earl of Wycliffe, Plymouth.*

"I suppose I should feel sad about leaving this place," Topper said, fanning himself with his new purple silk tricorn. "I arrived here thirty years ago and all this was French." He motioned to the brighly coloured houses built down to the banquettes of the harbour.

Smiling, Abdee contradicted him. "Thirty years ago, Fat Fox, this was still English." He had grown fonder of Topper over the last few weeks but he still refused to let him embellish on the truth. His clothes, yes. But fact, never.

Fluffing the two curls of his new tie-wig, Topper snapped, "What do you know? You were not even born thirty years ago?" Then, plopping the tricorn back onto his head, Topper mumbled about the inferiority of provincial wig-makers. He had asked specifically for a "Cadogan."

"It seems to me that the Fat Fox can not wait to get away from his beloved island paradise?"

Reaching for a lace handkerchief in the fashionably low-placed pocket of his frockcoat, Topper mopped his forehead and said, "Only because of you, dear boy, only because of you staying behind to carry on my tradition. It is like leaving the South Sea Company in the hands of a capable son."

"Don't take offence, Fat Fox, but I doubt if I will live out my days here as a trader."

Glancing around for the flunkeys to carry his luggage aboard—the wig-maker had caused his delay—Topper said disinterestedly, "I have had such little time to listen to your plans, dear boy. You are always dashing here, dashing there. And when I do see you, if you are not tasting some rum to see that I am not swindling you, then you are sulking. No, you must really develop your sense of humour, dear boy. Look toward the lighter things in life if you want to survive."

"I leave the joviality to you." And now it was Abdee's turn to add: "Your Lordship!"

"You do think I am silly, don't you? Secretly? Confess it."

"On the contrary . . . I thought it was quite obvious that I have always thought you were a fool."

"You don't mean that!"

"I do. But I also think that you have schemes in your head that even you aren't aware of. But, don't fear, I'll never come looking for you. I'll never regret the day that you took that burden off *my* back."

"To you it was a burden," Topper said, looking again for the carriers. "But I must confess that I have been seriously thinking of going into politics when I get back to England. Lord Wilberforce is making quite a name for himself, so why shouldn't I?"

Throwing back his head, Abdee laughed. "You do have a better sense of humour than me, Foxy. Politics! Wilberforce!"

"What's so funny about that? He's causing a stir and he doesn't even know horse beans about the Africans."

Shaking his head, Abdee said, "Here. I don't want to keep you from your destiny." Bending to lift one of Topper's hampers, he said, "I will give you a hand with these."

But Topper's malacca cane came cracking down against the hamper. "No! You forget that you are a white man. If you are going to amount to anything here—anything—you must remember who does the work."

"What happened to Wilberforce?" Abdee asked.

"Wilberforce is in England. You are here."

Sobering, Abdee said, "So that is the rule, then, is it? Who does the work?"

Topper was adamant. "That is the rule."

Abdee looked him coldly in the eye, saying, "Perhaps that is one of the reasons you never got the South Sea Company off the ground. You had that damned idea of colour in your head. The whites and the blacks. Who does the lifting and who does not."

Annoyed, Topper again doffed his tricorn and said, "You sound just like Geoff Shanks!"

"Who?"

"My partner, Captain Geoffrey Shanks. He had the same attitude, too. Work, work, work. Everybody works. Nigger, whiteman, Chinese."

"You never told me you had a partner."

"If Shanks had lived, he would have been just one more item on your list of acquisitions—three hundred casks of rum, fifty acres of land, and one not-so-good English sea captain."

"You had a partner in the South Sea Company?"

"God rest his soul."

"How long ago was this?"

Flicking his cobweb of lace, Topper said, "Now, don't get that killer look in your eyes, Abdee. There is nothing to worry about. He was written out five years ago at least. He sailed from here a good decade ago and some Dutch sailor returned two years after that with the sad news—tut, tut—that Captain Geoff got himself chopped up during one of the raids on the Gold Coast."

"And what exactly was a partner of yours doing on the Gold Coast? The South Sea Company didn't have a hand in the slave trade, too?"

"Don't look so optimistic, Mister Abdee. It wasn't a hand. It was more like a finger. One tiny, little finger. But, if Shanks would have stayed here where he be-

longed and helped me develop the exporting side of the
company, he would have never got the axe. But he was
always the adventurer, the stubborn old swine, and so
serves him right if the savages made a stew out of
him." Looking anxiously around, Topper said, "Curse
those lazy niggers. Don't they know who I am!"

But Abdee pursued the subject of Geoffrey Shanks.
"You do know for certain, though, that he's dead?"

"Of course I know for certain. Do you think a man
would stay away from his rightful due for five long
years?"

"If that man was, say, being held prisoner, yes, he
might."

Now it was Topper's turn to laugh. "In Africa? A
white man held prisoner in Africa? You dear, silly,
naïve boy. In Africa, the savages don't 'keep' people
prisoner. If prisoners are kept too long in that heat they
spoil. The Africans *cook* them while they are still fresh.
They *eat* them. By now, poor old Geoff Shanks is probably nothing but some shrivelled hunk of nigger turd,
rolled into a brick, holding up some hougan's hut."

Narrowing his eyes, Abdee said, "Mister Topper, if
you weren't such a big, fat, soft, sonofabitch, I would
smash you right in the face."

Holding himself aloft, Topper said, "May I ask you
why . . . and, please, in the future, kindly refer to me
with the correct title."

"For not telling that you had a partner, Your Lordship."

"You must stop being such an alarmist, dear boy.
You have not inherited a partner, so that is that. Geoff
Shanks is dead, I tell you, DEAD!"

Finally, the roustabouts came to carry Topper's belongings.

And, as Topper began waddling up the gang-plank,
the bird swinging from his arm, he called over his
shoulder to Abdee, "And then there's America, too."

"Captain Shanks could be in America?" Abdee
called.

Continuing up the incline, Topper said, "No, no,

dear boy. Shanks is dead. I'm talking about me. I might make my mark in America. I understand that English titles command great respect in the south!"

"You had better change ships!"

"The Atlantic has been conquered, Mister Abdee. We traverse it at will," Topper said, and then disappeared into *The Pearl of Manchester.*

Standing alone on the wharf, Abdee thought: Is it strange that I have never thought about America for myself?

Maybe he would go there some day.

But, turning toward the tall, narrow, white buildings which crowded the *quai,* he was determined to try his luck here first.

4

Petit Jour

Contentment—a shifting, changing, suspicious contentment, but contentment all the same—came over Abdee in the days following Topper's departure.

He still visited *Chez Naomi* but his appearances there were becoming less frequent. The organization of a bawdy house was losing its appeal. And, lately, most of Naomi's time went into organizing her theatrical evenings, the dramatic orgies held in her cellar.

Naomi tried to coax Abdee to take part in her midnight exhibitions. But Abdee refused. Flatly. He had his new life to discover.

He was spending his time now in the *quai*-side taverns, cultivating a taste for *taffa*.

He went frequently, too, to the cock fights on Cayon Street and seldom lost.

And, as another part of his immersion into the locale, Abdee asked around the island and found that he had enough stock to open that roadhouse which he had imagined on those early morning rides around the island.

But something was the matter with the roadhouse plan. He felt that there was something bigger for him to do, another way in which he could take advantage of St. Kitts.

One afternoon, when the rest of the population was asleep from their midday meal, Abdee was riding Irish along a dusty road shaded by drooping palmettos. The air was thick and heavy, perfumed by the orange blossoms. When Abdee reached the gate post of the French estate, Petit Jour, he decided that he would lie down and take a snooze himself. This was his boundary, too.

His breeches clung to his thighs with perspiration as he dismounted and, tying Irish's reins to a naseberry bush, he unbuttoned his shirt as he began looking for a suitable napping spot.

But, first, he decided to have one more look up at that Frenchman's house.

Sauntering over to the locked but unguarded wrought-iron gates of Petit Jour, Abdee saw the road gracefully climb up a hill toward the white mansion which perched atop the green knoll. Both the front and the sides of Petit Jour were lined with a double tier of columned porches. Fan-topped windows ran the length of the house and, on the roof, eight peaked windows ran along the yellow slate roof like points on a diamond tiara set upon golden hair. The magnificent house looked brilliant and aloof to Abdee. Set high on the knoll about the lay of the entangled jungle, Petit Jour seemed virginal, protected, unsullied by the rest of the life on St. Kitts. It was the house he saw in his sleep. The plunder. But, as Petit Jour seemed so unattainable, it came to him lately only in anxious nightmares.

Despondent again, Abdee moved slowly along the iron and stone fence which bordered the two properties, looking inside for any signs of life at Petit Jour. But he saw nothing. Not even a house slave scurrying in the yard. The house was too well-maintained, though, to be abandoned. But when Abdee had continued to make enquiries in town about the owners of Petit Jour, no one ever seemed able to tell him more than what he had learned before. That they were French. They moved in a small, select circle of friends. And that in French, Petit Jour meant "twilight."

Twilight, Abdee thought as he plodded through the thick foliage. To him, the house looked more like a big burst of sunshine.

By now, he had wandered deeper into the wilderness. The stone and iron fence continued to guard the property of Petit Jour from any intruders. And, by now, Abdee was knee deep in the marsh of his own property.

Overhead, he heard the jeering of a cockatoo. Then, as he moved deeper into the green, a parrot shrilled at him.

The bastards are laughing at me, Abdee thought, laughing at the way I'm gawking like such a fool at that Frenchman's house.

Disgusted, he turned back to the road.

Suddenly, though, another sound broke the hot stillness.

Abdee stopped to listen more closely.

But, now he heard nothing. When he looked overhead, all he could see were those tree-top red flowers, the Flame of the Forest.

Thinking that he had just imagined a noise—or that he had heard a bird which now had flown—he continued to slush back to where he had left Irish chomping on some blossoms.

But he heard the noise again.

Listening, he distinctly recognized the noise now as singing. People singing some kind of a song.

Moving back into the tangle of lianas, Abdee began to hear a certain pattern to the words of their song. But the words were not English. Then, remembering that—of course—the owners of Petit Jour were French, he listened to hear if it was a French song they were singing. But, as the words became clearer, Abdee could clearly hear that what they sang was neither French nor English. But he was certain of one thing, though: the afternoon songsters were either women or children. Perhaps even both.

Cautiously, he moved past some ceiba trees to listen more closely.

Then, suddenly through a curtain of drooping willows, he saw the party. There were four. A white woman and three young Negresses. The white woman was seated on a rattan chair in a mossy clearing and, at her feet, were gathered the three black girls who could not have been more than eighteen or nineteen years old. The skirts of their gingham dresses were spread out around them on the soft, mossy grass like petals of huge flowers. With their heads lowered, the three black girls traced the words in a small black book as they sang:

Tan-tum-er-go-sac-ra-men-tum . . .

Of course! It was Latin. The European woman was teaching them a Popist song. She was a Roman Catholic. French. And those were her maids. Her slave girls. But, as Abdee studied the three Negresses, they began to look more like chocolate angels dressed in yellow, blue and pink candy frocks. His mouth watered, and he became aware of the movement inside his perspiration-soaked breeches. Now, he was standing so close to them that he could see the intricate designs into which the girls had plaited their black hair. And, struggling with the Latin words, they used their full breasts as stands for their hymnals.

Abdee next studied the white woman herself and saw that, although she was older than the black girls—even older than himself, she must have been in her early thirties—she was none-the-less attractive. But it was the black skin which immediately tempted Abdee and he imagined rolling with one—or all three of them—right there on that soft grass. The white woman was too reserved-looking for that. And, although Abdee was not usually attracted to handsome and so-called "older" women, he conceded to her the honour of being one of the most beautiful of that particular breed. Her soft, blonde hair was delicately curled and pulled softly back from her smooth face. Her eyes were large, perfectly placed on either side of her fine nose. And the yellow of her silk dress was not bright enough to be gay— nothing like the brilliant hues which the black girls wore—but hers was soft, elegant and befitting to the regal way she held herself in the rattan chair. By the arm of her chair, rested a white parasol which, he guessed, was to protect her smooth, ivory skin from the sun. He wanted her, too. But she was to be conquered. Not necessarily enjoyed.

At that moment, the French woman lifted her soft eyes from her hymnal and spotted Abdee standing behind the curtain of willows.

She let her eyes linger on him—as if she was not certain if she were looking at a real person, or merely seeing an apparition—but then she held one hand out to the girls.

In a soft voice, she called, "Bonjour, Monsieur!"

"Excuse me," Abdee said, parting a way for himself through the paradisiac branches.

"Ah! You are English," she said.

"Yes. But please do not let me disturb you."

"Did you perhaps stray from the main road, Monsieur?" she asked, looking at his muddy black boots. Then, raising her eyes, she unavoidably lingered on the crotch of his breeches which still clung to him. And when she did raise her eyes, they only got as far as the last button of his opened shirt.

"No," Abdee answered as he watched her quickly grab for the gold crucifix around her neck. Then, reaching to button his shirt, so she would not think that he was going to rush out and rape her, he said, "You must be the mistress of Petit Jour."

More collected now, she answered, "It belongs to my . . . husband."

"Your husband?"

She answered quickly, to dispel any doubts. "*Oui.* Pierre Jubiot."

Bowing, Abdee said, "Excuse me for disturbing you like this, Madam Jubiot."

Firmer now, she said, "You did not answer my question, Monsieur. Have you lost your way from the road?"

"Oh, but I did answer you, Madame," he said. "No. I have not lost my way."

Sitting rigid in the chair, she said, "Perhaps, then, you were looking for my . . . husband?" She said it like a threat. Polite, but a threat.

"Nor was I looking for your husband, Madame Jubiot. I was merely looking at my new property," he said, motioning at the untamed wilderness behind him.

"The swamp?" she blurted. But, then, quickly checking herself, she added more softly, "That is our name for the land."

"A good name, too, Madame. It's nothing more than a swamp, is it?"

Much more genteel now, she said, "But I am certain that Monsieur has great plans for the land if he has bought it. Something no one else has realized."

Staring at her straight in the sapphire eyes, he said, "You can be sure of that, Madame. I have great plans."

Abdee was then surprised by how long she held his gaze. Judging from her general manner, she was not flirting with him on purpose. But she did not seem able to remove her eyes from Abdee's.

The three Negresses had noticed their mistress's conduct, too, because now they were bending their heads together, giggling.

Quickly snapping out of her daze, Madame Jubiot said, "Ta-Ta! Sabine! Ambrosia! Do not be so silly! You act as if you never saw . . . a stranger before!"

The girls lowered their big eyes to their flared skirts, trying to drown their mirth by fidgeting with the scalloped hems.

Raising her eyes to Abdee, Madame Jubiot said politely, "Then I wish you good luck with your new property, Monsieur." But, again, she was toying with the crucifix around her neck. Abdee wondered if that small golden cross was to protect her from strangers? Like a chastity belt, locked on her by a jealous husband?

"Forgive me for not introducing myself," Abdee said, stepping even farther out into the clearing. "I am Richard Abdee. I have only just arrived on St. Kitts."

"Then, welcome," she said. But instead of extending her hand she reached for her parasol. Quickly rising, she said to the three Negresses, "Come! It is getting late. We must go back to the house. Sugar Loaf is making some of her American pound cake for our tea. Come!"

But Abdee did not want her to go. Not yet. He wanted to find out more about her and Petit Jour. Why she and her husband were such a mystery to most people on the island. Quickly, he called, "I am sorry, Madame, that I have no house to invite you and Monsieur to, around for some tea with me!"

Turning, looking at Abdee with a strange expression—was it anguish, or only shock at what might be some improper hint to be invited to their house—she said, "How kind. But we mix so little, Monsieur." She then added a little too gaily, "*Bon jour!*" And with a snap, she raised her parasol, disappearing through the willows on her side of the clearing.

When one of the three black girls turned to him, Abdee shrugged to her: Help me! She was the cheekiest girl of the trio.

"Come, girls," Madame Jubiot called as she continued forward.

And Abdee saw that one Negress understood vaguely what he had meant. But, taking it as a compliment for herself, she quickly lifted up her pink skirt and showed him the black patch between her chocolatey legs.

Wanting that, too, Abdee grabbed his crotch with both hands, signalling that he was ready.

But the Negress in pink—was it Sabine?—quickly dropped her full skirt and ran giggling to catch up with her mistress and the other two girls.

Soon, they had all disappeared toward Petit Jour, the virginal house on the knoll.

5

The Spoils of Fig Tree Bay

Abdee saw the Negro girl again. But not before he met the hauntingly beautiful French woman.

The second meeting with Madame Jubiot also took place by accident, at Fig Tree Bay, an English-owned plantation on the west side of the island.

Fig Tree Bay had been put into the hands of its creditors. But the reasons for its bankruptcy were contradictory. One story held that the owner, Andrew St. John-Burton, was too lenient in his handling of slaves. The other story which circulated among the gossip-hungry islanders was that Fig Tree Bay lay too close to the Slave Market on Mt. Misery, that a voodoo god had put a curse on the property which neighboured the mastiff-patrolled pens.

But there was no soil on St. Kitts richer than the fields of Fig Tree Bay. Also, the house itself reigned supreme as one of the island's unique edifices. A driveway of waving palms led from the main road down to the sprawling, flamingo-pink mansion built in the style of the Pantheon. Mister St. John-Burton was a bachelor and had meticulously maintained both the exterior and interior of the fifty-room house.

Some neighbours said that he had even gone too far. They claimed that an indulgence in opulent luxury was what had broken Fig Tree Bay and reduced it and the furnishings to be auctioned at public. Abdee knew well the circumstances of foreclosure. But now that the creditors were not his—his family, Thornhurst—he could take advantage of it. This was his new life.

Many carriages had already arrived for the late morning auction when Abdee rode up in front of the towering, pink columns of Fig Tree Bay. He handed Irish's reins to a groom dressed in the green and black livery, and scanned the facade of the house, its formal gardens sloping to the sea. He thought, hell, the upkeep on this place alone must cost hundreds, thousands—even with slave labour!

Slowly climbing the steps toward the front doors, he was confronted with even greater expense. Savonnerie carpets lay lapping over one another on the flagstone terrace. Crystal chandeliers tinkled at neat intervals between the columns of the porch. Sturdy silver chains hung limp but ready to lower the chandeliers if a strong gust should rise from the sea. And, where the shudders were attached to the outside of the French windows, generous folds of fuschia brocade were tied-back with gold cords, forming a rich backdrop for the blue Chinese porcelain tubs of yellow orchids.

Inside the house, a scurry of people raced up and down the gold and black staircase at the far end of the white marble hall. From the vaulted salons to the left and the right of the hall, women and men ran screaming as they greedily spotted more items which they wanted to take away to their own homes.

But it was not the costliness of Fig Tree Bay which staggered Abdee. Nor was it the avariciousness in which these white people were conducting themselves. He realized that all the money which had originally paid for these possessions had been made right here on St. Kitts. That another man had done all this, so why could not he?

In the four or five weeks since Abdee had arrived here, his skin had darkened to a rich sienna and his hair lightened to a paler gold. Also, in his new beige waist jacket and breeches, there was no chance that any of the people would recognize him as the Dragonard. Not that he cared but he did enjoy the anonymity.

He had come here specifically today to enquire about the gate-lodge at the main road. Thinking that it would make a suitable building for the roadhouse he was still contemplating to open, he had proposed to submit a modest bid for it. But on the list which the hoary-headed Negro major domo had handed him at the door, Abdee saw no mention of buildings—only the furnishings and decorative effects of the house were being offered today. The numbers on this sheet coincided with numbers inked on white tags which he now clearly saw attached to everything: the silver candelabra, the services of Sèvres china laid out on shining mahogany tables, the Watteaus in ormolu frames.

Perhaps there is a second sheet, Abdee thought, a list for outer buildings. Also, he realized that there must be a separate auction, too, for the slaves. But, turning to find the major domo who had given him this first sheet, Abdee suddenly spotted another latecomer through the tall, double doors.

Of course! He *knew* that person. It was the same woman whom he had not been able to get out of his mind. The cool mistress of Petit Jour. The owner of those three buxom beauties. And that house.

Quickly moving toward the door, he called, "Madame Jubiot!"

Turning her head, and being taken completely by surprise, she called, "Richard Abdee!" But, then, realizing what she had done—that she had addressed a stranger by his Christian name—she blushed, lowered her head, and murmured, "Good afternoon, Mister Abdee."

But she had said enough. Abdee knew now that she, too, had been thinking about him. That she had not only remembered his name, but both names. He asked, "Have you come to find yourself a treasure today?" He knew how to be polite, and when.

On guard again, she answered, "I am afraid I have come here out of curiosity, Monsieur. It is rather morbid, I know, when a man meets this end. But—", she paused, looking around the room, "—but, this gentleman is said to have several beautiful objects."

Abdee laughed. "Several! It looks more like hundreds."

"Hundreds," she repeated, as she glanced up at the ornate panelling. "But much here is too—how shall I say—colourful for Petit Jour."

"You think it's vulgar? Gilt on the lily?"

"But that sounds so snob, Monsieur."

"Not at all, Madame Jubiot. I am sure that your tastes are much more subtle than this. For a start, I doubt if you would carpet your verandah."

"Ah, but there is a great lady of reputed taste in France at this very moment who goes much farther than that! At Trianon, there are even carpets for the cows!"

"But Mister St. John-Burton," Abdee said, "he is English. He should know better."

"Poor man. I know what the rumours say about him. That he is either cursed by a black god or that—"

Abdee broke in again. "Or that he is too good to his niggers and doesn't get enough work out of them."

She looked quickly at him. Was she surprised to hear him use that word, "niggers"? Or did she believe in a gentle handling of Africans? Glancing toward the people streaming in and out of the room, she said, "All the same, I am surprised to see so many people here today. But I do wish the ladies would close their parasols. This is still a gentleman's home."

"No longer. It is only one more outing for bored people."

She nodded. "I suppose it is because of your Government cancelling their function in Basseterre."

"What function is that, Madame Jubiot?"

"In The Circus," she explained. "I do not go, of course, but every month the planters from all over the island send their . . ."

"Ah! You mean the Dragonard!"

"*Oui*. It is the first Saturday of the month. And the day for that is today. But my . . . husband, he tells me that there is no more the Dragonard. So the people, they must come here to amuse themselves. Pick like vultures at Fig Tree Bay."

Abdee asked, "So is that why Monsieur Jubiot is not with you today?" He was certain that she did not have the slightest notion that she was actually standing right next to a Dragonard—the reason that these people here today had no amusement in Basseterre. He asked, "Like other planters on the island, must Monsieur Jubiot deal with his own problems now?"

"Fortunately, at Petit Jour we do not have many problems. My . . . husband. He is very kind."

Brightly, Abdee asked, "How did your black girls sing in church last Sunday?"

"Ah!" she said, obviously happy to change the subject to something more ladylike. "The girls are not ready to sing for Mass yet. But I am pleased you remembered."

"Of course I remembered."

"Perhaps some Sunday you would like to come hear them when they are ready?"

"In Church?"

"Why not?"

"I would rather pay a visit to Petit Jour."

Fumbling with her fan, she struggled for some excuse.

But Abdee had not spent all this time chatting brightly with her for nothing. Becoming more specific, he said, "Now that I am your neighbour, why don't you invite me to your home?"

Yes, he could see that he was plainly embarrassing her. But, why not?

Pressing, he said, "I suppose you will say you do not 'receive' much."

"No," she said. "No, I do not." Then, quickly correcting herself, she said, "No, *we* do not receive much at all."

"Then, why don't I break the tradition?"

"It is very difficult, Monsieur," she faltered still polite.

But Abdee would not let her escape this time. "Why

is it difficult, Madame Jubiot?" he asked, standing, closer. "Is your husband some kind of a three-legged monster and you are embarrassed of people seeing him?"

"Monsieur!" she said, gathering her skirt with one hand.

But, before she could turn, Abdee put a hand on her glove. "Why can't we both go there right now? There is nothing for you to see here. As you implied, it is all vulgar and ostentatious."

Her voice hardening, her oval-green eyes burning like sapphires, she said, "Mister Abdee. I do not think that it is wise for you to talk about what is vulgar and ostentatious."

"Mister Abdee!" he repeated. "When you came in a few minutes ago, you called me Richard. And you called me Richard because that is how you have been thinking about me since you last saw me. Admit it."

Her cheeks flushed to a bright scarlet as she made a strong effort to move away from him. She did not look old now at all. She could have been twenty. No, Abdee decided, he would not let her get away from him. So, gripping her wrist tightly now, he said, "Come, let me get your carriage for you."

Now, her voice was quaking. And Abdee saw that her slim hands trembled. "Please," she pleaded. "People will *see!*"

"The hell with people!" Abdee boomed. Then, watching her nervously glance around to see if they were creating a spectacle, he said, "They are too intent on sacking this place to notice what we do, anyway. Come on!"

"But what would my ... husband, what would he think?"

"Ah! So there! You *do* want me to come back with you."

"I did not say that!"

But, by now, Abdee was already leading her out the door, across the Savonnerie carpets and down the steps.

Madame Jubiot struggled less when they were in full

79

view of the people outside. But, when Abdee asked which carriage was hers, she angrily whispered, "You can not call for my carriage. It would be a scandal!"

"Then, damn it, you call for it. And I will follow at a safe distance. But do not forget. We will meet by your gates. And if you are not there, I shall pound and clang on them until somebody lets me in. Even your husband!"

With her green eyes blazing, she said, "Why are you humiliating me in this way?"

Taking her hand, bowing, he said, "Do not be frightened, Madame Jubiot. I am not a bandit."

"I asked why are you humiliating me like this?"

Rising erect, Abdee smiled—flashing his teeth—and answered softly, "Perhaps you should ask me that question in three months from now?"

Then, turning, he went toward the groom who waited with Irish.

As they both departed from the sea-bent gardens—Abdee paced well behind her carriage—two women emerged from behind one of the columns.

The first woman asked, "Arabella, who is that man following your friend, Madame Jubiot?"

"He is not following Honore," Arabella Warburton quickly answered. "She does not let men follow her. They are probably both leaving together by chance. Pay no attention." Then Arabella Warburton took her friend by the arm to lead her into the house. She felt a pang of jealousy at first, and was even tempted to let Honore Jubiot learn that she had witnessed their mutual departure. Also, Arabella was tempted to tell Honore Jubiot what that handsome young Englishman had done for money when he had first arrived on St. Kitts. But, no, Arabella Warburton quickly reconsidered. It could suit her quite well if that simpering Honore Jubiot made friends with the lean, blonde, hungry-looking Dragonard chap. Arabella had felt a hunger, too, since she had first met him on that day in Government House.

At Petit Jour, the kitchen was the first to hear that Madame Jubiot was entertaining a stranger—alone.

Sabine sulkily slammed the door between the kitchen and the servants' hall and shouted to the gregarious, fat black woman who stood in front of the cookstove. "Sugar Loaf! Mistress wants a pitcher of lemon-lime."

"Fix it yourself," she answered, turning over thick slices of ham in an iron skillet. "Can't you see I cooking early supper."

"I no kitchen help," Sabine snapped.

"Thankful for that, too," Sugar Loaf answered, reaching to stir the syrup for the baked pineapples. She had been brought to Petit Jour from the Star Plantation in Louisiana. The mark of The Star—a pair of small, silver star earrings—still hung on Sugar Loaf's pierced ears, twinkling under her white turban. But, more than a turban, Sugar Loaf's spotless head-dress was intricately tied and blossomed above her like some giant, swaying gardenia blooming on top of her head. In her six years at Petit Jour, Sugar Loaf had never been seen without her earrings, or the swaying, multi-yardage *création de tête*.

Many West Indian plantation-owners sent their favourite house Negroes to learn the art of *haute cuisine* in Paris. But Pierre Jubiot had purchased an American trained Negress for his kitchen with a special purpose in mind. Sugar Loaf's cooking was often too rough for his palate—grits, ham, roasts, endless rice dishes—but a Negro from America was often considered to be more trustworthy in the kitchen than a West Indian purchased slave. The main explanation for this was that Africans in the American colonies practiced less voodoo and witchcraft than they did in the Caribbean. And the plantation kitchen was the prime target for the slow poisoning of the whites. Deadly herbs and obeah charms were plentiful in the West Indies. Often, when laced into the food, they left no trace in the corpse.

But the only damage which the American Negroes perpetrated was their manner of speaking, their "niggerese"—a bastardization of the King's English. But even that was welcome in the West Indies as a guard against an African tongue which no white person could understand, a language which could plot a revolution. From kind-hearted Sugar Loaf, though, the only maliciousness which poured was her impatience with other Negroes who had pretensions above their station. She said to Sabine now, "If I remember right, Miss Upstairs Nigger, I sees you squeeze a few lemons before. What the trouble with those pretty little fingers today? Too much of that white lady paint on the nails? Too heavy to lift few lemons?"

So Sabine began to explain the reason for her temper. "Madame Jubiot! White mistress! She got her that man."

"What man?" Sugar Loaf asked, more interested in the pineapple's syrup.

"That same white stranger man we tells you we sees last week over-west."

Returning to her skillet of ham, Sugar Loaf said, "Time too Mistress gets her some man visiting around here. Thinks she gets tired just visiting with that Mistress Arabella Warburton. That Mistress Warburton not all that good of white woman."

But Sabine asked, "What about white Master coming back and catching her with stranger-man?"

"Mistress just have to fight white Master for stranger-man, that's all." Then, dropping her fork into the skillet, Sugar Loaf turned to ask, "You telling me truth that Mistress got herself another white man under this roof?"

"Swear she has. Mistress comes back in her buggy from auction sale and stranger follows right behind on horse. He remembers my name, too, when he sees me on the front porch. He says, 'Hello, Sabine! How comes all your church singing, Sabine?' "

"You lying nigger! Why can't you be honest girl like Ta-Ta? Thought all you upstair girls supposed to be special. Even your lies. They ain't so special."

"No, Sugar Loaf. I swear. But white stranger man

didn't do again what he did back-west when Mistress made us all run away."

"What he do back-west?"

"He grabbed himself, Sugar Loaf. White stranger-man grabbed himself when Mistress turns her back and he wants to hump me right there!"

"White man grabbing his pecker! Ha! White man's pecker so small you can't see what he's grabbing at."

"Not his pecker, Sugar Loaf. His pecker big like old Kaiser."

Sugar Loaf snorted. "Old Kaiser's got himself a good sized hunk. But nothing likes Calabar got. Calabar got the biggest hunk of black trouble on whole island."

But Sabine swore, "This white pecker just as big as Calabar's, too. And we catches Mistress gawking at it. Right through his white breeches. Mistress sees it plain as day."

Sugar Loaf's white head-dress swayed as she shook a knife at Sabine, scolding, "You tells one more lie, Nigger Girl, one more lie and Sugar Loaf cut that lying tongue clean out of your mouth!"

"I swears! Stranger got biggest pecker I ever sees on no white man. Sees it, too. Clean through the sweat on his breeches. Mistress can't believe her eyes, neither."

"You just mind your own business. That white pecker not meant for you, anyway."

She turned back to her cooking.

"Why not? Not first time no white man takes a shine to no nigger girl—except maybe around *here*!"

"No talking neither about your white Master like that. You start fixing that lemon-lime Mistress wanting and get out of my kitchen. Those bucks be here any minute and when they hungry they eat the whole place."

Sniffing, Sabine said, "Those pretty nigger boys can have me if they hungry."

"Thought you crazy over white pecker now?"

"I am. But Mistress, once she sees stranger, shining up to me, she sweetens herself towards him like day to night. Mistress awful huffy when she first comes up through the gate—like she no wanting stranger around our property. Then, when Stranger sees me looking all pretty on front porch and Mistress sees him shining at me, calling, waving, saying 'Hello, Sabine! How's your church singing going?' then Mistress changes her tune like lightning. Mistress says to him, 'Well, now you here you might as well come inside!' Then once Mistress gets him inside, she turns to me and says, Sabine, you get us something cool. Get us some lemon-lime."

"And Mistress every right to do that. She your mistress."

"But not takes stranger when he wants me!"

Sugar Loaf turned from her cooking again. "Listen, Nigger Girl. Your Mistress, she a white lady. White lady wants, she can takes your nigger life away from you. Remembers that. But remembers, too, that our white Mistress be a saint. Be what her religion calls a saint. She not going to take any nigger life away. She not even taking no man away." Shaking her head, Sugar Loaf said, "Yes, our white Mistress is what her religion calls a saint."

"Saints crave screwing, too!"

Sugar Loaf turned in disgust from Sabine. "Shows how much you knows about white man's religion. You nothing but upstairs slut. And that's what you always be. Upstairs slut. Now, you want your hands on something, starts squeezing those lemons and limes in that basket under red table."

So, stooping, slowly picking up a few lemons, Sabine continued to grumble to herself.

But Sugar Loaf warned, "Don't thinks neither you lay around my kitchen till pretty bucks come in and you makes eyes at them, too. 'Cause you ain't!"

Sabine complained, "Don't look no white strangers. Don't look no black boys. Who I to look at?"

"Not around heres you ain't looking no black boys. Anyway them black boys. Master's pretty boys. They nice niggers all the same. They can't help doing what they have to be doing. They just follows orders. So don't get juicy for them, you hears. You knows the stories about what happens to poor Stallion. Stallion one of Master's prettiest pretty boys a few years back. But Stallion gets tempted by nigger bitch like you. And nigger bitch costs Stallion his nuts. No, Master don't likes his pretty boys toying with no wenches. They his. Seed and everything. And wench gets caught toying with poor Stallion, she sold for field labour. Six months time she cold dead. Dead from plucking sugar. She upstairs girl, too. Just like you. So learn your lessons from that and hurry up with them lemons and limes."

"I hurry, Sugar Loaf. And don't fret. I don't tease those pretty boys. No buck's no good with no nuts. Not even for master."

"You just shut your mouth and stop wasting time."

Sabine explained, "Can't get back to sitting-room too soon. Mistress ain't have enough time for stranger to feel her titties."

"About time, too, some man feels that poor saint's titties," Sugar Loaf said, bending to open the oven door. "When I owned up there on Star Plantation, that's all they ever do there. They really titty people, those American whites. Screws lots, too. Says don't do much screwing back in country they comes from but up there in Louisiana, they screws like crazy."

"Don't you think Master *ever* screws Mistress, Sugar Loaf?"

But their conversation was abruptly interrupted. Behind them, a voice suddenly hissed, "What Master does. What Mistress does. None of your business, understand!"

Sugar Loaf and Sabine both spun around.

And there, standing in the kitchen doorway, they saw a small, lean Negro. On his upper cheeks were African tribal marks cut deeply into his prune black skin. He wore a pure white linen suit. And, in one hand, he carried a riding crop.

"Calabar!" Sugar Loaf exclaimed. "You scares the juices right out of me, Calabar, you does."

Walking into the kitchen, Calabar asked, "What were you two niggers talking about?"

"Nothing," Sugar Loaf answered, busily applying herself to the ham and pineapple.

But Sabine, not one to keep a secret, said to Calabar, "I just telling Sugar Loaf about white stranger-man Mistress sitting with in other room now. He no Frenchie, either. Stranger an Englishman. Almost pretty as a black boy, too," Sabine said. But, then, looking more closely at Calabar, she added haughtily, "Anyway, pretty as *some* niggers. And as big in certain places as other more ugly ones!"

Sugar Loaf shot Sabine a quick glance.

But Calabar asked coldly, "Is this stranger a friend of Master Jubiot?"

"Don't think so," Sabine said, tilting her head.

But, to stop Sabine from saying more, Sugar Loaf said, "Calabar, I thinks you go to Basseterre this morning to sees that freed nigger lady you knows."

Turning on Sugar Loaf, Calabar said, "*When* I go into town. And *where* I go when I gets into town. And *whats* I do when I get there is not your business."

"Hummmmmph!" Sugar Loaf said, throwing up her chin.

Turning back to Sabine, Calabar asked, "You says the stranger in with your Mistress now?"

"Uh-huh."

Then, as suddenly as Calabar had entered the kitchen, he disappeared.

And, as soon as he was out of earshot, Sugar Loaf turned to Sabine and scolded, "Big mouth nigger girl! What you tells Calabar for? You knows he's meanest nigger alive and runs tells Master everything."

"I don't say nothing wrong."

"Like blazes you don't say nothing wrong. You don't knows what you started."

Considering that she might have gone too far, Sabine carefully asked, "Should I tells Mistress that Calabar finds out she's got company?"

Sugar Loaf widened her eyes in disbelief at the girl's naïveté. "And have Calabar whipping you for running to Mistress? Don't be no fool, nigger girl. You just keeps your mouth shut about white people's business. Learn to protects your own black ass. Now get that drink ready." Turning back to the cookstove, Sugar Loaf wiped the perspiration from her forehead and muttered to herself, "Guesses Mistress has rights to entertains folk as much as any white woman ... Least should have." Shaking her head, her head-blossom of white linen tilting from left to right, Sugar Loaf muttered, "A saint. That woman a saint."

And behind her, Sabine was quietly hurrying with the lemons. She knew that she had gone too far this time.

But she could not help from feeling glad that she had let Calabar know that he was no longer the champion pecker holder.

6

Fire!

Abdee had not seen Honore Jubiot since Saturday, that afternoon he had followed her back to Petit Jour. Their parting had been plainly torturous for her. To his mind, she was already in love with him.

Richard Abdee could not remember ever being in love himself. Nor was he in love now. Certainly not. But he did recognize Honore Jubiot as something special for him, an available subject for his attention. The only flaw which he could see in her so far was the patience with which she bore his impositions. He knew when he was being a bully. It took a majority of such flawed people, though, to create the hierarchy of his own particular breed.

Also, Abdee realized that Honore could not merely be classed as a rich, married woman over thirty who endured anything to attract, even keep a dashing young lover. She had resisted his pure physical advances too vehemently for him to think that. But the afternoon alone with her at Petit Jour had told him a great deal about the kind of sheltered life Honore Jubiot led. Her anxious state, those quick glances toward the windows and French doors, that persistent toying with her gold crucifix, all betrayed the more than basic attraction he had for her. But from the way in which she did not once lower her eyes beneath his cleft chin, Abdee knew exactly where her mind secretly explored as she sat so pristinely across from him, in front of her rosewood spinet. She would not let herself look, though. And Abdee resisted the temptations to rub himself, to *make* her look down at his bulging breeches. He had to keep reminding himself that he would have all the time in the world for that later.

So, not to push his luck that afternoon, he decided to leave her there in her sitting-room before the husband returned. Rising slowly from the chair, he said, "I can see that I have caused you enough misery for one day, Madame." He patted his flat stomach, heaved his chest.

"You go now?" she asked, still refusing to look at his sinewy body, the new clothes clinging to him like his own natural skin.

"I think so."

Her eyes widened and she said angrily, "First, you barge in here uninvited. Then, you rush away without even taking the refreshments I send my girl to prepare. What kind of rude man are you?"

"I wanted to see the kind of life you live up here at Petit Jour," he said lightly, motioning to the pale blue silk on the walls, the white lacquered tables around him. "Now I have so I can leave."

"Oh, I see! You come to inspect. And do we pass as suitable neighbours for the gentleman from the swamp?"

He smiled at her attempt for self-preservation: "*You* pass."

"I am glad," she said in a clipped voice, rising from her chair, too. "And I suppose you conduct these enquiries wherever you go."

"No," Abdee answered, not removing his eyes from her. He knew she was regretting his presence here—the risk had not been worth it.

But, then, as suddenly as her anger had flared, it waned. And, as her eyes unexpectedly flooded with tears, she turned her head from him. He could just see the pearl clips holding her golden hair into soft curls. He realized that the clips were very expensive to have been hidden under a straw bonnet. "Now what is the matter?" he asked, watching her surge of emotions. "Do you want me to stay? Do you want us to be rude to one another even more than we have been?"

She shook her head. He noticed then that the clip on the crucifix was encrusted with diamonds. Petit Jour must be a very rich plantation.

Moving closer to her, he said, "Let's set a date to meet again. Someplace more private next time."

Shaking her head, she repeated, "No more. No more. Today is a mistake. No more."

Abdee rested both hands on her slim shoulders and felt her tremble under the lavender silk. But, before he knew what was happening, Honore had turned, had flung both arms around him and was kissing him. Her mouth was sweet but it was not a gentle kiss which she pressed on him. She was plunging her tongue in and out of his mouth, wildly working her violet-tinted lips. It was the desperate kiss of a woman who had been without a man for too long. A starved, undernourished kiss.

Pulling back his head, Abdee grabbed her chin and said, "I was not expecting that!"

Shamelessly, Honore stared up at him with her large green eyes, studying his face. She said, "This is madness. These last nights when I dream about the stranger in the willows, we are the same. Equal. But when I see you now, here, you are so young. So independent. So . . ." She stopped, and, biting her lip, she shook her head. "No, this is madness."

Looking around at the open windows, Abdee said, "It is also a little dangerous."

"Oh, not for you!" she said. Was it with irony?

"But what about yourself? Isn't your husband jealous?"

Contemptuously, she said, "My husband!"

Then, suddenly, it all became clear to Abdee. Or he thought it was. And, reaching for her again, he said, "Your husband! Of course! He does not make love to you, does he? That's why you need me." He had said—told her—the word *need*.

And Honore did not object. Her lips were parting. She was beginning to speak, to confide in him. She checked the indiscretion, though, and quickly turning, she fled from the room.

But Abdee did not follow her. He did not know if she was leading him, intending him to chase after her like a lovesick schoolboy. For some reason, though, he felt that she did not want that. What she was playing was not a coquette's game of hide and seek.

Slowly, he left by an open French door and looked for the groom who had taken Irish.

And that was how he had left Petit Jour on Saturday: one feverish kiss, what he considered to be a small insight into the Jubiots' marital problems, and the realization that he had found a very rich, beautifully matured, impeccably discreet woman who was an ideal candidate for his doting mistress. He also considered her forebearance with pain. As Irish cantered down the drive, Abdee saw Honore Jubiot fulfilling no larger role than that in his life, a convenient female and perfectly timed. But reaching the iron gates, he did neglect to look toward his own marshy property. Instead, he turned in his saddle and gazed one more time at the virginal whiteness of Petit Jour, the stately columns, the wide porches, the eight dormer windows lining the yellow slate roof like diamond points on a tiara. In the unconscious recesses of his mind, he had already begun the plot.

On the next day, Sunday, he rose late and rode up to a tavern at Half Way House. He intended to make enquiries from the keeper as to where he could purchase large quantities of *taffa*—that potent Negroes' drink which most taverns on the island refused to stock but which Abdee planned to buy in plentiful supply for his proposed establishment. He was certain, too, that Honore would provide him with any extra capital he might need for this business venture. He already saw her as easy game.

The tavern-keeper was a large Welshman, built like a bear with bushy, black sideburns. Leaning across the rough oak table toward Abdee, he readily admitted that he himself always kept a small supply of *taffa*. "For tough-livered blokes like you. Oh, I take the odd slug of it myself. But most white men never touch the stuff so if you intend to buy as much as you say you do, you'll find, my friend, that you'll be running a nigger parlour and you don't want that. A freed nigger means nothing more than a nigger without a regular meal." Shaking his head, the keeper said, "No, my friend, they make bad customers. In fact, I have a rule when it comes to niggers: Niggers are not welcome in my place of business and only in my bed when they've been boiled for three hours!" Holding his nose, he said, "Whew! Do those nigger wenches have a stink to them. I've only a stomach for the young, tender ones—before they get ripe. But, after eleven, twelve, I don't want them near me."

Abdee found it difficult to imagine this good-natured man imposing himself on a helpless Negro child. Abdee knew, though, that it was commonplace for the local whites to practice such habits but he could not bring himself to agree with it. But, then, he had not come here to discuss raping. He quickly brought the subject back to *taffa*. "If you say it only draws freed blacks, then why, down on the wharf, do the British sailors drink it by buckets?"

"If it's a dive you want, my friend, that is your concern. I would guess off hand, though, that a handsome strapping young buck like yourself would have his eyes set more on a respectable trade. Attract some of the island's restless carriage set." Leaning closer toward Abdee, he confided, "Surprising, too, how many of these swells are stopping at all hours of the day and asking for food. Oh, they're not hungry. And when I do provide them with some fare, they leave their plates near enough untouched. No, their bellies ain't empty. They just want to waste their time. And money as well. So, to my way of thinking, it's a kitchen you should be considering, not a cellar of nigger juice!"

Abdee quickly debated with himself whether he should explain to this gregarious tavern-keeper about yet another plan of his—to cask *taffa* like rum and sell it to the ships as a sea-going brew. Abdee had devised a ruse, too, of side-stepping the government tax. But, suddenly, both he and the keeper were distracted from their conversation by the sound of a rider galloping up to the tavern.

Bursting through the door, a dust-covered young boy called in breathless spurts, "Fig Tree Bay— The niggers locked themselves in— The constable going to start a fire—burn the niggers out."

Rising from his chair, the keeper said, "Slow down, lad. Slow down and get your breath so we can make more sense of what you're saying."

Gasping, the young boy doffed his cap and blurted, "Constable Dunne is burning Fig Tree Bay, Sir."

"You mean the big house, lad? The house whose outside is all coloured the very inside pink of a fig itself?"

"No," the boy answered excitedly, holding his stomach. "The big house is safe. It's the gate lodge. The niggers locked themselves inside the gate lodge. Say they won't be sold off. Say their Master was good to them. Say they don't care if he's broke. Say they won't go. Afraid they be sold to America, I guess. Rather die."

"Stupid blacks," the keeper grumbled, sitting back down to the table. "Complain about America when they will probably end up in the dark mines of Brazil. Never see light again down there. But none of it's no worry of ours. The niggers and neither Fig Tree Bay. That's the next parish up and, even if they do have a fire, it won't spread down to us."

But Abdee was already moving from the table. The gate house at Fig Tree Bay was the one building on the island he wanted. They could not burn that. And it was the perfect location for the venture he had been debating with himself about whether or not to tell the keeper—to run barrels of contraband and *taffa* down to the sea and smuggle them out to the ships.

Irish took to the road like lightning.

But, even from the tamarind tree at the fork in the

93

road, Abdee could see the sky already blackening with smoke. Also, he saw a collection of buggies and waggons near the blazing, two-storied house. People stood back from the scorch of the heat, pointing up at the flames which lapped from the windows.

First, Abdee heard the onlookers shouting that the Negroes were still inside the burning house. Then, dismounting, he could hear the slaves themselves. They were singing. Chanting.

In a low mournful chorus, voices rose from the belching furnace.

Abdee could not make out the words. To him, they were nothing but rhythmic African grunts. But when the roof timbers started falling, he began to see the black people themselves crowded together into the small building like dark, sweating tapers.

As the rafters fell, the Negroes did not scream, run, or try to escape from the flames. They clung to one another with their eyes closed, raising their chant as the fire licked closer.

Whilst Abdee stood staring at their impassive faces, someone tapped him on the shoulder.

But he was too engrossed in the hideous spectacle to notice the tap. The man next to him was saying that Negroes were not frightened of dying, that they believed death would carry them back to Africa.

The hand prodded Abdee's shoulder again.

On the third contact, Abdee finally turned.

He saw a man, a stranger dressed in dove-grey, wearing a tall black hat.

"Yes?" Abdee asked.

Not answering, the man handed Abdee a sealed letter.

Looking at the letter, Abdee asked, "Who's this from?"

The man's only words were: "Petit Jour."

Abdee suddenly smiled.

But solemnly, the man poked the letter into Abdee's stomach.

So, taking it, thinking that it was probably word

from Honore, that she was trying to arrange another meeting with him, he quickly broke the blue seal.

But the letter was not from Honore.

The sender was Monsieur Pierre Jubiot. Her husband.

He—dishonoured—was giving Richard Abdee the choice of weapons. The time was set for tomorrow at dawn. Abdee could choose the place.

"A duel?" Abdee asked, looking up.

But the messenger in the tall black hat had gone.

Behind Abdee, the top floor was collapsing.

7

An Answer From Our Lady

Abdee immediately thought of the old, tatty, but very enthusiastic Frenchman whom he had met in The Circus—that armaments pedler who now dealt in whips, canes, peculiar sexual apparati . . . and duels! So, without delay, he set off for Basseterre to find Gerrard Delon.

With success, he located Delon in a dark, cramped cellar under a tobacco warehouse in Paradise Lane. The squat walls of his subterranean headquarters were lined with cat-o-nine-tails, chains, manacles, thumb screws, and iron collars with sharp prongs. Delon quickly explained to Abdee that these iron gadgets were yet another facet of his trade—instruments of discipline which he sold to the white slave owners—and, then, clapping his hands in delight, he repeated that he would be proud to offer his assistance to Abdee. Delon even went further, explaining the complete eitquette of duelling on St. Kitts. He gave Abdee the invaluable insight on how to escape the laws. "First, Monsieur Dragonard, you must answer this note he has sent. You must name the place you are to meet. That, of course, will be Dieppe Bay."

"Any special reason for Dieppe Bay?" Abdee asked, intrigued with the old man, his dome-shaped cellar, his collection of iron equipment, and especially his ready knowledge of the duelling arts.

"Most certainly there is reason for Dieppe Bay. It is there that the boundaries of two parishes meet in a field. The constable, if he should catch word of this affair, he will come for your arrest. But when you see him, you merely step over the boundary into the next parish. *Helas*! You are then out of his jurisdiction and he must go write out another warrant. By the time he returns, one of you is dead!"

"And you suggest I take pistols."

"Do you know the foil?" Delon asked like a headmaster interviewing a candidate for advanced study.

Abdee shook his head. "Not to deal with an expert."

"But you shoot?"

Abdee nodded.

"Then you shoot. And it just so happens that I have a very fine pair of pistols on the premises. The case, too, is *par excellence.*"

"I'm not so worried about the case."

"Ah, Monsieur Dragonard!" Delon sighed, shaking his head. "You offer a gentleman a weapon from a feed bag and he spits in your face."

"Then I fight him with my fists!"

"Fists only put you in the prisons. No, Monsieur, for you it is pistols. *Et honeur*!"

"First, though," Abdee said, holding back the old Frenchman from rushing off to fetch the pistols. "When and how do I answer this challenge? This note I was handed?"

"Leave that to me," Delon said, winking. "You wisely have come to the right man. All you do now is to spend a good night sleeping so you have a steady hand tomorrow for the trigger. You want we should practise?"

"It might not do any harm at least holding one of your pistols."

"My pistols, Monsieur? No, they are yours. As am I! I do what they call 'preside.' I am your second."

Abdee asked, "Does that mean you're the one who stays behind after it's all over and buries me?"

"No, I do not bury Master La Dragonard!"

Abdee reminded him, "You know, I'm not the Dragonard any more."

"Monsieur Ab*dee*," he said, lifting his arms to the iron equipment on the walls around them. "A man like you is always the Dragonard. I see it in your eye the first day you flog in Basseterre. You do it with grace. *Savoir-faire.* A knowledge! But if it is not with the Government's Dragon's Tongue, well ... you make your own beasts, *oui*? You come to me and we make them together!"

Abdee realized that Gerrard Delon was one man who approached understanding him. And, so, with the comfort of having that ragged, old rascal on his side, Abdee took his advice and left to have a good night's sleep—or a good night and perhaps some sleep later. He went to see someone whom he had been neglecting, he headed straight for *Chez Naomi*.

It was the hour of early dusk now in Basseterre. And the time when the town began to throb with life again. The leafy Banyans were filled with millions of swallows swarming the branches in a loud, chattering congress. The shrill, more piercing cry of a parrot cut through their din while flocks of Kiskidees transferred from tree to tree, their small yellow wings quickly filling the sky with a noise like crackling paper.

People, too, came out into the street at this hour. And, as Abdee strolled toward Barracks Lane, he passed Negresses with large baskets of freshly sliced pineapples for sale. Little piccaninnies walked barefooted, their arms outstretched and strung with brilliant pink camellia necklaces for anyone to buy. And above the narrow white streets, the jalousies began to push open and European faces peered down at the activity on the street below.

It was at this sundown hour, too, that Abdee enjoyed a cool drink. Forgoing *taffa*, he anticipated the taste of rum poured into a fresh coconut. At *Chez Naomi*, it was young Nero who mixed these unique refreshments for him. And Abdee thought, too, how he and Naomi could take their coconuts out into the seclusion of her back garden.

But when he was let in and pointed upstairs, he found Naomi in the first stages of her toilette, preparing for one of her theatrical evenings.

She relaxed in a zinc bath, the bubbles rising up around her slim, black shoulders. With a yellow silk scarf wrapped around her head, she lay back in her white, perfumed froth and beckoned one long finger for Abdee to join her in the bath.

He looked quickly to the maid standing beside the tub—a squat black Negress dressed in a starched white cotton smock and a spotless kerchief tied around her head. She held a large, brown sponge in each hand.

Laughing at Abdee's reluctance, Naomi said, "You worried about Zenia? Hell, Zenia has seen more white men's bare asses than probably even me!"

The maid's broad face spread into a grin as she moved toward Naomi with her sponges.

Arching her back for Zenia to scrub, Naomi asked her, "You wouldn't mind washing two of us, would you, Zenia?"

"No indeed, Miss Naomi," she said, working the sponges in simultaneous movements. "Haven't seen a white gentleman shucked down in a long, long time."

"He's no gentleman," Naomi said, leaning her head forward so Zenia could get to her long neck.

Zenia chuckled, saying as she rubbed, "Then I enjoys it all the more, Miss Naomi. Maybe he lets me plays with him, too."

Abdee smiled. "Anytime."

"But maybe Miss Naomi don't likes that, though," Zenia said, laughing.

Splashing her with water and bubbles, Naomi said, "I've never kept anything from you, Zenia. The trouble with you, is that you haven't got that mama idea out of your head. Any man you see, you want babies from him. And we don't have room for any babies around here, Zenia. You've got to get that into your head."

Reaching for Naomi's feet now, Zenia said, "Sure do like babies, Miss Naomi."

"Well, you can't have any. That is, unless Mister Abdee here is willing to buy you off me. Then he's the one who has to put up with your breeding."

Abdee said, "I might not be around to buy Zenia, babies or anything."

Naomi looked up at him.

"I've been invited to a duel." He bowed, mockingly.

For a brief moment, Naomi stared at Abdee. But, suddenly, her mouth opened and she broke out into a laugh, falling back into the tub.

"Yes, I thought you'd be this concerned for my safety!"

Then, as Zenia tried to straighten Naomi's body in the tub, to hold her still so she could finish bathing her, Naomi explained, "You do get yourself involved in everything, don't you? Tell me who it is?"

"A Frenchman."

"And you've been sniffing around his wife? I knew it, too. That's why we haven't been seeing you around here, isn't it?"

Abdee nodded.

"Does she have money?"

He grinned.

"That's my boy," she said, looking at him now, appraising the way in which his dusty clothes covered his lean, hard body, and still arriving at the same conclusion as always—that Richard Abdee was the only white nigger she had ever met. In fact, regardless of the good times that they had in bed, she sometimes even felt as if he might be a brother to her. They had so much in common. They both wanted their freedom. They both respected each other's ability to stand alone. Also, there was their common bond of power. They knew but never questioned that some people were stronger than others. But when she and Abdee were together, there was no master, no slave. To them, her house had been like Mount Olympus and, in their way, they were the god, the goddess. She said now, almost in a sisterly fashion, "Well, I don't want you losing, do you understand me?"

"Neither do I!"

"What I'm talking about is *me*! Here!" she said, pointing at the floor, her house. "You still haven't made an appearance at one of my *soirées*, you know, and I don't want you getting your head splattered all over the ground before we make a little exhibition of your certain other parts. In fact, maybe when you agree to strip down for all the white perverts, that will be the first time that I'll take part in the activities myself. I always did want people watching you and me make sparks."

Behind her, Zenia said, "If Miss Naomi wants, I watches!"

Splashing her again, Naomi said, "You even stand slobbering at dogs!"

Zenia chuckled.

Then, Naomi hurried, having little time left before her first batch of gentlemen would begin to arrive. She explained to Abdee that she also had that certain outsider coming in tonight, a black man from an estate up north, a Negro whose particular endowments occasionally added to her intimate gatherings. Also, she told Abdee to sleep in her bed but that she would probably not join him until late. "On second thought," she said, stepping out of the tub, "perhaps I will not climb in with you at all. You probably need all the rest you can get tonight so you have a good, clear eye for the morning."

Sitting on the edge of her bed, Abdee began to pull off his boots. "It could be some time before I see you again, though."

"If you miss, friend, I'll *never* see you again. Not at all!" she said, standing as Zenia covered her thin, agile body with huge, soft flannels.

And, as Zenia carefully pressed the absorbent fabric against Naomi's tender skin, she said, "I stays with him, Miss Naomi."

Swatting her, Naomi said, "You'll get your black ass downstairs, that's what you'll do. And put out those white hand towels for the gentlemen. I'm not having them spilling themselves all over my new carpets. And, sister, are they going to be grabbing for little white towels when they see the black titties I've got lined up for them in tonight's little show!"

Zenia chuckled as she led Naomi to a chaise longue. And Naomi closed her eyes for a little rest while Zenia finished drying her legs, arms, hands, and feet.

Abdee, too, spread out for a nap. And for the rest of the night, too, he slept alone on Naomi's bed. But he went to sleep knowing that she was probably the best— if not the only—friend that he had. And like any good friend, he knew that Naomi would always be there for him to see, no matter how long the interims might be.

Morning came early.

Abdee shared a cup of coffee and some bread downstairs in the kitchen with Nero. Having become fairly good friends with the pleasant youth, Abdee shook hands goodbye with him and told him to concentrate on his guitar playing. Then, he walked down the six wooden steps in front of *Chez Naomi*, not knowing when—or how—he would return to Barracks Lane.

The morning was still dark and Abdee walked quickly to the inn. He had Irish stabled nearby. And Delon joined him there, mounted on a dappled horse which he had hired with money that Abdee had advanced him.

Together they rode north to Dieppe Bay. Neither of them was nervous, but they did not do much talking.

As the orange sun was rising behind the soft hills illuminating the cane fields, Abdee and Delon left the main road, following a faint trail across dewy sweetgrass.

Neither man spoke until they emerged in a clearing. A copse of tamarind trees stood on the left of this secret opening. And at the far end, two men waited by their horses.

"Jubiot, he is here," Delon said under his breath. That was all.

Then, they dismounted.

From where he stood, Abdee saw that Pierre Jubiot was a tall man, perhaps even taller than Abdee. But he looked older, too. Jubiot was perhaps even fifty years old and his face was so strongly featured that Abdee could discern his cragginess. Also, the fine, straight nose. When Abdee and Delon had first arrived, Jubiot was wearing a black greatcoat with a cape to the waist. Now, he had stripped to only his white, full-sleeved shirt and breeches. Studying him, Abdee could not imagine Honore marrying such a clean-moving but cold man. He was striking and self-assured. But, in some strange way, he and Honore looked too much alike to be husband and wife. Even apart from that clean-lined nose. So what was the attraction?

Abdee forgot then about Honore. Delon and Jubiot's second were exchanging words.

They withdrew. They each walked to their alternate sides, the duellists. The time now belonged to the challenge. And the acceptance.

And now, walking across the field toward Jubiot, Abdee began to see the look in his eyes. Like Honore, his eyes were also green. But they did not look like the eyes of an angry man, the challenger. They did not look like the eyes of a man who fights to cling onto every possession he owns, especially his wife. And this was the first time that Abdee realized his own circumstance and asked himself: Do I want enough from Honore to risk my own life? Even against that dewy-eyed Frenchman?

Reckless courage was his answer. And ambition. Freedom for himself.

As Abdee and Jubiot met in the centre of the field,

Delon joined them and opened the red-velvet lined case. He extended it to them like a platter of blood.

Pistols were chosen.

The nod, purely form.

Then Delon began counting, as agreed, in French.

The men paced.

. . . *dix-sept, dix-huit, dix-neuf, VINGT!*

They turned, fired.

A dense, grey smoke clouded Jubiot from Abdee's vision. But he felt a pain through his shoulder. At least he was still standing. Then, as the smoke whitened and lifted, Abdee saw a body lying face down on the grass. The lump of a man's body. He had killed his first man!

Jubiot's second rushed forward to lift the limp body to his lap and, as he did, Abdee saw a dark river gush from between Jubiot's eyes. Blood. And Abdee now had forgotten about the killing, excited by hitting his target.

"Monsieur! Monsieur!" Delon called, rushing victoriously toward Abdee. But, when a sudden sound of a buggy clattered across the field, Delon stopped to stare at the person who had unexpectedly emerged from behind the tamarind copse.

Delon turned to run.

Smiling, though, remaining where he stood, Abdee dropped his pistol to the ground. He saw that it was Honore in the buggy. And she was racing not toward the body of her dead husband but for Abdee.

She drew the reins for him to jump in beside her. And taking them from her gloved hands, Abdee said, "Petit Jour."

But she did not reply. She only clung to his arm as he snapped the whip over the head of her chestnut mare.

It was not until they were on the main road west that she finally noticed that the other sleeve of Abdee's shirt was scarlet with blood and she quickly leant to inspect the wound. But he pushed her away, sluffing it off as a slight graze.

Then, neither of them spoke until they reached a large and gnarled oak set behind a white stone fence.

"Turn here," Honore said.

Without questioning her, Abdee pulled right, and Honore fell silent again, still not offering any explanation for her unexpected appearance in the field, nor why they had turned by the gnarled oak.

The road soon ended abruptly in front of a small, freestone building. On its peaked roof, Abdee saw a wrought-iron cross. It was a chapel.

Moving to step down from the buggy, Honore said, "I will not be long."

Abdee jumped from the buggy, too.

"You don't have to come in," she murmured, pulling the hood of her light blue cape over her head. "I have a small promise to keep."

"Who do you owe a promise to here?"

Her mouth moved to speak. She tried to explain. But she could not and, patting his arm, she said, "You have much to learn about me and Petit Jour."

"Can't you begin telling me now?"

"I am only able—" Then she paused, biting her lips. Again, she was struggling with herself. But, finally, widening her eyes, she stared up at Abdee and said, "Pierre was not my . . . husband. We are—were—sister and brother." Turning, she moved toward the church.

But Abdee grabbed her.

Looking up at him, Honore smiled gently and assured him, "No, it was not what you are thinking. We did not live together like *that*. Pierre, in fact, does—did—not like women at all. In no way. He preferred . . ." But she stopped, shaking her head. "You will know all this soon enough. Please, let me go inside now, I will not be long."

Abdee repeated, "But who do you have to see here? Now?" The revelation of their relationship was too unexpected for him to question quite yet. Too out-of-hand.

But Abdee's enquiries of her visit here stunned Honore. She thought that she had explained enough. But quickly realizing his unawareness of God, she said patiently, "I have made a prayer. I have made a prayer for as long as I can remember. It seems eternity since I have been praying to Our Lady that some day she would help me out of this terrible problem. This lie. That someday I, too, would be free to—"

Abdee understood now. And, finishing for her, he said, "Free to be married."

Her breast heaved under her cloak. "Yes. But I could not. You see, by law, Pierre could only own Petit Jour if he was a married man. Since the *Code Noir,* no French colonial can receive a land charter here unless he has a wife who can bear him children. Establish the family. So I posed as that wife. Certificates are no problem. It is only the charade that tires you. And, as far as the death—the duel—I think it was how he wanted it. He was tired, too, you see. I think it was suicide." Her eyes were dry.

But Abdee did not care about the duel. The death. That was over. He had won, suicide-wish or not. But now he wanted to know just a little bit more about what he had won. He asked, "You mean you sacrificed yourself so your brother could have that plantation?"

She protested. "But I love Petit Jour, too. And before Pierre came here, he was a good brother. He never liked the normal things, true . . ."

Softer now, Abdee said, "But it is all yours now, isn't it?"

She shrugged. "Yes."

"And your prayer?" he asked, nodding toward the rough door of the chapel.

"Not to own Petit Jour myself! My prayer to Our Lady was for love. Happiness. A true family. You will certainly laugh but I am already thirty-three years old, Monsieur!" She looked at him with fear, as if she expected him to run away at her admission.

But Abdee did not run.

"And would you be shocked if I told you more?"

Abdee remained still.

"I am still a virgin."

His eyes not even flickered.

Seizing this silence as an excuse for a total confession, Honore said, "And that is too late—too long perhaps to even have children!"

Holding her tightly now, he repeated her name as she buried her face against his chest. Then, kissing the soft folds of her hair, he said, "Hurry with your thank-you. I want to take you home."

"To Petit Jour?" she whispered. She was asking him.

"To Petit Jour," Abdee repeated, then paused discreetly before adding, "But you must promise that we will come quickly back here. I cannot wait much longer, Honore. But if you have saved yourself up to now, my love, then why throw away that honour?"

Pulling away, she looked up at him. "I knew you were good."

"Hurry now," he said, kissing her hand.

Then, after Honore had rushed into the small, freestone chapel, Abdee leaned against her buggy—his buggy—and smiled.

What luck, he thought. A devoted and untarnished bride. A spreading sugar plantation. And a houseful of ripe black girls. *Helas*! And, yes, he knew that his proposal for marriage had not been too hasty. Nor was he doing wrong to let Honore cling onto her virginity until they were married. In the meantime, he could amuse himself with—what was her name—yes, Sabine. Sabine! Ta-Ta! Ambrosia! Yes, as old Delon would say, *Helas*!

Suddenly, thinking of Delon, he bolted from the side of the buggy. He remembered Irish! He had left Irish behind in Dieppe Bay.

Damned woman, he thought. I don't want to lose a good animal on account of her hysterics. He quickly realized, though, that Delon would take care of the horse. But he was still angry with Honore for snatching him away from there in such a hurry. He thought, what I've got, I want to keep. Multiply. Build.

Then, he settled himself again in the warm morning's sun, waiting for his bride-to-be to come out of the chapel.

Hell, he thought, bolting upright again. Hell, I'm in the nigger business now, too!

Everything was going his way.

And on the doorstep of thirty.

So he must hurry. But, already, he was a long way from England, the life he had wanted to shed, and the feeling was delicious.

With the eves of a new man, now, he looked overhead and saw flocks of gorlings. They were small white birds which flew in V formations every morning to the north end of the island. From now on they would be a familiar sight.

Book II
SMOKE

8

Married Life

The story still held—after seven months—that Pierre
Jubiot had been thrown from his horse near Black
Rocks. The body had not yet been recovered, due to
the north-eastern tide which supposedly carried him out
to sea. Even a few treasure-hunters from nearby
Sadlers Village and Sandy Point Town rowed out to
Black Rocks in hope of finding rings, the watch, or a
valuable fob still clinging to the decay of Pierre Jubiot.
They believed that his corpse could have caught on
those thick, dark boulders thrusting upwards in the
crashing sea.

But Honore knew different.

Richard Abdee did not care what the neighbours believed had happened to Pierre Jubiot.

And the Negroes at Petit Jour, who enjoyed a good
tale, were too busy now coping with the transformation
in their own lives. They had little time to discuss what
had or had not happened to their former white master.
In the last seven months, the new white master demanded all their attention, was the subject of all their
free time gossip.

The upstairs maid, Sabine, was only one obvious example of changes occurring at Petit Jour. On this hot,
late-summer afternoon, she sat sulking by the workta-
ble in the kitchen. Gone was her bright pink gingham
dress with the scalloped hem. Now Sabine wore an un-
distinguished, loose-fitting linen shift. But what angered
her more than the change of garb was the transforma-

tion under the new dress. She bulged seven months pregnant.

With her arms folded across her new belly, she whined to Sugar Loaf, "Just when those pretty bucks start to fancy us upstairs again, here I go popping with a sucker."

But Sugar Loaf still had no patience for the girl, pregnant or otherwise. Rolling a thin sheet of dough across a floured cloth, she said, "You the one in such a hurry to let New White Master pester you. You don't listen to old Sugar Loaf saying let Mistress have first pickings. No, you rush in there before their wedding night and get tasting. Serves you right you finding yourself that way. You have to leave those pretty boys alone now. Maybe let few other wenches around this place have some pleasuring, too. Big nigger hog all sowed up now, ain't she?"

"Not likely you gets any."

"Don't say I craves to. Got my own hands full coping with all other changes happening around here lately. Like waking up and finding myself in whole new world."

"Ruined our place back-west, too, he did," Sabine pouted.

"You talking New White Master down now that you swelled out like some spoiled peach."

"No talking nobody down. Just don't think it's right for New White Master tearing down willows and ruining our place back-west. No need to drain old piss water out of that stinking no good old swamp of his. Plenty land here for anybody."

"That New White Master got himself a lot of ambition in him, he has. Goes morning noon and night like ten men. I gets up an hour early since he moves in. Wants his breakfast before cockcrow stands on the fence."

"Works those pretty boys too hard, too. What they know about working?"

"I say better they working than lay around buggering *Old* White Master."

"Bet now she wishes she had Old White Master back instead of living with new one."

"Don't you go talking like that. Going to be already a year soon they married. They probably happy as two bugs on a stick of sugar cane far you knows."

"Happy! You no hearing fighting like I do. Down here you not hear nothing. But I hears him hits her. Old Master, he never hits her."

"New White Master do lots of things Old Master didn't do. You living and walking proof of that, black bitch. You and about ten, twelve, other wenches around this place. Pretty soon whole place be carrying around his suckers."

"He not so good."

"Being good nothing to do with it. Being done is important."

"He mean! Black boys ain't like that. Black boys don't hit and slap like he do. Black boys don't hurt."

"Black boys hurting something terrible. Arms and legs hurting black boys now like they never hurts before. Using every muscle they never knew they had. Yes, those black boys you got your eyes on are so hurting tired when they drags back at night from swamps they too bushed to be mean or nice or anything to anyone or anybody. Yes, are they learning to work fast! Good for them, too. Once they get used to working, they be prettier than they ever be. Then, when they gets that work done they start on other work. Work they sure going to enjoy."

"What other work?" Sabine asked suspiciously.

"Just other work. That's all!" Sugar Loaf answered airily.

"You know something you not telling me, Sugar Loaf?"

"I know something I don't know if I should be telling you, that's what I know. And I not telling you because I know how much you tell around things and I

don't know if New White Master wants whole plantation to know about what he planning for nigger boys
next. Probably don't want all those wenches getting too
excited about what they going to be getting."

But Sugar Loaf had said enough for Sabine to guess
the rest. "New White Master going to breed pretty boys
with field wenches?"

"Not all field wenches. Just prettiest and most
comely. Calabar tells me so and Calabar not too happy
about new plans like he ain't too happy about rest of
what happening round here. But Sugar Loaf! Sugar
Loaf as excited as a spring flower to see this place
jumping and crawling with whole new batch of little
black suckers." She stood back and clapped her hands
with joy.

Sabine grunted. "Most likely half of them be not
black but yellow. Be yellow suckers from sap of New
White Master."

"Man got sap, let him sow it. Good market for yellows these days. People call them 'fancies' and keep
them around the house just to look fancy. New White
Master knows what he's doing when he seeds you black
girls."

To keep one step ahead of Sugar Loaf in plantation
news, Sabine said, "Plenty white women, too, trying to
get him pleasuring them. Mistress just about drives herself crazy keeping all hungry white women away."

"Now I know you make up lies. Nobody comes up
that drive no more. Never used to be many callers before. Not like we had at Star Plantation. But Old White
Master here always kept us near enough locked up
from rest of world. But New White Master even worse.
Mistress don't hardly invite any her white friends up
here no more and don't dare sets foot outside herself
without New White Master right there by her side.
Mistress Warburton, she about only white lady ever
sets foot inside our property no more and now I hear
it's mostly little pink notes passing back and forth from
our plantation to theirs. White ladies sure do like writ-

ing blue words on pink papers. Must be their favourite colours. Me, I choose red if I knew writing."

Sabine still would not let Sugar Loaf win. "Mistress Warburton worst white woman of all. Mistress Warburton wanting New White Master most. Course Mistress Our House being so blind she can't see it. Thinks Mistress Warburton is best friend. Best friend! Ha! Mistress Warburton nothing but scrawny little white hen. Mean, pecking little white hen poking around everyplace and wanting nothing better than pestering with New White Master. That's what Mistress Warburton wants. Don't have to tell me nothing about pink and blue notes!"

"Don't you talk disrespectful about white ladies like that. Fact, don't go passing on what happening around here to nobody. None of your business. None of mine. If Mistress Our House marries him and makes over what's belonging to her to New White Master that just her doings. Not ours. Not up to us to judge. Not niggers."

"Not just me talking," Sabine said, staring down at her growing shape. "Every nigger talking. Every nigger changing their ideas about New White Master. Some niggers saying if he keeps working them like this, they going to run."

Sugar Loaf poohed the idea. "You listening to wrong niggers. I hear niggers takes to him. And if some niggers crazy enough to run like you saying, then, where they running to when they run? Run down hill to ocean? Then what they do? Run into fishes? Don't talk crazy."

"Calabar has a place to run and Calabar likes New White Master least of nobody."

"Calabar! Calabar has a freed nigger whore in town to run to and that's the limit of his running. Calabar only grumping because Calabar ain't high and mighty as Calabar was year ago. Still head house-nigger but now he got nobody to whisper stories to anymore. Never did trust none of those Fanti niggers. Mean niggers they are. Bad ways. Don't listen to what no Fanti tells you. Ever. They do strange things. That's all I saying but don't trust being with no Fanti alone."

But Sabine preferred gossiping about white people. She said, "Mistress, she getting her fill of New White Master, too."

"Mistress don't tell you no such thing herself, I knows."

"Not in words."

"Then you don't know, do you?"

"I hear their racket," Sabine said.

"You hears their racket on bed, too. Even white ladies puts up with few tiffs long enough she gets her bed racket. No, I don't think Mistress swaps places with old days for one minute."

"Then why I don't hear bed ricket no more? Why then she say she going to leave him?"

"She not saying that!"

"She do! She saying if New White Master changes name of our place she leaving him."

"Name of what our place?"

"Name our place here. Name New White Master aiming to call us. Aiming to call us 'Dragonard' now."

"You lies!"

"Don't lie. Swear. New Master wants to name us 'Dragonard' now."

Sugar Loaf dropped her rolling pin to the thin sheet of dough. "You sure you hears that? That Frenchie who whips poor niggers down in middle of whole town? The New White Master wants to call us that?"

"That's what I hearing. New White Master used to be one, too, didn't he? New White Master not Frenchie but sure was Dragonard!"

"Sure hearing that story," Sugar Loaf said, unconsciously fingering one of her silver-star earrings. "Hearing stories that New White Master used to be one himself. But not hearing stories about New White Master wanting to changing our name—" Sugar Loaf stopped and looked more closely at Sabine. "You sure you hears right?"

"Swear!"

"Dragonard!" Sugar Loaf repeated, staring into space. "Our house! Name right here!"

"That's why Mistress saying she leaving him. Saying she don't want her house being called no 'Dragonard.' Saying she leaving him before she allowing that disgraceful name on her place here."

Sugar Loaf was talking low now, serious business. "Mistress leaving do no good. Law says place his. New White Master. Do what he wants to do with it. But, Dragonard! He changes us to that, you and me and other niggers can't leave. We stuck under that name. Live right under that name like living under big, dark old storm cloud threatening down on us day and night."

"That right," Sabine said smugly, pleased to have impressed Sugar Loaf with at least one of the stories she had heard upstairs.

Suddenly, a bell tinkled over the spice cupboards.

They both looked toward the board of numbered bells hanging high up on the wall.

"His room!" Sugar Loaf said, clutching her sagging breasts. "New White Master never in the house this time of day! What wrong? What he wanting now?"

"Where's Ta-Ta?" Sabine asked. "Let Ta-Ta go see."

"No! Mistress orders that Ta-Ta not go near that room. You know that."

"Why Ta-Ta so special?"

"Don't ask no questions. Just do like mistress says. Maybe it not him in the room. Maybe it is, too. You just run along and see who rings that bell."

Dragging herself up from the chair, Sabine said, "He ain't pleasuring me if that's what he wanting now. Has to wait till planting before he pleasures me again."

Then, as Sabine sluffed out of the kitchen, Sugar Loaf stood staring into space.

Her mind was still spinning with the news.

Dragonard.

She shuddered all over.

Richard Abdee was making his progress in slow but definite strides. Mostly, he concentrated on the outside of the house but, among the few changes he began to make on the inside, was the rearrangement of Pierre Jubiot's bedroom. For a start, Abdee had moved the bed to the front of the double windows. It was a wide, shiny mahogany bed with brass eagles decorating both the head and foot boards. From this new position, he could look out over the east slopes of Petit Jour and see the workers in the neatly divided "plats" of the sugar field.

Usually, he was awake and dressed before the five o'clock bell clanged down in the slave cabins at the back of the big house. And, at night, he did not climb into this particular bed until after the bell had clanged again at nine o'clock. Abdee slept better, though, and more secure realizing that he could wake up and look out at his own fields whenever he wanted. They were his. In a few months he would know them better, and the mills, the boiling houses. But, even in these early days, they were his.

Abdee was not usually in the house during the afternoon. But today he had come back from acquainting himself with the fields to settle an important question with Honore.

He had left word with Calabar to tell the Mistress to be in his bedroom at three o'clock. At three-thirty, he himself sauntered up the wide staircase and down the Oriental carpeted hallway. When he opened the bedroom door, he found Honore obediently waiting for him on a chair. It sat next to a French door which opened onto the upper porch.

Over the last months, Honore had become thinner and more pale. The first flush of married life had gone quickly. The loss of her virginity had been physically painful but not as painful as the waiting had been, the waiting for her husband to return to her bed for the second time. But when he did eventually come back to her bedroom, it was with a third kind of pain for her, a surge of authority which repelled her. Honore soon discovered that she had married a man who made love with a brutality which she never knew existed between people. And that was only on the occasions when he chose to visit her. For the rest of the time, she had nothing. She was never allowed in his bedroom, unless formally invited. Today was one of those rare occasions.

Abdee himself literally glowed in his new position in life. The hard work had kept his body lean and trim. His cornflower blue eyes had taken on an extra lustre. His constant presence in the sun, too, had bronzed his skin almost to the colour of an octoroon. But, without that colouring, new lines would be more apparent along his cheeks and across his brow. They were the hard lines of determination, the deep furrows which come with fulfilment.

Honore had not been meek, easy for Abdee to handle, not like he had originally anticipated. Recently, he had to fight with her for everything. But, slowly he was getting his own way again.

As the bedroom door opened, Honore lifted her head and said, "If someone asks me to meet them at three o'clock, I expect them to be prompt, too." Although her voice had hardened and her face thinned, she was still clinging onto her beauty in these early days. She still took care of her dressing, her *toilette*. Today, she wore a dove-grey faille dress with light-blue panniers. An opal necklace hung gracefully over her white lace bodice.

Frowning at her, Abdee crossed the room and dropped his riding crop to the bed. He stood looking out his favourite window. Planting would start next month. That was what excited him now.

"Can't you forget about work for one minute and

talk about us?" Honore asked, moving to the edge of the chair.

Still, he was silent. He was wondering about an overseer. So far, he had not found a white man he could trust. A man who understood discipline but still did not strip the meat off the workers. Abdee was learning how to get the most from the Negroes, how to spare the whip and his temper—at least, outside the house.

"Richard?"

"Yes," he said, turning.

"Richard, what is happening to you?"

"Me?"

Staring at him anxiously, Honore sighed and sank back in the chair. It was no use. These last few weeks, months, he always reacted the same. Constantly sidestepping the questions when they were leading up to their personal problems. And Honore knew that that was what he was doing now. She had wondered, at first, if he was finding her less attractive. That could have explained his brutality, too. But then she had slowly begun to think that he had wanted more from her than herself. Or, perhaps, he had not wanted her at all. She merely was part of the territory.

Abdee folded his hands behind his back now and slowly began to pace his tall-ceilinged, almost Spartan bedroom. He liked it bare this way. Except for the large bed, a few chairs, a writing table, and the one campaign chest, he had removed all Jubiot's possessions from the room. Pictures. Busts. Lounges. In fact, Abdee was fastly removing Jubiot's entire imprint from the whole of Petit Jour—but that was what he wanted to finalize this afternoon: Petit Jour. The name. If this was to be his new life it had to be all his.

He began, "Honore, I'm riding down to Basseterre tomorrow."

She sat silently.

"I'm leaving early to keep an appointment at Government House."

Still, she did not move.

"I am taking the deed with me."

She looked up at him, her slim nostrils flaring.

"We have been through this before, Honore. I know your feelings about alterations, changes. But, frankly, I think that it's all sentimental rubbish."

"Do you not think you have changed enough?"

His heels echoed against the bare floor as he walked toward her, and then, facing out the French windows, he asked, "Have you noticed the work going on down by the gate?"

"Of course."

"No. Not the work in the swamp. By the gate posts themselves. Have you seen the digging? It has just started today." He knew she had not seen it.

Quickly, she raised her head.

"The new posts I've ordered should be arriving tomorrow. It was too hard a job for old Kaiser to forge the iron here so I had to go to a friend of mine in Basseterre—Gerrard Delon. He got what I wanted and the new gates should be in by the end of the week at the latest." Still staring out the window, he continued, "I've seen them, too. Part of them, at least. The iron lettering. Looks very nice in the style old Delon and I chose." Then, moving his hand in the air, as if he were scrolling, Abdee slowly pronounced, "DRAGONARD."

Honore flew from her chair to strike him. But as she brought back her hand, he grabbed her.

"Easy, *Madame Abdee*," he said, mocking her French accent. Mockery was another path to subjugation. To break Honore meant Petit Jour all for himself. And that spelt "Dragonard."

She spat at him.

Dropping Honore's hand, Abdee wiped his face and laughed at her.

Quaking with anger, Honore said, "You think you are the saviour of Petit Jour. You think you are so young and strong and you give to Petit Jour all it needs. And you think now that you are changing Petit Jour, you can change the name. I know you never

121

liked the name. You, you told me once that instead of twilight, Petit Jour looked more to you like sunlight! Morning! It was too fresh for 'Petit Jour.' But what do you think calling it 'Dragonard' will do? Do you think 'Dragonard' will suit it better? Does that make it sunshine? Does that make it daybreak? No! The answer is no! All your name does is to glorify yourself. Glorify you. Show the world how strong you are. You, the man with the whip! What you are doing is stripping me of everything I love and whipping me with that name."

Not denying it, he said calmly, "Still angry that I did not tell you sooner what I did before I married you?" He turned his back.

"Not only what you did," she shrilled, following him. "What you are! You are disgusting. It is disgusting to call a home after a professional *fouet*! You whipped poor, helpless people for money once and you do it again. I hear stories, too, how you treat the Africans who work here."

"Then you are hearing lies. And please do not call them 'those poor, helpless people.' Those poor, helpless people were part of your dowry. Your brother bought them. Not me. And you played wife to him so he could keep those 'poor helpless people'."

"Yes, my dowry! I see long time ago that you marry me for my dowry. Those slaves you blame now on me, that is all you wanted. And the land. But, now, Monsieur Dragonard, once a man starts doing things for money, he can never stop. He can never see the real things. You, you are blinded by money. Blinded by power. By the strength you think you have in that body. But you are the devil, that is what you are. The Devil!"

No, she did not understand him. She did not know what his freedom meant, how he had to be. He said now, "I thought that that was the name you saved only for your beloved late brother, *le diable*."

"At least Pierre was honest with people. He did not lie and try to hide the truth. He did not come slithering around like you do. He did wrong things but he did it with honesty."

"Don't I?"

"You? You do not know the word 'honesty.' You only know the word 'hell.' And that is what you are making Petit Jour. Hell! I used to think that someday I would be happy. Someday that Petit Jour would be a home. A real home. Heaven! But now you want to turn it into a public spectacle. Already people are laughing at us—"

Interrupting her, Abdee said, "If people laugh, Honore, it is you they are laughing at. Not me."

"And a woman as foolish as I have been deserves to be laughed at. Let me be a lesson to all the women in the world. Do not marry someone younger than you. Do not trust a handsome, smooth-mannered *fouet*! Do not be taken in by that talk. It will only turn against you. Be thrown against you. Make for you a hell out of your own home."

"I have seen you crying once or twice for some more of that hell," he said, smiling at her.

"Yes, I cried! I cried only because I want love. Some attention. You make me cry. Beg. But still I do not get it. The only way you know how to give love is to be brutal. But let me tell you this. What you give is not love. It is sickness. Sickness! You are the worst lover in the world. And I do not want it from you. Ever. Save it for your black girls who have to put up with it. But not me!"

He slapped her.

Reeling, Honore slipped and fell to the floor. Holding her face, she said, "See, that is what I mean. In anger you act the same way you act in love. A bully! A mean, greedy, clumsy bully! I wish I never met you. I wish my brother were here and life was as it used to be. At least then I had pride."

"Slut! Every slut whines for pride!"

"I am only how you see me. What your eyes are capable of seeing."

"I see you as a pitiful, whining slut. And that's how I've always seen you. That's how I see you now. And that's what you will always be to me and to the rest of the world as well. A pitiful, whining slut clinging to her rosary beads and alabaster madonnas. But a cock-happy slut all the same."

"Get out of here!"

Quietly, he reminded her, "This is my room, Honore. Our house and my room."

"You *are* the devil."

Staring down at her sprawled on the floor, his eyes quickly glazed with an idea. Turning, he walked to the wall and pulled the blue silk chord. He would show her dependancy.

"What are you doing?"

"Shut up," he said.

Honore tried to raise herself but as Abdee's boots moved to stand next to her face, she sank to the floor. Burying her head in her arms, she cried, "Someday you will kill me. I know."

Bending, Abdee gently stroked the back of her neck. He saw that her skin was already looking older. He noticed for the first time how lifeless her hair was at close inspection. Then, watching her tired, quaking body, he quickly unclasped the necklace from around her throat.

"Take everything. I do not care any more."

Behind them the door opened.

"Yes, Master Sir?" a voice cautiously asked.

Turning, Abdee saw Sabine. But he had not wanted her. She was already swelling with a child from him. He asked, "Where's Ta-Ta?"

"Ta-Ta?" Sabine repeated, staring at Honore sprawled on the floor.

"Get me Ta-Ta!" Abdee ordered.

Then, looking at Abdee, Sabine noticed the opal necklace hanging from his hand.

"I don't know where Ta-Ta is, Master Sir. I don't see Ta-Ta all day."

"GET ME TA-TA!"

"Yes, Master Sir," Sabine said, slowly backing out the door, gently closing it, but keeping her eyes on Honore all the while.

As the door shut, Honore pushed herself up from the floor. Grasping onto the side of the chair, she lifted herself to stand, gasping, "Leave Ta-Ta alone. She belongs to me."

"Sit there," Abdee said, nodding toward the chair. "You are going to watch what you tell me to do only to my nigger wenches."

"Ta-Ta is mine!"

"Look at you! Fighting over who belongs to who? What's happened to all that 'poor helpless people' talk? Now, sit there!"

Honore glared at him. But, being too frightened of him to fight, she sank into the chair, murmuring, "God will punish you. God will punish you."

Then, a rap came on the door and, when Abdee shouted, the door slowly opened again and Ta-Ta sheepishly entered the bedroom. She was still Honore's personal maid, the one who slept on the pallet in Honore's bedroom, the constant attendant. Her gingham frock had been replaced by a sober white dress. She looked soberly beautiful, too.

Now, as she obediently slunk into the room like a sleek but frightened cat, her eyes were wide, expecting the worst. Her devotions were all toward her mistress.

"Yes, Master Sir?" Ta-Ta said to Abdee but staring at Honore sitting as pale as a ghost.

Holding up the opal necklace, Abdee said, "How would you like this, Ta-Ta?"

Immediately recognizing the necklace—indeed, Ta-Ta herself had fastened it around Honore's neck that very afternoon after washing and brushing her hair—she answered, "It is not mine to have, Master Sir."

Stepping toward her, Abdee said, "Did I hear a slave contradicting me?" He spoke the words for Honore's benefit.

"No, Master Sir. I mean, Master Sir ..." Ta-Ta's mind was working as fast now as her hands were trembling. "The necklace looks so beautiful around Mistress's fine skin, Master Sir. It is a shame to ruin it on me, Master Sir."

"That's for me to judge," Abdee said, moving to fasten the necklace around Ta-Ta's smooth brown throat. Then, standing back, he said, "I could see it better if you took off that dress."

Ta-Ta looked quickly at Honore.

And Honore nodded reluctantly, as if to say: Do what the mad man asks!

So, slowly, Ta-Ta bent to lift the hem of her white dress up over her head. Like all the girls, she wore nothing under her dress. Neither did she wear shoes. And, as she stood in front of Abdee now, completely naked, the bib of opals and diamonds glimmered against her rich skin and formed a V between her taut, brown breasts.

"Ta-Ta, have you ever been with a white man before?" Abdee asked, looking at her slim waist, those plump thighs, that nice little patch.

"No, Master Sir."

"First time for you, is it? Well, this is not the first time for me to be with a nigger girl. You've seen the ones already pregnant by me, haven't you? And if you take, Ta-Ta, if in nine months' time you give me a nice little nigger baby, that necklace you have around your throat right now is yours to keep for ever and ever. You might even buy your freedom with it. That is, if your mistress does not set too high a price on you."

Ta-Ta reached for the necklace.

By now, Abdee was pulling at his waistband. And nodding to the bed, he said, "The trouble with me, Ta-Ta, is that I'm lazy. I don't like to do too much work."

"Oh, no, Master Sir!" Ta-Ta said, glancing quickly to Honore. "Everybody knows that you, Master Sir, works the hardest of anybody here. You works the hardest of anybody on the island, Master Sir."

"Are you talking back to me?"

"No, Master Sir."

"Good," Abdee said, smiling again. "But that's not the kind of work I meant, anyway." Then, suddenly, becoming stern—that manner which Honore had only seen since their marriage—Abdee said, "I meant that I want you to get your black ass on that bed and wrap your legs around me, understand? And if you don't get to work on me fast, I'm going to give you a nice sharp lick of that riding crop there until you do. Just like I give the field hands, Ta-Ta, when they don't work. Understand? Now, get your ass on that bed." Abdee cracked the crop against his boot as Ta-Ta scrambled onto the bed. Then, as she lay quaking on her back in front of him, her legs spread, he said, "And another thing, Ta-Ta. You get walloped, too, every time your mistress there turns her head away from us. But if your devoted and kind mistress keeps looking at us and you keep working on me, then you don't get whipped. But if either one of you fails me . . ." Abdee whapped her one thigh as an example.

Then Ta-Ta moved herself back and forth, working her thighs, gripping him into her.

And Abdee looked to see if Honore was getting a good view. She was. She was holding her breath, staring at them in horror.

Looking down at himself disappearing in and out of Ta-Ta's pushing patch of black wool, Abdee laughed and gave her another crack to help her along.

Late that night, from the pallet on the floor in Honore's bedroom, Ta-Ta whispered, "Mistress?"

Honore was still awake. "Yes, Ta-Ta."

"If I have a baby and Master gives me the necklace, I don't want it, Mistress."

Quietly, Honore answered, "You earned more than the necklace, Ta-Ta."

"I don't want the necklace, Mistress. It is your necklace."

"I don't want it either," Honore said, staring blankly across her pillow. One hand lay palm-upward on the pillow. A rosary of pearls hung from her fingers falling down to the lace-edges of the pillows. Quietly, she said into the space of night, "What I want, Ta-Ta, is what you have. I want what's beginning to grow inside you right now. And that's the only thing I ever wanted, Ta-Ta. Ever."

Then, closing her eyes, Honore tried to hold back the bitter, lonely tears. Her mistakes. The thoughts of wasting her life. And the fears, the horrors, the grotesque images which even her rosary could not chase from her mind.

Honore had prayed all her adult life for a family, for a man who would give her children. But the men in her life were nothing but that—men! Not fathers. Not husbands. Just males!

When Honore thought about men now, she only thought of one aspect of their masculinity, that appendage on which they seemed to centre their thoughts.

To this day, she still suffered from nightmares about the afternoon when she saw her brother holding himself in one hand, fondling his God-given organ while he knelt subserviently in front of another male. He was a stocky black man who had lowered his breeches down to his knees and was lounging back with his arms folded as he watched Pierre feverishly stretching his lips, trying to consume him down to the patch of black wire.

Another time, too, Honore had been strolling backwest and accidentally saw Pierre lying on the ground. His clothes sat in a pile beside him. But this time Honore was spared the sight of actually seeing her brother's maleness. Instead, Pierre's white and finely developed body was supporting one Negro—offering the black man the nearest answer to the feminine orifice—while he simultaneously buried his head into the groin of a second Negro male, again seeking that oral satisfaction which had come to rule his life.

In Honore's eyes, though, Abdee was no better than Pierre. Perhaps he was even worse because today Abdee had deliberately taunted Honore. He knew she was seeing him. He had *forced* her to watch. And that sight which Honore had come to dread, that cylindrical hardness of a man now probed not her body but her brain. And she could still see her husband holding Ta-Ta's legs wide apart, sinking himself into her soft, black gates, watching her stretch to hold him, and then pulling himself out to the crown of that—that false value which, to Honore, seemed to rule all people's lives. And if not by its ready accessibility, then by its absence. No, she could think of nothing else except that monolith of sacrilege. But she prayed to God to condone this afternoon's sinful act and grant Ta-Ta a child. To Honore, a birth was one positive step forward from perversion.

And, as the night grew later, Honore continued to toss in a half-asleep state. Her prayers, her justifications, and the humid air of the night provided little respite from her one true wish.

9

A Resurrection

The great dining salon had not been used in the last months. A Holland bag hung over the chandelier. Dust sheets covered the long table and thirty-six tall backed chairs. But the mint-flocked walls were still daily brushed and the silver scounces kept gleaming. The beeswax candles for them, though, had not been brought out for over a half-year now. And the silver trays and domed covers not moved from their places on the sideboard. But early every morning, the shimmering green brocade curtains were drawn and the French doors opened to allow the air to circulate and prevent the island's ever-threatening menace of mildew. But, apart from the four black women who worked in the dining-room daily, the only other activity in here these days came in the shape of a brown-tipped butterfly which had slipped in through the voile panels, or a grasshopper jump, jump, jumping from the lawn, across the eastside porch until it found itself on the gleaming parquet floor of this now forgotten salon.

Lately, Abdee and Honore took their meals in the breakfast room off the centre garden inside the house. And they did this only when they wanted to break the monotony of separate trays brought to their own bedrooms. Guests for dinner were unheard of these days at Petit Jour—or, Dragonard, as the new iron lettering over the gateway now announced in its thick, Gothic chunks. And the rare meals together in the cheery yellow and white breakfast room did not fulfil the usual companionable function of dining *en famille*. Without conversation, or even an occasional comment on the food—that nobody in the world makes a souffle like Sugar Loaf, or, "Is your creamed chicken a bit salty, too?"—they both endured their meals in silence. The forks scraped with loud echoes across the china plates. Setting tumblers made comparative rumbles. And beside the crystal-door cabinet, Calabar stood with his tribal marks stretching in controlled rage as he watched the two white people consuming their food. Abdee knew that a man with Calabar's past liberties as head-house Negro hated to be made—forced—to preside over his master's meals. And that was exactly why Abdee insisted on it. More basic than mere discipline, he was introducing something more natural. Abdee recognized Calabar —as well as all the other slaves—as being not merely a white man's property, disposable chattel, but men and women themselves. And like all men and women, these Negroes, too, would serve his best under the best consideration. Often he was sparing the whip these days. He found that often the answer was to subject. Like he was subjecting Calabar.

This morning when Honore walked into the breakfast room she was surprised to find the round table laid for two. She had thought that Abdee had eaten and left hours ago, that she at least could enjoy the morning having her fresh pineapple, her one egg, a thin slice of toast in the leisure of her own inner garden.

Silently, and more than slightly annoyed by this intrusion, she unfolded her napkin and slowly began to pick at the lemon-flavoured chunks of pineapple which Calabar had placed so stoically on her silver plate. Across from Honore now, a great bowl of porridge steamed in front of Abdee as he sat studying conversions sheets. For weeks now he had been planning to convert the wind-powered mills into steam.

His shifting of the crackling sheets was the only break in the silence. And Honore's fork.

Suddenly, there was a knock on the door. But, before either Abdee or Honore could respond—when Calabar himself had only half-crossed the small-tented room—the door opened and the young Negro, Paw-Paw, rushed forward with excitement. Abdee had brought Paw-Paw into the house from the shed where Pierre Jubiot had kept his special reserve of handsome bucks. Most of those young males had been put to work draining Abdee's swamp. But he felt that Paw-Paw would be of more service inside the house, to act as Abdee's personal servant. Paw-Paw was a handsome but delicately boned young man. Abdee guessed that he had only been picked by Jubiot for the size of his maleness. But, as Abdee had predicted, Paw-Paw was proving himself trustworthy, obedient, even quick to learn the necessary European toilet habits which were required to live inside the big house. And if Abdee had not purchased any Negroes of his own yet, he still felt free to mould, re-arrange, and improve the ones at his disposal. And, as of yet, he had not caught one rumour of complaint.

Rushing to Abdee's chair, Paw-Paw forgot his recently-learned decorum and blurted to Abdee, "Stranger here, Master Sir. Stranger with sickness all over face. Says he want to see Master Sir!"

Abdee quickly looked at Honore—the first time this morning. His eyes quickly asked if the caller could be someone who had not heard the news? That Pierre Jubiot was now dead? That, as well as a name, there was a new master at what once had been Petit Jour?

But turning back to Paw-Paw, Abdee asked, "Who exactly does he want to see, Paw-Paw?"

"You, Master Sir! Asking for you by whole name. Said Master Richard Abdee at home?" Then, wrinkling his large lips and shaking his shaved head, Paw-Paw pointed at his mouth and said, "Teeth! No whole ones at all. Just little tiny pieces of teeth there."

Honore quickly dropped her fork.

Calmly, Abdee inquired, "Did you ask him his name, Paw-Paw?"

Paw-Paw quickly nodded. "I asks him who he was, just like Master Sir tells me to say."

"And?"

"He said you, Master Sir, and him have something like—" Then Paw-Paw hesitated and, looking up at the rosette in the centre of the tented ceiling, he squinted his eyes and continued slowly, "Stranger says you have something like . . . yes! That's what! Stranger says you, Master Sir, and him have friend by name of . . . Frankland?"

"Franklin Topper?"

Paw-Paw's eyes danced with pride. "Yes, Master Sir! Yes! That right. Franklin Topper!" Then, nodding proudly over his good memory and his progress with house English, Paw-Paw continued, "I brings him to you, Master Sir, if you wants me to. But Paw-Paw really thinks we scrubs stranger first. Feathers on stranger's hat and his old coat and boots all looks full of bugs, Master Sir . . ." Then quickly looking at Honore, Paw-Paw wrinkled his upper lip and smiled at her—as if this were the first opportunity he had to recognize her presence—he added, ". . . and Mistress Mam."

Honore did not return Paw-Paw's nod. But not from contempt did she ignore the boy. Clutching the napkin to her breast, she sat staring aghast at the apparition which had appeared in the doorway of the breakfast room.

And, now, Abdee and Calabar, too, were looking at the stranger.

Paw-Paw excitedly pointed at him, screeching, "That him, Master Sir! That him!"

Sweeping a purple-plumed hat from his head, the stranger bowed deeply, saying, "Madame! Monsieur! I am Captain Geoff Shanks." Then, as he held his over-courteous bow, long and greasy grey-black chunks of shoulder length hair toppled forward and exposed smooth, bald patches dotted unevenly around his scalp. Rising, the stranger continued, "I have a cargo of priceless merchandise waiting for your inspection in

Basseterre harbour, Monsieur!" Then, setting the wide-brimmed hat back on his head, he added, "That is if you *are* Monsieur Richard Abdee, friend and successor to our mutual acquaintance, Mister Franklin Topper."

But Abdee was too stunned by the condition of the man's face to answer him immediately. The face of Captain Geoff Shanks was riddled with disease and brown marks spreading from his forehead down to his throat.

Impervious, though, to the inspection, Shanks stood waiting for an answer.

"Yes, I am Abdee," he said, pushing back his chair. "I also remember Topper telling me about you, Captain Shanks. But, Mister Topper also said that ..." Abdee hesitated, his eyes focusing blankly on the mismatched buttons of the Captain's frockcoat as he tried to remember precisely.

"Dead!" Shanks said for him. "Topper thought I was dead. Sunk to the bottom of the sea, no doubt. And so I was, in a manner of speaking," he said, gesturing to the condition of his face. And, as his hands moved upward, Abdee saw more ulcers on his wrists and fingers. But, again, heedless to the curiosity which his appearance aroused, Shanks continued, "Now, though, my original mission has been achieved and I return to Basseterre with what I set out for."

The story of Geoffrey Shanks suddenly all came back to Abdee. He had disappeared on The Gold Coast. Also, there was a business arrangement. Or had been. Abdee asked, "You and Topper were partners, weren't you?"

"A lenient sort of partnership. Nothing too binding," Shanks said, his face cracking into a crooked smile as he shook his head in good humour at Honore now. She could clearly see those remnants of teeth which she had heard about from Paw-Paw. She knocked her tumbler of water across the table.

But Abdee was intrigued with him. "You were on

the Gold Coast, Captain Shanks, if I remember correctly."

"The Gold Coast. The Ivory coast. And as far as the good River Niger has ever taken an Englishman. Yes, Mister Abdee, Africa was my home for these last seven years."

"But I distinctly remember Topper telling me that you disappeared *ten* years ago."

Sticking both hands inside his wide leather belt, Shanks said, "Eight. Ten. Could also be twelve. In Africa, time is not counted."

"But you say you have brought back what you originally set out for?"

"Oh, much more than I originally intended, Mister Abdee. Not so much in number now, I agree. But in rareness, I have fared twenty times better. On arriving here, though, when I enquired for the whereabouts of Franklin Topper himself, I hear from Government House that the South Sea Company has been taken by you. But, judging from your fine situation I see now, you have obviously diverted from whatever business you first arranged with dear Topper. I did think, though, it might be worth both our time, Mister Abdee, if I should come straight to you with the news of my arrival." Smiling again, Shanks added emphatically, "And success with my mission."

Abdee understood fully. "You say you are at Basseterre?"

"Yes. And not begun to unload. The wind is right to take us leeward to Barbados. But perhaps the prospects will prove best here. I have only hours to make my decision, you see, Sir."

But, unconsciously, Abdee had already begun making his decision. And consciously, he definitely wanted to see the cargo. If he were to offer a deal to Captain Shanks, to honour his old partnership with Topper, he might not do wrong for himself, either. But that would all come later. Curiosity, though, was too great for him to let a slaver fresh from the middle voyage escape

135

through his fingers—especially a slaver which could be said to be partially his! Wasn't that part of his early ambitions, too?

Quickly, he told Paw-Paw to send for Irish to be brought to the front of the house.

Shanks repeated his deep bow to Honore—who nodded her head only an inch, she was so frightened. She had understood nothing about which she had just heard. But recently, Honore understood nothing at all—happening inside or out. Every action, every move, every word constituted danger. But, never before, though, had she been faced with such a horrible man as Captain Geoff Shanks! His appearance confirmed her suspicions of Abdee's life outside the house, his past.

Before Shanks left the room, though, he faced Calabar and, eyeing the tribal marks on his face, he said to Abdee, "You've got yourself one Fanti already, I see. And I bet I know how that crafty-looking git got himself over here."

Then, with the turned-down tops of his boots slapping together, Geoff Shanks followed Abdee and Paw-Paw from the centre garden.

Quickly, Honore rushed off in the other direction.

But Calabar remained.

And, slowly, he walked toward the spot where Shanks had been standing in the doorway. Looking down, Calabar saw the flakes of dead skin, small particles which had fallen from Shanks's face and clothing. Wetting a finger with his tongue, Calabar bent to the floor and carefully gathered a few of the pieces with his moist finger. Rising, he slowly walked to the table and, taking the slightly-used napkin from Honore's place, he dropped the brown flecks to the white damask. They looked like grains of coarse sugar. Then, folding the napkin, Calabar slowly put it into his pocket and exited from the centre garden, too.

Honore had fled to the sitting-room as soon as Abdee had ridden off to Basseterre with Captain Shanks.

It was the same room in which she had received Abdee on his first visit to Petit Jour. It seemed like years now since she had met him that afternoon at the Fig Tree Bay auction, an eternity had passed since he had first bullied himself into her life.

But, now, as Honore sat soberly on the edge of the piano stool, her back to the keyboard, she remembered how she had undeniably thrilled at his brash, cavalier advances.

She had to admit that Richard Abdee was a very exciting man. His blonde hair, his haunting blue eyes, the square jaw still excited Honore—or could, if only he would not be so domineering, if only he would consider her feminine emotions and gentle needs.

As she sat staring helplessly into the lap of her full skirt, these painful thoughts of a life lost—or never achieved—were suddenly disturbed by the sound of a carriage trundling up the driveway. Quickly rushing toward the open window, Honore stood on the toes of her slippers to see if Abdee was already returning from Basseterre. Her heart beat anxiously as she wondered what hideous people he might be travelling with now. She hoped, she implored the Blessed Mother that Abdee was not bringing that unsavory captain back to the house.

But seeing a small carriage stop in front of the pillars, the white livery of its driver, Honore saw that it was *not* Abdee. Her spirits instantly lifted when she recognized the familiar, petite frame of a dear friend. Yes, Arabella Warburton had come to pay her a visit!

Honore greeted Mrs. Warburton as if she were an angel from heaven, immediately settling her in the bright, sunny end of the sitting-room, surrounding her with tea cups, plates of fluffy pastries, and all the comfiest silk cushions she could find in the room.

At first, Arabella Warburton accepted Honore's generosity as natural hospitality. But, being an astute woman, she noticed a nervousness in Honore, a desire to share, perhaps something other than cushions. Yes, Honore was vexed.

Arabella tilted her head, the lace brim of her pink bonnet touching the bell-sleeve of her organdy dress, and she asked candidly, "Honore, what is troubling you?"

Honore acted surprised. "Why do you ask *that*, Arabella?"

Setting down her tea-cup, Arabella moved to the edge of the settee. Taking Honore's slim hand in hers, she asked directly, "It's about you and Richard, isn't it?"

Honore tried to be strong, to hold her eyes on Arabella's sharp, inquisitive blue pupils. But she stammered.

"You do not have to hide the truth from me, dear Honore. You have made a mistake, haven't you?"

"A mistake?" Honore asked, pulling her hand away from Arabella's as she rose from her chair and swiftly turned her back.

But, clutching the lacy edges of her georgette stole, Arabella rose, too. Putting one hand on Honore's shoulder, she said, "My dear, you are not a strong woman. But that is no reason for shame. That is part of your sweet, docile nature."

Honore stood silent, her head lowered. She had not seen Arabella for so long—had seen no one, socialized with none of her old friends—but she did not want to pour out her troubles. But were they that obvious? Was her distress so apparent?

Arabella proceeded in her low, crystal-clear voice. "I appreciate the fact that you have probably not recovered completely from the shock of losing Pierre. It is not easy for a woman to lose one husband and then try to . . ."

Honore reached to pat Arabella's hand resting on her shoulder. She shook her head.

But Arabella continued to draw her out. "So this is no surprise to me at all. Why do you think that I have left you alone, Honore? Oh, so many times my dear husband has asked me, 'Arabella, why have you not been to see your cherished friend, Honore?' Or, 'Arabella, don't you think we should invite the . . . Abdees to dinner?' But, I said no. I did not think that the time was right. And I did not contact you because I did not love you, Honore. Nor because we don't accept Richard. If I can be explicit with you, Honore, let me say that by now everyone knows what Richard was when he first came to Basseterre. Where he first worked. The Dragonard. And everyone knows that you did not allow yourself a period of mourning for Pierre. And if I can be more blunt with you, Honore, let me say that there are even rumours of a duel. No, no, NO! Stop quaking. Do not quiver. There is no need for shameful tears now. Those friends who truly love you do not care about such things. Those few friends who love you deeply are friends like myself, people who have patiently allowed you a period of adjustment. To become accustomed to your husband. We want to give you both a chance."

Quickly turning, Honore flung both arms around Arabella, burying her head in one shoulder.

Patting her gently, Arabella consoled, "There, there, my dear. We silly women all make mistakes. But we don't give up easily, do we? No. And I'm certain that Richard will prove to be the right person for you after all."

Pulling back her head, Honore said, "I am going to ask you something which I have never asked another person. Not even myself, dear Arabella."

"What is that, my friend?"

Fumbling with her gold crucifix, Honore asked, "Am I the right woman for Richard?"

Arabella's sharp eyes suddenly—but only momentarily—dilated into a hard blue. And, arching a thin eyebrow, she said quietly to Honore, "But you give Richard everything he requires, don't you?"

Honore's breast heaved. "I try. Oh, dear Arabella, I *try!*"

"Then you have nothing to worry about then, do you? Unless you are . . ."

"Unless what?" Honore begged.

Now Arabella sighed. "Often men go to other women, Honore." She was speaking carefully now. She knew that, among other things, Honore's religion had made her so ignorant about the ways of the body.

But Honore confessed, "I do know that some men keep mistresses, Arabella. Yes, I even know that men on this island, in our society, meet with their black . . . servants."

"Negresses!" Arabella said sharply.

Honore lowered her head, nodding.

Arabella said, "Not at Warburton Field, they don't! But then I—" She paused, her voice softening.

Honore raised her moist, green eyes. "You what, Arabella?"

Arabella smiled blandly. And shaking her head, she said, "You and I are so different, dear Honore. But that is why we are such good friends, isn't it? And please, *please* promise me that you will never change. Not even for your husband. Do not forget, Honore, that a woman's first and utmost responsibility is to herself."

"Is that true, Arabella?"

Looking Honore straight in the eye, Arabella answered, "Yes, my dear, that is true. A woman's first responsibility *is* to herself." But Arabella did not elaborate. She did not explain what such responsibilities involved, nor how each woman could arrive at her own interpretation of such a rule. Arabella Warburton recognized Honore as being not a very demanding woman, not in a sensual way. Arabella even thought at times that Honore would have been happier in a convent, living as a nun, to lead a life without men. Everyone on St. Kitts knew that Pierre Jubiot had preferred men to women—but even Arabella's own knowledge of the Jubiots' arrangement was complete only to that one suspicion, and not including what Pierre and Honore's true relationship had really been—but Arabella Warburton knew that Honore had not been satisfied in a normal, conjugal manner. Or Pierre, by her. But, being friendly enough with Honore and, being a clever woman, Arabella knew her own limits as a friend. No, she could not suggest that Honore should take a lover. Nor could she explain the arrangements which certain white ladies on St. Kitts had made to ease the physical drives which this oppressive heat only aggravated. Yes, more than a few white women had found release from a Negro, a tactful black man with a fine body and devoted will. Of course, such measures were practised with the most discretion, and away from both public and household scrutiny. But if something *were* to happen, if someone should discover a white lady in such an uncompromising alliance, there was always an escape for her. She could scream that the brutal Negro had taken her by surprise, had forced his enormity upon her, and the lady could prove her innocence with tears and the insistence upon a bodyguard from that day forward.

Arabella herself had had such a succession of Negroes. But she did not like them to be too young because she felt that youth—even in brawny Africans— was not readily adaptable to her specific requirements. And her black men certainly could not be called lovers because there was no exchange of emotions. A woman did not love Negroes. It was merely a matter of roles, and in Arabella's particular assignations, it was a reversal, of the slave becoming the master. Despite any of her oaths of loyalty to them at the moment, it was a completely physical arrangement, entirely a concoction for the moment and then forgotten. But, in return for her Negroes' unflagging services, she had discreetly arranged for them to do less work at Warburton Field.

But Arabella had the advantage, too, of being married to a man who rode daily to his offices in Basseterre, giving her the freedom to make clandestine meetings with the Negroes of her choice. And then,

whatever physical demands which her husband—tired
from a day's work—would make upon her later that
evening, she would be refreshed and quite capable of
satisfying his meagre requirements. But in her eight
years of married life, Arabella had had not one experience with her husband which could match the hearty,
torrid performance from a shiny, black man. Where her
husband might hesitate, be overly cautious of ill-
treating his fragile wife, a Negro did not hesitate one
second. There was not one moment of reluctance in a
Negro male; there was no act, no movement, no deed or
debasity to which a Negro male would not readily apply
himself. But a woman's appetite for sex soon grows, becomes a norm, and those tender caresses dispensed by a
devoted husband soon become annoying, begin to have
an irritable effect on her ivory skin. Many times, Arabella found herself held limp in a marital embrace with
her mind drifting back to the strong, overpowering
grasp of a Negro male. Arabella had to admit that once
a Negro stands over a white woman, asserting his domi-
nance, both physically and with rough words, that
woman soon grows to look for such treatment, to become addicted to that brutality like some savage drug.
But Arabella realized that she could not expect similar
co-operation from her husband. Apart from being repelled by even the suggestion of such activity, he might
also become suspicious of her source of knowledge.
Yes, Arabella was too clever to risk her position, both
in society and in terms of being turned out of her own
home.

Consequently, Arabella had divided her mind like a
two-sectioned jewel casket. One compartment contained
the dutiful responses of a devoted wife and the second
section held the unbridled passions of an extremely sen-
suous female. This morning, for example, after a frus-
trating and sleepless night, Arabella had risen early and
stood in the doorway of Warburton Field to wave
goodbye to her husband. As soon as he had disappeared through the gates, she grabbed a shawl and

rushed to a cote where the slave, Muley, was supposed to be working. Muley was far from Arabella's ideal of masculinity. He was short—not much taller than Arabella herself—and had a pot belly. And no matter how much she ordered him to scrub himself, the taint of musk still clung to his black skin. But Muley also had a natural sense of survival. He knew that if he performed well for his mistress—and kept his mouth shut about their activities—he would not have to work as hard as the other slaves. He knew that his mistress would see that he was kept on the job of white-washing the out-buildings of Warburton Field, and working at his own ease.

Sure enough, when Arabella opened the door to the lattice-walled cote, Muley was there painting the centre pillars. The white canvas curtains were drawn around the octagonal room and only a faint shaft of morning light broke through the roof. When Muley saw who it was at the door, he quickly uncinched the rope around his trousers and let them drop to his ankles.

Closing the door behind her, Arabella secured the hook latch and moved toward Muley without the slightest word of salutation. Her eyes sought nothing but the lower half of his body, the zone beginning where the curve of his belly gave way to kinky, black wool. Falling to her knees, Arabella extended both hands toward this dark and sinister grotto.

But Muley slapped her hands away.

Arabella gasped. But this morning's gasp was more than her usual theatrics. She had tossed on her bed all night in anticipation of this moment. Her body—and her mind—longed for this nourishing visit.

Again she reached toward Muley's phallus. It was standing now. And the reservations which Arabella had had about its shape—not smooth and straight in its erection but bent too much upwards—were gone from her mind. And Muley's quickness, too, to learn what Arabella wanted to hear from him compensated for his lack of physical perfection. Muley did not merely repeat the words he had learned at former assignations with his mistress. He invented new phrases of derision. He created alternate ploys by which Arabella had to crawl, beg, cry, or work for the mere touch of his none-too-handsome body.

As if Muley, too, could read Arabella's mind, he often made her concentrate on the parts of his body which disgusted her the most—his excessive foreskin, the stench from the wiry pits of his arms, the perspiration which had caked onto that dull-black skin.

This morning's punishment was a double torture for Arabella. Not once did Muley let her touch his erection and when, at last, he worked himself to the explosive excitement, he caught the white seed in the palm of his left hand. And, then, bending down, he smeared it over his feet like balm. If Arabella wanted her reward, she must fall to her face and take it from down there on the floor. She must use her tongue.

She did. Simultaneously, she performed on herself the female counterpart of the act which had brought Muley to his explosion.

When Arabella eventually left the cote, her mind was lighter and her tensions eased. Now, she could tackle the day ahead of her. The chores and her engagements. But there was still a feeling of frustration at the back of her mind. She longed for such conduct in the privacy of her own home, at night, in her marital bed. She wanted to break down the walls of her divided mind and live as one complete person. But Arabella realized that if she were to have any complete satisfaction from a male, a man she could take as a lover, someone who would be able to provide for her both home and a constancy of pleasures, such a man would have to be white. Negroes emancipate a white woman but only a white man can offer total security. And Arabella knew only one such white man, only one male who could completely satisfy the appetites which she had developed here in the West Indies. And that one man was Honore's new husband. Everything about Richard Abdee was perfect for Arabella. She had seen that long ago—that one day at Fig Tree Bay. Abdee was arrogant, assured of himself, well-built. He was the perfect master for her. But Arabella was playing a very patient and long term game. For the moment, she had her black men like Muley to satisfy her. But she also had the hopes of offering herself to Abdee.

Arabella stood now in the morning sun of the sitting-room, consoling Honore, convincing her that she must try to give Abdee a chance to improve, to fall into the gait of marriage. Indeed, it was to Arabella's best advantage if Honore's marriage did not dissolve. Where might Abdee go then? She was bright enough to know that it was too soon to make her intentions known to him. So, Arabella was willing to wait, to amuse herself with the musty blacks as long as there was some hope for getting a white version of her cultivated tastes. And she suspected that her chance for him would come through none other than dear, docile Honore.

So, Arabella gladly bolstered Honore's courage.

And, with her arm around Arabella's thin waist, Honore thanked her for coming to see her, for being so helpful, so lucid about her marital problems. And Honore said that this lull in their friendship had gone on too long.

Arabella quite agreed.

Then, the two ladies took their seats again, on either side of the tea table, and Arabella reported to Honore about her uneventful life at Warburton Field. Her garden. The new carpet in the salon. The set of Sèvres china sent to her from France. The drawings of the latest fashions being worn at Versailles. The more discreet, respectable styles from London.

It was not until Calabar brought fresh tea into the drawing-room that Arabella paused in the conversation of her idle, domestic life.

This was the first time that she had noticed *that* about Calabar! But she tried not to let her eyes linger on her discovery.

The protruding shape, though, bore a striking resemblance to another she had seen. Yes, Arabella quickly realized that Calabar was tucked into his trousers similarly to his new white master. He and Abdee had the same rise in their dressing. Arabella distinctly remembered that Abdee had more of a prominent crown whereas Calabar seemed to be, yes, smoothly hooded by his skin. But both were long, smooth and even.

"Lemon?" Honore asked.

Quickly looking at her, Arabella answered, "Yes, of course." And she promptly checked her thoughts. She told herself that she must not become over eager. She returned the subject to Warburton Field but not its Negroes.

On the ride to Basseterre, Captain Geoff Shanks began explaining the *Alexandria* to Abdee, and how he would willingly take her on another thousand league journey.

But it was not until they reached town that he began the full rhapsody about the trustworthy lady and her precious cargo.

Four hundred and fifty tons in weight, with the strength of thirty guns, the *Alexandria* weighed anchor in the harbour, looking shabby, tired from travel, and badly in need of repair.

But Shanks only saw her beauty.

"She's a good ship," he bragged as he walked more easily now, not on land, but on the realm of his own deck. "Six hundred and fifty niggers we finally sailed with from Whydah, logging two-months, ten-days ago. Three hundred and fifty niggers I lastly traded for there. Another fifty I picked up at Jaquin. Another odd ten and twenty from a petty *caboceer* at one inlet or other. But, ah, Mister Abdee, the original two hundred I gathered, picked with my own hands on the Upper Niger, those are the only strong-hearted pigs who remain alive with me to this day."

Quickly totting and reducing figures in his head, Abdee said, "You mean to say you lost four hundred men in the last two months?"

"Ah, not only men, Mister Abdee! Bucks. No, half of them wenches. Piccaninnies made up a good bulk, too. Slim choosings toward the last, so that's why I don't set no sorry store on my losses." Then, stopping, Shanks pointed, saying, "There, poop deck! That's where piccaninnies are fed once we get to sea. Wenches on quarter deck with us. But, for safety, bucks always fed over on main deck and forward. And always some of the crew standing by to blast if they decides to jump. These niggers jump even when we get from land to sea. We keep them shackled down in the hold till we're well out of sight of old Africa. And only at sea do we dare bring them up for some air. But on the fourth day out, eight, ten manacled in pairs, jumped overboard. Shouting and screaming and laughing they were in the waves, thinking they had escaped us. We had no choice—nor taste—except to hold our course and, sure enough, soon all their merry cries and laughter slowly died down and we hear nothing behind us but the wind. The soft slapping of the waves. And the wind. But for protection's sake—more for protection of our investment than our necks—we dragged up two scalawags who cahooted with the escapers and we blast them with shot so their black skins run red in full view of the others. A lesson for them all not to try jumping themselves. And, as I say, for protection of our investment. Sacrifice a few at first to scare some sense into the others. Niggers got to see to believe. Niggers are like dogs."

Kicking a huge copper tub then, Shanks said, "Dabbadab we mixes and boils in these for the niggers to eat. Dabbadab being a mixture of finely ground corn, throw in some salt, a little palm oil, and of course, your *malagetta*." His eyes twinkling, Shanks looked at Abdee and asked, "Know what that be, *malegetta*?"

Abdee shook his head.

"Pepper! Keeps down the flux. Main threat on the

middle voyage. Flux. And distemper. Distemper not so bad because spreads only to them. Has the same symptoms as our human variety, but nigger distemper never spreads to the crew. Then, of course, there's also the threat of what happened to us. Rare and heard of it only twice before."

Abdee said over-awed by it all, "The men jumping overboard?"

Shanks promptly shushed that idea. "Overboard! No, that is minor, Mister Abdee, minor. Overboard is no problem at all. That's the underwriter's loss. Like I said earlier to you on our way back to town, it was good luck I could get my hands again on this faithful old tub after I returned to Whydah from my long voyage inland. But, before I set up the Niger, I had safely taken precautions and tucked away the contract which Topper and me signs with Lloyds for our insurance. Still held, too, eight years later all true. And the fact is, I think we threw thirty-eight, even forty niggers overboard straightaway. See, a few weeks out and you can already spot which ones are weakening with flux or any other natural disorders which would keep them from fetching much of a good price here in the islands—so, yes, over they go! We figures that the underwriters might as well as take the loss over us. But food! Ah, the corn mash first getting soaked and then washing overboard is the story of the first month out. And that was the worst of any captain's blight."

"First month out? How did you feed the ones left if you lost the corn meal in the first month out? You still had six weeks left. And how many, four hundred to feed?"

Shanks tipped back his hat and answered, "Oh, we had a few horse beans left. Niggers love horse beans. And that gave us a week or two. Serve a nigger up some horse beans and he beats his chest and shouts '*pram, pram*' . . . good! good!"

"But what did you do when the beans gave out?"

"Lost more niggers for part," Shanks said, and narrowing his eyes at Abdee, he said, "You don't know all you would like to know about the nigger business, do you, Mister Abdee? The shipping side of the animals?"

Abdee could only agree that he did not.

"No, not many do. Not many of you white planters do. Course, not too many care to learn much, neither. They see it as commerce and leave it at that. To most, niggers are the strength of their fields. But the fact is that if many a white man took a closer gander at the hauling side of this business, perhaps he would get squeamish! Even start having bad dreams! Judging from you, though, Mister Abdee—as fair-haired and young as you are—you still have that faraway glint in your eye that craves to learn exactly what makes you your gold. Am I right?"

Abdee smiled, not telling this amiable old pirate how right he was.

So Shanks began his brief primer: "You see, the business of niggers all starts in Liverpool. Anyway, most of it does. Liverpool itself figures to make four hundred thousand pounds a year out of the nigger business without stepping one foot onto African soil. The place is a right bazaar with trinkets to haul off for the black man, to tempt him into selling his neighbour to the white man, and the equipment to hinder the nigger once he finds himself sold! So, from that shipping capital of England goes what we call the 'first voyage,' the ship brimming with goods to catch the black man's eye. Some iron. Some cloth. Anything shiny and everything cheap. And, like I say, Liverpool provides the thumb-screws, the fetters, the shackles which keeps all the niggers in tow. Liverpool has the whole thing organized like one big bazaar. And in Africa they have their factors waiting, the trading posts, the open mud fields which we call the 'guinea yards' where you see hundreds of Africans penned-in like so many black pigs, and squealing like pigs, too, as they are being bought up in lots. Course, that is the easy way, the guinea yards. If you choose to operate outside the code, then you deal direct with the *caboceers*, the African dealer who sells you his folks direct instead of kow-towing to the local factors. I say 'his folks.' Most often they never laid eyes on the niggers they're selling. It would be just like the people in Liverpool rushing to Manchester and, grabbing a few hundred citizens there and throwing them in chains, then selling them, say, to the Chinese! No, to the *caboceers*, he just sees the niggers as a mile-long gaggle of blacks brought down some river or out of the jungle from another *caboceer* farther inland, another black who wants shiny mirrors to see his ugly face, or a trunkful of glass beads to shut up his wives. Course, the *caboceers* and the chieftains, they are getting wise, too. And you are having to pay higher prices these days along the Ivory and the Gold. It's not just us English there. It's the French and the Germans and the Spanish and the Dutch. They are all buying niggers and all pushing up prices. So, you see, that's why I headed myself up the Niger, to fetch me some right bargains. But, here! Listen to me! I'm going on teaching you what I can fill you in on later. You know what's called the 'middle voyage' is the run from Africa to here. And the 'last voyage,' the final leg, is back across the Atlantic to England. Then, the holds have been dismantled and scrubbed free of disease and the nigger musk and then crammed full of sugar. But, like I say, maybe I will be telling you more about the business later and my last voyage will wait. But I have something for you to see here that I won't keep you waiting for." Shanks stopped and, grunting, he bent down. With one hand on his hat, he cautiously peered down into a half-exposed grating. In almost a whisper, he said, "There they be, Mister Abdee. The first I got still holding strong to the last. From the Niger they are. And all the way up!"

Now, Abdee stooped, too, to peer through the iron grill.

First, he saw nothing except darkness. Then, as Shanks pulled back the canvas from the metal latticing, daylight shafted down into the ship's hold, and the darkness below began to shine. And, then, the shineness began to move. But, only in places. And Abdee slowly began to see the shapes of people. Of Negroes. They were still chained together spoon-fashion—one Negro's head pressed against the next Negro's feet—but they were moving.

In Abdee's ear, Shanks chuckled, whispering as if he were exhibiting a cargo of precious stones, a holdful of gems, black rubies. "What do you say, then, Abdee? You and me partners?"

Abdee still looked.

"Beautiful sight, ain't they? Shiny black meat! And to think! The first stayed to the last. All Fantis, too. Two hundred strong. The Hausas. The Mandingoes. The Ashantis. As much as those niggers are bragged up over here, they be the ones who kicks off the first. And now, just me left and the Fantis and ... ah, look at you, Mister Abdee! I see that you do enjoy a good sight yourself! The smell's none too strong for you, neither. You're like me! The strong smell of sick and hardship is perfume for the purse, ain't she?"

No, before Shanks had mentioned it, Abdee had not noticed the odour. But now that he was aware of it, he definitely did notice the strong, hideous stench of sick, sweat, and excrement wafting up from the dark hold. But it was not strong enough to still his excitement.

Shanks continued in Abdee's ear, "Course, I don't know about my profits, Mister Abdee. Probably won't have any profits to speak of, even with our insurance. See, I've got the crew I took on to pay. And there are the owners of this ship to consider. For eight years she sat in the harbour, for eight years she weathered uprisings, changes, and storm. She's a tough lady but, like all tough ladies, I am endebted to her for the use."

Abdee answered, keeping his eyes on the blacks, "We can even *buy* the ship."

Laughing, clapping Abdee on the shoulder, Shanks exploded, "I knew you would agree, Mister Abdee. I knew the minute I seen you with my eyes, I knew you be a man to love the Fantis like me. And they'll be your pets, too, I tell you, Mister Abdee. They'll be your pets."

But Abdee was still looking through the iron grating, intrigued by the sight in the hold. He was watching the Negroes reacting to the first shaft of sunlight. They were stirring. The limbs of their ebony bodies contorting. To Abdee, it was like looking down into a dark hole churning with sluggish, black snakes beginning to wiggle, slither, squirm.

And they were his. Those people down there belonged to him. Not Honore. Not Petit Jour. But to Dragonard.

10

The Captain's Story

So Abdee gave them a home—Captain Geoff Shanks and the Fantis—and the biggest personal adjustment which Abdee had to make was in regards to the old captain himself.

Geoff Shanks never stopped talking.

Abdee suspected at first, though, that Shanks was telling him all those untiring accounts about Africa not merely out of excitement for his last eight years there. Abdee wondered if he was trying to distract his attention or divert his eye from some other matter.

But, for the first days, Abdee let himself listen to Shanks. Then, as the days at Dragonard stretched like the pustules across the very face of Geoff Shanks, Abdee learned that much of what he was telling him was true. One or two of the Fantis themselves, ones who had learned basic English in rare forays from their village, upheld the stories of Geoff Shanks. But where Shanks was loquacious, the Fantis went in the other direction to a fault, too. Cold, seemingly emotionless people, they settled quickly into the impromptu wattle huts which Abdee had thrown up for them on Dragonard. And the Fantis readily accepted the fact, too, that the other plantation Negroes refused to have anything to do with them. The rest of the Africans openly shunned the Fanti tribesmen. And the only other Fanti already here, Calabar, also remained as far away as possible from the small group of shacks at the end of slave's row. The Fantis kept their dirt-floored and palm-roofed houses neat and tidy. And their only domestic decorations were the few bones they rescued from the large communal stews provided for a common feeding.

From the Fantis emerged a leader, a spokesman, a tall black man who spoke English. Shanks's name for him was "Manroot," and so it stuck. If the Fantis communicated with the other Negroes at all, it was through Manroot. A tall, broad-shouldered giant, Manroot spoke little and worked hard. He asked Abdee for no favours for either himself or his people—except to continue to keep Calabar away from their huts. Even if Calabar would decide to strike up a friendship, Manroot asked for him to be kept away. He did not explain. Abdee did not ask.

But it was from Manroot, too, that Abdee verified his suspicions for the cause of Shanks's bad skin.

Manroot said that the disease covered not just the body. It went in, too. The disease had first come to Africa with the white man and, because some blacks held great esteem for those mirror-laden, European traders—white gods rich with glass beads and colourful cloths—the Africans also accepted the other rarities which they brought to their villages. Abdee learned from Manroot that, in his village, syphilis was thought to be a gift of the gods and bestowed only on a chosen few. Captain Geoff Shanks had contracted his case from Queen Fa-Da-Lono.

Shanks himself explained the royal black lady to Abdee during one of their drunken evenings. Shanks also enjoyed drinking *taffa* and he complimented Abdee on the thick brown brew which he was now producing on Dragonard. So, in one of the late hour sessions which were becoming more and more part of their routine, Shanks related the story of Queen Fa-Da-Lono:

"She was a Fanti, the size of two of those barrels over there," he slurred, pointing across the lantern-lit tackroom where they had stumbled together tonight. Around them gleamed black leather saddles, oiled bridles, and lines of glistening harnesses. "Yes, the fattest woman I ever saw. But one of the shrewdest, too. She is Manroot's sister, you know, a sister out of the same father, King Kula. But because Fa-Da-Lono's mother was more in favour with King Kula than Manroot's black ma, Fa-Da-Lono took the throne when King Kula died. And how she filled that throne, too. Six elephant tusks had to be added to each side! And twenty ostriches hunted and killed to get feathers to enlarge her canopy. Yes, if whales had tits that woman would be dodging harpoons!

"Now, let me tell you, political uprisings happen in Africa as frequently as they do in our Europe. And Fa-Da-Lono was always guarding her position. Say, as if the Fanti territory was Spain. And Fa-Da-Lono represented the house of Bourbon. Understand? Then, Manroot, he might be called the pretender? Understand? Well, before me there was only one other white man who had been as far up the Niger. But he was not English. No, sir. I was the first Englishman. But the first white man was a German, a factor called Huysman. And along with Huysman and his canoes of black guides and wenches and beads and whatnot, he also brought the plague. The disease. This . . ." Shanks said, motioning to his face. "Manroot, being nobody's fool, he sees that the black wenches travelling with Huysman, and he sees the condition of Huysman himself. And also Manroot has seen other white men before and he knows that they aren't all covered with sores like the barnacles on Huysman. Or me now, too. So, with the ingenuity of a human—or a very crafty animal—and the knowledge of what some other blacks believe, Manroot tells the voodoo priest that Huysman had a very honourable infliction. Yes, he calls it an honour. And he tells the voodoo priest not to tell Queen Fa-Da-Lono to bed with Huysman because she will get the eternal strength if she does. See, the voodoo priest was supposed to be an ally of Manroot. And this was his way of testing him, too. But, just as Manroot suspected, the priest runs straight to Fa-Da-Lono and tells her about what she is missing. Now, as you know or you don't know, this curse strikes men in all different ways. So far, I myself feel no madness settling into my brain. Except from this *taffa*. But I have learned to live with the looks of it. I suppose that comes from living so long with that lie spread by Manroot and based loosely on the Fantis's traditions and tales. But, maybe I, too, gullibly see it as an honour. The particular physical effect that it has on me, though, is that if even some wench would let me plow my crusty cock inside her, I could not! I can not! I can not get it up anymore. Huysman, though, was as randy and capable as a sixteen-year-old buck and he and Queen Fa-Da-Lono spent two nights and three days in the hut together with food sent in and drinks sent in and they never broke once. Manroot, of course, thinking now that all he has to do is to sit back and wait. The best weapon against Fa-Da-Lono has been supplied by nature itself. Greed for cock and the plague! Well, it had not! No it had not! First thing Fa-Da-Lono does, she bellows out from the hut and orders Huysman strung dead. She wants no other woman catching this disease, by God! No, the honour is hers and she is going to keep it. And she kills all the wenches who've come up the Niger with Huysman, too. Then, to get her own pleasure from then on, she starts her succession of studs. But, tiring of them fast, as those native sows do, instead of letting them go picking elsewhere when she's through with them, no, she orders them killed dead and takes her the next one. I suppose like us humans, too, the blacks thinks that he's the one and only who can satisfy a wench. That she will keep me! Oh, yes, she will keep me! So, they be waiting in lines in front of her hut. But, royal black wench being similar to royal white human wench, does not keep them. Queen Fa-Da-Lono went through a hundred leagues of black pecker like a dose of salts, being the only one to hold onto the royal privilege. And having that strength of the elephant, which she looked like, too, she showed no signs on her body, either. Not a scab or a blemish. But, then, came my misfortune because at that time I paddles along and she takes a new white man past the ostrich plumes of her hut. And, as I always fancied a good, fleshy wench, having the equipment to deal with those fat folds, and her looking juicy enough to me, I readily accepted the royal invitation and spent my two nights and three days inside the hut, too. Even a bit proud of it, I was at the time. Proud to be getting such uncommon treatment.

"The treatment, though, about came to an end when I emerged on the third night because, to credit the story I later heard tell, that Queen was about to have *me* killed, too, to prevent *me* from spreading around the particular gifts I might hold in my spunk. And when I sees this happening, I thinks that I have a lot more to live for, and I didn't know then what I'd caught from the royal garden. In fact, I still don't want to die to this day. This scabby complaint has given me a freedom that good health keeps from a chipper man. In good health, a man is always a wreck, wondering when is something going to strike. But, like this, I have nothing to fear. Let it strike! I have the worst! But to proceed with the story, I now do my trick. At least, I thought it was my trick. And, in the end, it turned out to be. But the end was much farther away than I first imagined at that time. Oh, ho ho! That was *her* trick.

"I slowly began to explain to Fa-Da-Lono, about taking niggers across great, blue stretches of water. She listened with her eyes as glistening as sugared pies as I explained to her how other tribes got rid of their enemies by capturing and selling them to white men who took them away from there once and for all. Fa-Da-Lono knew that there was a trickle of truth in the story because some of her people had disappeared not so much earlier and stories came back, some saying that they had been taken in great huts of wood which moved on the water by magic white sheets! In fact, that's the parcel of Fantis which your head-nigger, Calabar, most likely came over on. It landed in Nassau from the town of New Calabar itself. But to make certain that I was not telling her lies, waiting to see if the earlier captives did come back, Fa-Da-Lono keeps me in her village. If they did come back, I'm a liar. But they didn't. And days go by. Months go by. I don't know how many months and years go by. The only wench I am allowed to touch is her and even she is beginning to see the crust gathering on my pecker and my abilities to get the big thing up is petering out on me too. Also, being of the womanly vanity which thinks that it's not her attractions that's failing, but my constitution, I am thus allowed a little more freedom. Guards kept on me at first but I roam more now. See things.

"Their times be peaceful. The only battles they have they wage themselves on niggers shorter than them. Nothing with much excitement. But also, during this time no other white man arrives up the Niger. And lucky for me that they don't. And, I suppose, lucky for them. In this time, also I see what they do with their captives. I learn why no niggers ventures in the way of a Fanti—what they do to other niggers. I can't tell you now because you might be too scared to hear the next. Or go off them as your pets. But during this time that my brains is supposed to be shrivelling, I am instead learning more and more about everything every day and also I see the trouble between her and Manroot. That was my name for him. Her name for him I could never pronounce—my tongue not able to turn so high up to the roof of my mouth—so I call him Manroot. I tell Fa-Da-Lono that the peckers which touch hers are the tools of God—she likes that god talk—but I tell her her enemies only have the cocks of mere men. She likes everything explained to her in pecker language, too. Peckers and gods. And I say to her that her enemies have the peckers of the lowest order. Men root. Man root. And unbeknownst to me, I had accidentally stumbled onto some of their philosophical beliefs. Part of their feud. What Manroot was trying to squelch but what she was learning more and more from the voodoo priest about her divine gifts. I fills her up with my talk, too, and when she finally sees I'm going to do her no harm, she releases me. And with me, for a token of thanks and also to be rid of him, I was given Manroot. Fa-Da-Lono orders me to take him away from her in my magic ship and to sell him and all of his people and some of her own followers, too, whom she'd been feeling suspicious of lately. So, there I be, loaded down with cowries and niggers and she lets me take back the chintz and the metals I had arrived with, and I was thankful for that, too, because by the time I reached Whyday, I used those supplies not only to hire me whites to take up where her guides left me, but bought me other niggers to sell. The Hausas. The Mundingoes. The Ashanti. And I still had enough resources to rig up the *Alexandria* and set sail. So, you see, my friend, I bring you enemies in one tribe but in one tribe I bring you one entire nation broken off from another. They have their differences, too, some of them being Fa-Da-Lono's people, some Manroot's. But what dogs don't scrap among themselves . . ." Then Shanks sat staring at Abdee. His eyeballs were red from the *taffa*, his belly winded by the long story.

Abdee always held well whatever liquor he consumed. And, after hearing Shanks's story, he was more sober than he had been before they had both started drinking tonight.

The Fantis were his first very own slaves, he knew. He was beginning to see, too, that they more than added to the work force. They worked harder than the others. Also they bred well amongst themselves. But a certain mystery still clung to them. What was it? The fight within their tribe? Shanks would—could—not explain further. What was it?

By dawn, though, Abdee was certain of one thing. Shanks had told him on the first day that the Fantis would become his pets. And, no matter how much more he was to learn about these people, he knew that he already favoured them far above the others. They were his.

To assure Shanks, too, that there was still a place for him on St. Kitts—even if the South Sea Company had been consumed by Dragonard—Abdee made Shanks his overseer.

The syphilitic old pirate—liar or not—was the one man whom Abdee knew he had been waiting for, the man who would help him shape Dragonard into what it was meant to be.

11

Expanding Worlds

Like the newcomers—the Fantis—the other blacks on
Dragonard were from West Africa, too. The white
planters in the New World swore on those breeds: the
Ashanti, the Corromantee, the Mundingoes, the Hausa,
the Bantu. But, the Fantis, even on their first morning
on the plantation—awakened by the bell shaking the
walls of their shacks—looked no different than the
blacks who had been at Dragonard for one month, six
months, two years.

In the morning, all Negroes were sluggishly bent with
a common lethargy, frozen by the same chill of the
misty, pre-sunrise. The men. The women. The ten-
year-old children. The majestic Mundingo or the squat
Bantu. They all came out hunched from their low-
roofed huts to begin the long hours of work before
breakfast, limbering-up only after two hours in the
field, and then only by the crack of the lash.

But Abdee had more to learn about than blacks.
Apart from seeing how his slaves worked, he also dedi-
cated himself to learning precisely what they worked.
He did not want to become an indolent landlord—re-
tire to an estate in England and live on the riches of his
months-old plantation. He did not even want to lead
that kind of life here. He had come here penniless,
aimless, but starved for a new world. And, now, every
morning, he saw it lying there before his eyes, seeming
to expand with each day that passed.

Dragonard's crop was solely sugar. Coffee had been

a short-lived endeavour here on St. Kitts. The ashy, volcanic soil, though, proved to be ideal for the sugar cane. But there was more to growing sugar, Abdee learned, than just sticking a few shoots in the earth and waiting for the ships to carry it off across the Atlantic. Abdee discovered that growing sugar was one of the biggest gambles in the world. Discounting the hurricanes. Discounting bad crops. Discounting sickness among the slaves. Or even a slave revolt. The most important thing for a planter to learn was the care with which each small shoot must be placed into the soil.

Petit Jour had consisted of six-hundred and fifty acres of sugar land when Abdee arrived. His swampland, when drained, swelled that by fifty acres. And all his sugar acreage, either that in the first months, or the increases which he was to make over the next five years, were all divided into twenty acre "plats." The plats were bordered by narrow roads for the carts. And within each plat stood wooden sticks which further divided the ground into four-foot-squares. Each square was assigned to one Negro and his hoe. That Negro was to dig one six-inch-deep-hole and then move onto the next hole. But he was also expected to keep hoeing in line with the Negroes on either side of him. In one day, a single Negro was expected to dig no less than one-hundred-and-fifty such holes. And behind him came the men—or women—with the baskets of cane shoots. But, to assure the synchronization of both the hoeing and planting, a driver strode through each plat with his whip. And these men—the drivers—were hand picked from the plantation Negroes themselves. But to insure the efficiency of these black drivers, Captain Shanks rode as overseer among the plats to supervise the entire operation. And when the movements were efficient—as often they were—no one felt the lash against their back. But often, too, the movements were not, so they did. But like Abdee, Shanks knew when not to whip, how to preserve the property.

The planting took from late July to October, benefiting from the rainy season. But, as the planting took a twelve-hour work day, the harvesting often took twenty. And between those two periods of planting and harvesting, came the work of the manure spreaders, the weeders, the preparations for the next crop.

One day, toward the end of Abdee's first harvest, he went to one of the six sugar mills. They were flat buildings topped with a conical dome which held the slatted wings to catch the wind. On this afternoon, Abdee saw a small, wiry Negro driver lashing the back of a woman. Grabbing the whip from him, Abdee asked, "Does she deserve this? Or you?" He had found that the blacks often became drunk with newly-bestowed powers.

"Master Sir," the driver quickly explained, kicking at the prostrate woman, "this nigger falls against the crusher, almost falls into roller."

Abdee looked down at her. He asked, "How long have you been working here?"

The small-boned Negress, dressed in the traditional osnaburgh shift, tried to raise herself. But she could not.

Kicking at her again, the driver answered, "She knows not to fall in. This her six harvest."

"No," Abdee roared. "How long *today*?"

The driver shrugged. "Since morning, I guess."

Abdee stopped. He quickly counted the breaks which the Negress would have had by now. Tallying them, he realized that she had been working nine hours on this job—probably three hours too long for her to give her best concentration on this very important job in the sugar mill.

Brusquely, he told the driver, "Leave her alone for now. Put in the next." Then, walking away, he slowly began thinking that he must do something about rotation of workers. He saw that the Negress had been in danger of being killed. To Abdee, that represented a loss of a worker. So, he slowly saw the importance of alternating slaves from job to job. They must transfer tired Negroes to a job where a dimmer, a spent brain could function.

And, with revelations such as that, Abdee's knowledge of effective slave-driving increased. Also, he was adding to his knowledge of milling sugar:

First, the sugar stalks went to the crusher, being fed twice through the stone rollers. Then, the syrupy juices rolled down the troughs to a lead vat and sluiced next into the boiling house. There, mixed with lime, it was cooled, and sent to be cured.

But at the Curing House, Abdee could do nothing about the apparent dangers. In the Curing House, he noticed the Negroes with swelling faces and limbs, victims of the poisonous wastes. And when the swelling started to show it was too late to stop dropsy. But the Curing House was only one small hazard on the whole process of grinding and milling sugar. And Abdee soon noted that the swelling did not happen to every Negro who worked in the Curing House. In fact, of the Fantis he put there, none of them caught the disease. And they worked quickly, still with their own peculiar silence.

As Abdee's harvests passed, he collected more notes —both mental and logged—on how to improve and expand his world. He noted, too, that there was an abundance of young Negroes around Dragonard lately. The yellowish ones he presumed to be his. Shanks was impotent and no other white man was allowed through the gates. But the majority of the new piccaninnies were coloured a deep brown, almost an iridescent black, and Abdee knew that they belonged to the fertile Fantis. Most of the children were no older than three or four years old and, as of yet, could serve him little purpose. But, taking an old Negress who had grown too feeble to cope with the boilers, he placed her in charge of the young ones, apprenticing them for the cane fields by teaching them, first, to weed the vegetable garden.

Also, Abdee encouraged the slaves to grow their own small plots of produce. Apart from saving on his expenditures for the Negroes' few pints of wheat per head, Abdee was filling their spare hours. The news of the Jamaican uprising still travelled through St. Kitts and Abdee knew that a Negro with no time on his hands had no blood on them, either. Thus, his slaves rose at pre-dawn. They broke for breakfast at nine o'clock, eating the food prepared the night before in their huts. Then, they worked until their first large break at midday. At that time, they ate a corn and fish mash mixed in large tubs and, then, they worked until sundown.

Abdee himself was spending most of his time out-of-doors, too. He had little reason, or desire, to go inside the house. Instead, he preferred seeing this world grow, and, as he worked with the blacks, he also found that he could take more and more pleasure from them, too. And, as Honore was needing less help in the house, Abdee sent her girls down to the Workhouse, the Cookhouse, the Factory where they made cloth, moulded pottery, wove furniture. Abdee was making Dragonard a city in itself, a self-contained community which rose in the early mists of the morning and was locked up at the nine o'clock night bell. It was the perfect domain for a man to draw plans in the dirt with the butt-end of his whip, a draft for tomorrow.

The years passed by quickly for him.

And, as life passed—and prospered—upon the sugar plantations of St. Kitts, so did the passing of days bring gold to the businesses of Basseterre. Abdee had not seen his soulmate, Naomi, for many months now but she continued to thrive on Barracks Lane.

Naomi had not achieved her early ambition of enticing Abdee to appear in one of her theatrical evenings but those private shows still took place in her cellar.

Tonight, in that crowded lower-level of *Chez Naomi* —lit by wax tapers flickering in silver candelabra— she stood in the centre of the carpeted floor. She was surrounded by an audience of white gentlemen sitting in tiers of red plush banquettes. Tonight was a masked evening. Naomi had devised the idea of masks to increase her number of customers, to lure that clientele who might otherwise be frightened to attend such a bold spectacle. The small, black-satin eye-masks also added to the excitement of such a subterranean entertainment.

Sporting a mask herself, Naomi also wore a sleeveless black lace gown which clung to her gazelle-like body. An explosion of black ostrich feathers towered over her head, catching the soft glow from the candles. And, at this moment, she held up her slim, bare black arms to attract the gentlemen's attention, to coax them into momentarily ignoring her girls—passing along the banquettes with silver trays of champagne—and to give their undivided attention to her. The presentation was about to commence.

"Gentlemen, please! There will be more champagne for you all. And there will also be time to exchange ideas with the young ladies! But now I want to bring your attention to the subject which has brought you this evening to *chez moi.*"

Naomi was greeted with applause.

Smiling to the roomful of men, Naomi's teeth formed a shiny crescent under her black satin mask. She ignored, though, the black curtain hanging to the left. It was behind that curtain where she sat those people who would not chance—even with the protection of an eye mask—anyone learning their identity. For the most part, those overcautious members of Naomi's audience were white women. And Naomi had also provided separate booths behind those veils, an added consideration for the ladies' anonymity, and, if they so required, a male attendant to assist them through the evening.

Naomi continued, "And keeping in the tradition of a masquerade, I have covered the face of our main attraction this evening."

There was a sudden ripple of disapproval among the banquettes.

But Naomi quieted her audience with a smile,

saying, "But I believe that you will soon see that the hood over his head is quite in order. For one thing, it is made of the finest black horsehide . . ."

The men applauded her suggestive ingenuity.

Holding up her long, bare arms, Naomi continued, "There are also those among you who might recognize this actor . . . But all that I can tell you is . . . He is black . . . From a local estate . . . A black who is . . ." Naomi paused, careful not to use the word "man," to accommodate some of her customers' opinions that only whites were "men," ". . . an entertainer who has delighted a small number of you before . . . But tonight I want to share this Negro's talents with . . . EVERY-ONE!"

Bowing her headful of ostrich plumes, Naomi accepted her applause with a deep curtsy, signalling for the show to begin:

The first person to enter the small, candle-lit arena was a child, a young and naked Negress who appeared to be no older than ten years. Her unformed breasts were only small, swollen buttons on her light-brown chest. And the softness between her slim legs had not yet begun to coarsen with hair. The black wool on the child's head, though, was neatly plaited into the pattern of a slave. Her thin arms hung nervously to the sides of her pubescent body, her bony knees wobbling as she hesitantly moved out into the arena. And, apart from walking uneasily because of the fright caused by appearing in front of a roomful of masked, white men, the young child was also having difficulty in balancing herself because of the shoes which she had been made to wear: the young coloured girl was completely naked except for a pair of silver court slippers which were too large for her child-sized feet.

Next, a white lady entered. It was Clover, the blonde girl who was permanent at Naomi's. Tonight she was dressed in a pale yellow summer frock, a replica of the frothy, country dresses worn by English ladies on St. Kitts, except for the absence of a bodice. Clover's two

breasts burst forth naked, pendulous, her nipples pink
and spreading over her powdered whiteness.

And, seeing the black child in the silver shoes, this
"white lady" grabbed her by the slim shoulder and
shoved her to the floor. As she began to kick the child,
scolding her for stealing her silver shoes, a "British soldier" entered the arena—one of Naomi's Negress em-
ployees, dressed tonight in the red and blue British uniform.

The "white lady" mimed her explanation to the
"British soldier" who, in turn, unleashed his abuse
upon the quivering child until the "white lady" whispered something into the "soldier's" ear.

The "soldier" nodded and quickly exited from the
arena. He returned promptly with a slim, sinewy,
and completely naked Negro male—naked except for a
black leather hood on his head, a hood with long
gashes for the eyes. When the "white lady" mimed the
child's crime to the hooded black man, he reached
down to his groin and lifted his limp but excessively
long and thick maleness in his right hand.

The gentlemen in the audience immediately seized
upon the symbolism. They shouted, "The Dragonard!
The Dragonard!" And, in spreading participation, they
all began to call for the thieving child to be submitted
to the Dragonard.

By this time, the "white woman" and the "British
soldier" were holding the frightened child to her knees
as the "Dragonard" began to whip the child's face.

Slapping her soft cheeks with that part of himself
which looked like oiled leather in this candlelight.
Next, as he probed himself toward the child's lips, even
jabbing the crown of his phallus at her eye, he began to
expand. And his blackness began to turn blue, the
veins moulding into one enormous instrument of torture.
And when the child tried to hold up her small hands to
protect herself from this punishment—and to block out
the jeers rising from the masked audience—the "British
soldier" and the "white lady" grabbed the small girl's

hands and forced her to submit to adults's dramatization of discipline.

But, slowly, the audience's amusement began to turn into a desire to participate in the licentiousness. They grabbed toward the Negresses passing between the banquettes with the trays of champagne.

In the arena, too, the "white lady" had lifted her skirts and, as the "soldier" mounted her, she grabbed in desperation to feel the oily black equivalent of the fabled Dragon's Tongue.

By now, the only area of Naomi's cellar which was not visibly writhing—had not succumbed to the perversities which Naomi had supplied for their tastes—was the black curtain to the left. But behind that partition of midnight gauze—in one of the private booths—a white woman clasped her hand firmly onto the breeches of the young Negro who sat on the chair beside her. She was Arabella Warburton. And he was Naomi's youthful employee, Nero.

Arabella looked anxiously from the display of the "Dragonard" back to the crotch of Nero's snug white breeches. She reached toward him with her hand.

But Nero stopped her.

Arabella persisted in her quick grabbings. But, looking simultaneously back to the theatrics, she suddenly stopped. Removing her hand from Nero, she sat on the edge of her chair and stared at the hooded Negro. She gasped, "But I know that black! I'm certain it's . . . Calabar! I've seen him at . . ."

Nero asked, "Do you want *him*?"

"It can only be Calabar!"

"Do you no good if you want *him*," Nero said slowly. He was trying to remember the exact words which Naomi had instructed him to say to this new customer.

Sitting on the edge of her chair, watching Calabar's elephantine proportions, Arabella reached again for Nero.

But he shoved her away from him. That was part of the tactics which Naomi had taught him, too.

Pulling back her hand, Arabella said, "You young ones are all alike! Get out!"

But Nero did not budge. Although he *was* young, he was old enough to know what specialties this white lady wanted. And he had been learning from Naomi, too, how to cater to such tastes. And, so, Nero slowly began to speak, to abuse Arabella Warburton with the vocabulary he had learned from Naomi. But, as often as Nero had practised it, he still found the words hard to say, the cock-sure manner hard to assimilate. He was a basic minded youth. He liked to play his guitar, to relax with people, whether they be male or female. But to coarsen Nero for his new role in her brothel, Naomi had told him that he must think of how the white people had enslaved him in Brazil. How they had shackled his mother, his father, family and friends to work their mines. How entire tribes had been dragged from Africa by the white people. And, although Nero was not from the same tribe as Naomi—a Fanti—he had to realize that all Negroes were bonded together by the brotherhood of their skin.

So, only with such coaching, such lectures from Naomi, could Nero bring himself to do and say the things which were against his nature. Naomi had kept repeating to him that these activities were for the good of their people. She promised that there would be a change for the Negroes someday. That the Africans could not be enslaved forever. That the white people were basically a weak race and the blacks must feed the white man's weaknesses. And, in her propaganda, Naomi explained how there were many different kinds of revenge for the black people. She explained to Nero how Calabar—a Fanti like herself—hoped to inflict someday his own variation of revenge upon a white person. Calabar was even more fanatical in his beliefs than Naomi. But she told Nero that he must find his way, too, his method of vengeance.

So, reluctantly, Nero learned how to debase the white ladies who came to *Chez Naomi*. But he still hoped for another, more peaceful way in which to help his people.

Unlike the white men, these theatrical evenings were no fun at all for Nero. But he suffered them because that was the wish of his mistress. Nero did not question the fact that, although Naomi spoke of freedom for the Negroes, he was bonded to her. That freed Negroes owned slaves, too, like white people, was only one more confusing fact of life for Nero in the new world, whether it be in Brazil, or here on the small island of St. Kitts.

Now, as he sat in the veiled booth, he allowed Arabella Warburton to have her first touch of his firmness. He held his head upright as her cautious fingers explored the length and width of his hardness. But then, as her small fingers became more greedy, he shoved her hand from his leg. He grunted, "White slut. White *whore!*"

Arabella promptly fell to her knees, wrapping both arms around the bulging muscles of his thighs and begged for mercy. She implored him now in choked whispers. She acknowledged his supremacy to her. She confessed her unworthiness as a partner. As a woman. Even as a human being.

But her continued confessions fell upon deaf ears. Nero's attention was directed toward the spectacle beyond the curtain. In the arena, the black girl screamed as Calabar relentlessly drove into her small body. At the moment when the two women sat with all their weight on the girl's spindly arms, Nero closed his eyes. He could not watch any more of this torture. After one last painful cry from the girl, though, all that Nero could hear was Arabella's whispering down by his knees. And, opening his eyes, he saw the girl's small body lying limp, helpless, silent.

For her, this was finished.

Book III
SILENT FLAME

12

Signs of Age

Honore studied her reflection in the cheval mirror. She saw herself as an hour-glass. Gussetted in at the waist, she felt not unlike an hour-glass. And she stood wondering what half of the sand was running dry.

Her face. Her neck. Her shoulders. The skin all looked firm. But it was taking her longer to make up her face these days. Five years of married life had not been easy on her. Nor had age. Despite her refusal to go unprotected into the sun, the tropical climate had still found ways to her face. And, now, feeling under her chin, Honore grabbed at some loose flesh.

Beginning to fidget, nervously jabbing at her hair as if it also might start collapsing, falling out at any moment, Honore wanted to turn away from the mirror and run. Run like a mouse because that was exactly the colour her hair was turning. Like a mouse.

But Ambrosia, one of her former personal servants who now worked mostly down in the Sewing House, knelt on the floor behind her and pleaded for Honore not to move. "Please, Mistress! This is the fourth time we fits you for this dress. We have another four fittings to go before it even starts looking ready. This thin white silk so hard to works with!"

"I do not want to go now!" Honore said, her eyes quickly darting back to her face, her hair, that limp skin under her chin.

Ta-Ta stood patiently behind Ambrosia. She held the garlands of silk roses for the skirt of Honore's new gown. And, as she watched Honore, she assured her,

"Mistress, you have kept yourself away from gatherings for too long. You *must* go meet the new Lord Governor. Who knows all the old friends you going to be meeting at the ball." Unlike Ambrosia, Ta-Ta had kept her trim figure and the civilized ways of living in the big house. In the last five years, Ta-Ta had become even a bit matronly, falling naturally into the position of a woman's companion. But she still slept on the pallet in the corner of Honore's bedroom.

To Honore now, though, the Lord Governor's ball sounded more like an utter exposure of herself than a social gathering. It sounded like an exhibition for what a foolish mistake she had made by marrying Richard Abdee. Her whole life! So, to change the subject, to chase away those thoughts of people laughing at her, she asked, "Ta-Ta, where's Monkey?"

Ta-Ta answered, "Probably down in the kitchen with Calabar where he usually is."

"You know how I feel about that child spending too much time with Calabar. It is not right. Calabar is a hard, cruel man, and that child is too precious."

From the floor, Ambrosia said, "You talking about cute little yellow piccaninny from Miss Ta-Ta here?"

"Yes," Honore said.

"I see he's prettiest yellow baby I seen in a long time. But still can't understand how Mistress allows him to run loose around the house like he's a human baby. I ain't never seen him down in the pen with other piccaninnies. Knows it being Ta-Ta's sucker and Ta-Ta being your personal maid and all, but, still, sometimes in the day in this house here, I see that yellow piccaninny running through the house like—I just seen him around the house a lot, that's all I saying."

"What happens inside the house," Honore said with some attempt at authority, "is none of Mister Abdee's business, if that's what you are trying to say, Ambrosia."

"I not trying to say anything, Mistress. Just trying to get at this tuck if you stand still."

But, annoyed, Honore continued, "Nor is it anybody else's business as far as that matters, Ambrosia. You of all people should know how I feel about treating you—" Then, Honore hesitated. She still found it difficult to find a name for them. Africans? Negroes? Certainly not "niggers" or "slaves." Since Abdee had taken command here, she had become doubly conscious of the injustices of slavery but found no way to do anything about it. Except to be considerate. It was not that her husband whipped them mercilessly as she had feared he would, but his hand over them was so heavy, like iron! But one thing which puzzled her, though, was the new tax law about which he was constantly grumbling lately. It was levied against extra crops. So had he made Petit Jour—or Dragonard—more productive because he drove the slaves harder? Or was he really a very good manager? Come to be an expert planter? If so, that was still no excuse to be cruel to her!

Ambrosia said, "Niggers all say that Mistress is good white lady."

"I appreciate that, Ambrosia."

"Niggers appreciate you, too, Mistress. Niggers like Sugar Loaf down in kitchen, she's always saying how white Mistress is a saint of the white man's religion."

Honore smiled. It felt refreshing, almost strange to smile. Even if she was smiling now at what seemed to be a joke on herself. A saint of her religion! Imagine! She prayed to God to forgive her for what she had done but she did not know if she had been heard. But she did know that no saint would have allowed Richard Abdee through the front doors, let alone marry him, good planter or not! For Ambrosia to pass on to Sugar Loaf, though, Honore said, "And there is nobody in the whole world I appreciate more than Sugar Loaf."

"Poor Sugar Loaf, I really do laugh at Sugar Loaf," Ambrosia said, pinning a line up from the hem. "Lately, Sugar Loaf flat-out refuses to go down to vegetable patch for anything. Sugar Loaf says she never knows when one of those little Fanti brats going to hop out from behind a cabbage or something and jump right on top of her."

Preferring not to get into a discussion about the swelling numbers of Fantis on the plantation, or that her husband had put children to work, Honore said, "We do not have cabbages in our vegetable garden, Ambrosia."

"We might not have cabbages, Mistress. But we sure do have ourselves a big, new crop of Fantis. Other plantations hereabouts, they losing niggers, they are. Left, right and centre. But not us. We the only people getting more. Breeding all the time, too, those Fantis do. None of them running away or nothing."

It seemed ironic to Honore but these days most of her gossip came from the slaves. And as she had heard nothing about the desertions, she asked, "Have there been many escapes on the island, Ambrosia?"

Ta-Ta answered the question for her. "Few field hands just disappearing, Mistress. But not here." She made it sound unimportant.

"And not from here, though?" Honore said, looking in the mirror. It was unusual to hear Ta-Ta talking about plantation life. Her sole concern seemed to be the life in this bedroom.

"No, Mistress."

"But where do they go? Do they join the Maroons in the mountains? But there aren't that many mountains here? Or have the Abolitionists organized ships to meet them and take them to freedom?"

On the floor below her, Ambrosia said, "We have strict orders, Mistress. We niggers told most strictly never to mention that word. Threatens us with cow-hide whips and shackles and burning pokers if we ever say that word around Dragonard."

"What word, Ambrosia?" Honore asked. She was still nauseous whenever she heard the word "Dragonard" mentioned.

But not to be drawn out, Ambrosia said, *"That* word."

"Abolitionists?"

"You said it, Mistress. Not Ambrosia. No, Ta-Ta witness to that, Mistress."

Honore frowned at such fear and asked, "Were those orders from Mister Abdee or did Captain Shanks place that polite request on you?"

"Mister Abdee! If Master Mister Abdee has anytime at all these days, it's not to talk to us. It's to go down to fields or down to the Fanti shacks and see how they faring. No, it was that Captain Shanks who tells us to foget about that word existing. Says it makes more trouble for us niggers than we have now. And if we hear or see any outside nigger coming in here preaching that stuff, we reports that nigger and gets ourself a silver eagle."

"Captain Master Shanks," Honore repeated with disdain.

"Looks worse than he really is, though, Mistress. Field niggers don't really have no complaints about Captain Master Shanks. Not like some of those nigger-drivers they have."

Without thinking what she was asking, Honore asked harmlessly, "Do Negroes complain, Ambrosia?"

But realizing what *she* had just said—that she had talked about black life to a white woman—Ambrosia answered quickly, "Oh. No, Mistress. Field slaves don't complain. Not to workhouse slaves. Not to mill slaves. Not to nobody. Nobody complains, Mistress."

"Oh, you know what I mean! Do they talk? Compare? Now, Ambrosia, please! You must understand that I do not try to ferret information out of you to use it against you. I just want to know what life down there is like!"

"Let me just say this, Mistress. We don't have no *bamboche* before Captain Master Shanks arrives. As much as Master Abdee says that the *bamboche* only gets us niggers all together so we get ourselves excited and we fight and we scrap and sometimes even we do things worse than that, he says. But Captain Master

Shanks, he says we niggers used to having our good times and he says to Master Abdee that we works harder if we have something to look forward to, and that's why now the niggers have Saturday night *bamboche*."

"You mean those loud parties I hear on week-ends?"

"Yes, Mistress," Ambrosia said, her eyes beaming. "That's what you hear. *Bamboche*! That sure what you hear."

Honore caught the reflection of Ta-Ta's disapproving frown and she smiled. She thought how that, even among Negroes—the so-called chattel of the white people—there were levels of social hierarchy. Obviously, a Negress like Ta-Ta did not approve of the *bamboche*. She probably thought that they were common. Nigger stuff. Field trash. And this gave Honore one more piece of proof that they were human-beings, too, demanding better treatment, even to be freed! The difference between the Fantis and the other plantation Negroes also testified Honore's long-held but never spoken conviction. And, thinking about the Fantis, she suddenly asked her source of information, "Does Calabar take part in the *bamboche*, Ambrosia?"

"Calabar?" she said, sitting on the heels of her bare feet. "Calabar, some niggers say, is more scared than Sugar Loaf. Some says he ain't."

"Scared? What does scared have to do with the *bamboche*?"

"The Fantis, that's what. But some say Calabar scared of old niggers, too. Scared of them because he's been lording it over them all these years. Some say Calabar funny about everything these days. Except little yellow piccaninny boy."

"You mean Monkey?"

"From Miss Ta-Ta here."

Looking into the mirror again, Honore caught Ta-Ta's eye and said, "See! That child is spending too much time with Calabar. He's an evil and despised man!"

Ta-Ta shrugged helplessly.

It was Ambrosia, though, who clarified that situation for Honore, too. She said, "Mistress, you don't want Monkey trailing after Calabar, then, you must say so yourself, Mistress. None of Miss Ta-Ta's say. She might be your special upstairs maid still and all that, Mistress, but Miss Ta-Ta nigger same the rest of us. Who she to go bossing other niggers around, say who's to follow around who?"

"But it's her child."

Stunned, Ambrosia said, "Mistress! Yellow baby's *your* piccaninny. And Master's."

Honore caught her breath. The horror of the child's conception came back to her.

Fortunately, though, Ambrosia continued, "All niggers—black, brown, yellow or what colour is your property. Not for Miss Ta-Ta here to say who's to follow who around the place."

Lifting up her unfinished skirt, Honore said, "Then *I* will say something about it!"

"Mistress!" Ambrosia said, staring at her pins and needles being dragged from her hands.

But Honore could not care less about her new dress. She was half-way out of the bedroom by now. She knew that her husband was downstairs in the library and so she would go down and have a word with him herself. And right now! As she strode angrily down the burgundy-carpeted hallway, she thought that it had been too long since she had taken a firm hand in things. After all, the plantation was half hers. The old slaves were still deeded-out in her name, too. So, she would see her husband right now and make her demands. Yes, it seemed as if a new dress had been responsible for this new vitality in her. It was her first new dress, too, in five year's time.

Abdee had registered the passage of years more in Honore than himself. He saw her as his senior, at least in age. Still handsome, but more of a relic of her former beauty.

He saw that his own face was growing tighter, more intent with work. His cornflower blue eyes were sinking farther under his brow. But he was learning that it was not the material things in life which a man comes to concentrate upon when he begins to attain his ambitions. He only works harder. The material things become not so important in themselves. Not that Abdee was letting himself deteriorate physically like Honore was doing. But he did notice his absence of enthusiasm over the little things. Like a new suit of clothing, that vanity which young men have over their outward appearances. Older men conserve time. So, in the last five years, Abdee had settled upon a uniform—a uniform for his whole self—black boots, brown breeches, a nankeen shirt, and the face of an industrious man who grabs his meals when he can and his wenches where the desire takes him. And everything centred around Dragonard—a seized dream.

This late morning, Abdee sat working at the desk in the library. After the changes on his bedroom, he had attacked the useless frippery down here. The library was still as full of clutter as it had been in Pierre Jubiot's days at Petit Jour. But, in the new era of Dragonard, the library held useful things. Not busts and tapestries and alabaster statuettes and volumes of French poets. But maps and diagrams and plantation charts and the latest information about innovations in crops. Abdee was dedicating his entire life to Dragonard.

When the door opened, Abdee looked up expectantly from the table. He had been waiting for Shanks to arrive with the reports, some facts for that tax which the new Lord had levied against surplus output. But seeing Honore rather than Shanks, and seeing her in a half-sewn dress, Abdee stared bemused at the unexpected sight. He had not seen Honore for two weeks. He had not really talked to her for a month. But perhaps his suspicions were true. Perhaps Honore was slowly losing her mind, going insane. Those green eyes looked like the wild eyes of a crazy woman.

Now, Honore's heels clicked across the parquet floor as she demanded, "Why is Monkey allowed to spend so much time with Calabar?"

Abdee was surprised to hear Honore mention slaves to him. He asked, "Monkey?"

Her face grew red. She was appalled that he should forget the name of his own son. But, then, she remembered that he had at least a dozen more half-caste children running around the plantation with equally odd names.

"Ta-Ta's child!" she said.

"Oh, yes," Abdee answered, remembering the little boy now. "What about him?"

"Why is he spending so much time with Calabar? I do not approve of it."

"I'm sorry," he said, his voice dry with insincerity.

"You are not sorry. You don't even know anything about it so how can you be sorry?"

Yes, he knew that he was right. Madness was setting in. He answered her quietly, "Why come interrogating me, then, if you know so much more?"

"Because I have left you uninterrupted for too long. And now I want my say. And I want to start by saying that the child called Monkey is not to spend so much time with Calabar in the kitchen, do you understand?"

"The kitchen falls under your jurisdiction, Honore. You know that as well as I do. The only say I have in the house is what Paw-Paw does and says."

"Which is about everything now. That boy is power crazy."

"He seems happier in this job, though, than what your brother had him doing. At least he can feel he's a man."

"My brother still haunts you, doesn't he?"

"Not in the slightest, Honore. Why? Are you having nightmares?"

"Of course not. Anyway, not about *him*!"

"Well, let's try to keep the subject of your dreamlife away from reality for a while, Honore, and let us make some sense of your problems. Now, first, yes, I do agree with you. Paw-Paw is becoming somewhat drunk with power. As a matter of fact, I have been very seriously considering bringing Manroot into the house. I hate to lose a strong man like that in the field but he does understand people. I might just be wasting him out there."

"Is he one of your Fantis?"

Honore always made herself such an easy target for Abdee. He asked, "Since when do you know one black from another? Except who ties your shoes and who cooks your meals?"

"I will not have any of those Fantis in my house."

"So we have lost our sense of honour, have we? Gone is our sympathy for those poor, black people?"

"But they are different."

Abdee reminded her, "Calabar is a Fanti."

"I do not even like him around."

Abdee shrugged. "He is your property. You can do with him what you like. But before you do anything, Honore," he said, slowly motioning at her half-sewn dress, "I do wish you would finish dressing yourself. Word gets around, you know. And white ladies do get raped. Especially *mad* ones. They have black babies!"

"I was being fitted for a new dress," she said, tugging at the white lace *modiste* between her breasts.

"Oh, is that it? Well, I'm certainly glad of that. You can use some new clothes."

"Since when have you noticed how I look."

Abdee said, "I notice more than you think, Honore. Little oddities here. Little oddities there. Small weakenings." If she was not crazy, perhaps he could persuade her that she was. Nothing would suit him better than for Honore to be in a madhouse and he could be in sole possession of Dragonard.

Glaring at him, Honore said, "And, besides, this

dress is not for you. It is to wear to the new Lord Governor's ball!"

"You have personally received an invitation, have you?"

Fumbling, she said, "No . . . but we will get one."

"You think so."

"Of course. Arabella said everyone is invited."

"And Arabella Warburton thinks that we will be there, too. Our record for production will secure us an invitation?"

"Arabella is not so vulgar as always to think in terms of money!"

"Perhaps not vulgar like that," Abdee said. But, then he thought better than to continue. Instead, he said, "Not to shatter your hopes, Honore, but I doubt if we will receive an invitation. And, even if we do, I know that neither of us shall attend." He turned. His work was more important than Honore. Dragonard took precedence over everything.

"But I want to go."

"I said we will not."

Then, as he stood, almost hearing Honore's spirits crumbling, her sudden surge of power quietly slipping away, he said, "And I think you are getting yourself worked up for nothing. I assure you no invitation from any new Lord Governor will be arriving at Dragonard." Looking down at the papers on his desk, he added, "And why they send men like that here, I have no idea."

"Lord Rothwell!"

"I know his name, Honore. I know. You don't have to shout. And I know that he is also a Quaker and an Abolitionist."

"So that is why you will not go."

"That is why *we* will not go."

"Because of the slaves."

"The whole island has slaves, Honore. It is only those who extract the most from them who are most attacked."

"He knows you have them beaten."

"No one is beaten on Dragonard unless they need it."

"It has to do with that name, too, doesn't it? The English are ashamed of you! The English are ashamed that you keep that name alive. Still flaunting . . ."

Slowly turning, Abdee said, "Nobody is ashamed of anything, Honore. Except a man, if any one should see his wife in your condition."

"And who possibly could come in that door? Captain Master Geoff Shanks? Should I be ashamed how I look in front of that man?"

"Even Captain Shanks can be appalled at such a mad, distressed sight as you. Now, get out of here!"

She had lost again. And holding the skirt of her half-sewn dress, she rushed from the study. Her mind was a chaotic jumble of anger, humiliation, and those same, re-occuring phallic images which troubled her soul. She was trapped and still being tortured in this house which seemed destined to imprison females.

Captain Geoff Shanks arrived in the hallway as Honore rushed from the study in a flurry of *crepe de chine* and needles. He reached toward the brim of his hat but Honore sailed past him and ascended the stairs without a word.

Behind her, Abdee had moved to close the library door. But Shanks appeared in it before he had time. Shanks asked no questions, though, and Abdee still never offered explanations to anyone.

Sitting back down at the table, Abdee asked, "You got the figures?" His voice smouldered with irritation.

"Don't look too good. This year is going to be the biggest crop yet."

Abdee's fist struck hard on the table.

Shanks tried to soften what normally would be taken as good news. "Course, we could always hope that Lord Governor don't put in the taxation right at his arrival."

"Hope? What does hope do? Nothing?" Abdee was standing again.

"There could be other ways to beat it."

"If there's not, we will have to make some."

"Shame to burn the crops," Shanks said.

"No, we won't burn anything. Never destroy what you have," Abdee said. But, then, as if he were contemplating a compromise on that long-held philosophy—was indeed thinking about burning the surplus sugar crops upon which the new taxes would be placed —he added, "Anyway, they will have scouts looking for signs of that."

"Yesterday, down in Basseterre, I saw the whole laws posted outside Government House."

"We have those here."

"But never before did I take in that law about inheritance. It seems now they are changing the law and the new one says that if you die and your plantation is in aid of the colony and you have no next of kin or such, except your spouse—and if she be not English—then the plantation can be turned over to the government."

Abdee knew that law. He just hated to think about it.

Shanks continued, "Be a shame seeing Dragonard go to the King."

Abdee slowly began to realize, then, what Shanks was trying to say. So, to save him the effort, he said, "But if a note could be legally put down on paper that you, Geoff Shanks, were my partner, then the King could not get it? That is if, say . . . something happened to me?"

"That's one way around it," Shanks said, studying the greasy brim of his hat. The feathers were gone now.

As Abdee stood chewing his thumb, he studied Shanks and realized how that crusty old crook would murder him to get Dragonard. Abdee did not worry about Honore being left penniless. It was providing an opportunity for Shanks to get his scaley, flaking fingers

187

on Dragonard which bothered Abdee. Walking toward him, Abdee asked, "When's the Governor's ball?"

"Next week. Why? You not thinking of going, are you?"

"We haven't been invited."

"Seems with all the taxes you will be paying, you at least would get one of the invitations."

"I wouldn't go anyway, would I?"

Shanks shrugged.

Then, turning, Abdee repeated, "Next Thursday." He was thinking. He had a plan. And his thoughts became words as he said, "So next Thursday it will be."

"Planning something?" Shanks asked.

"Only something for Dragonard."

"If it's for the niggers," Shanks said, raising his eyes again, "don't forget they have their *bamboche* on Saturday nights."

"No, I never forget, Shanks, how much you get out of them with your devious ways."

"Devious? Who said I was devious?"

"Your own mother if asked," Abdee snapped. Then, sitting down at his table, he said, "No, I am not thinking about the blacks. I was thinking more about the 'white folks'." Then he reached to study the reports which Shanks had brought in to him.

Still standing behind him, Shanks said in a more relaxed voice, "That *taffa* has aged mighty fine. I have a few bottles set aside for whenever you want to taste it."

Abdee waved his hand. He was telling Shanks to go. Leave him alone. The days of *taffa* and midnight carousing were over.

"Just thought I would mention it."

Abdee said to himself, "And you just thought that you would mention the point about a partnership, too. So the place could be yours, you swine. But I'll get you before you ever have time to get me."

Today was one of those days for Abdee on which he thought that he had come so very far in realizing his dreams of dominating his own private world—but, at the same time, everything around him seemed to threaten his accomplishments. Honore was a meddling idiot. Shanks was a grasping, ulterior pirate. The Government was a leech, trying to bleed him. But the most ironic new fact was that, without their heirs, Abdee now could have no solace in his own ambitions.

Sitting alone at his desk, Abdee thought about his own family. He thought about his home at Thornhurst. He remembered the millstone of his own inheritance. How he had tried and *tried* to shake it from his neck to gain his own life. And had succeeded.

Abdee also remembered the words he had once said: *If a son expects more than the light of day from me, he is no son of mine.*

And Abdee still felt the same way. The days and nights of his life still belonged to him. Anyone could enjoy the same. Any weakling. But only a strong man can seize the appointments of life. The booty to be had in this grasping world.

13

The Lord Governor's Ball

On the night of the Lord Governor's ball, Honore left
orders that no one should disturb her. It was a meaningless command but the act of saying the words gave
her some sense of position. Not many people called at
Dragonard these days. But, at the back of her mind,
she had feared that Arabella Warburton might drop by,
just to show Honore her gown. Arabella would not
mean harm, Honore felt. She just liked to share. But
Honore was not even in the mood to see Arabella Warburton tonight. Sad and dejected, she had gone to bed
before sundown and lay watching the light fade
through the mosquito netting hanging between herself
and the porch windows.

She must have fallen asleep, though, because when
the door opened, she jolted up from the pillows.

"Ta-Ta?" she called, thinking that it was her coming
in to go to sleep.

But Honore did not receive an answer. And, not
seeing Ta-Ta's slim figure move in the shadows between herself and the windows, Honore sat high in bed
and reached for the netting.

Then, a hand touched hers.

It was Abdee!

"Richard!" she said, jerking back. What was *he*
doing in here?

But Abdee just looked down through the netting at
her. He had not come to harm her. He did not frown.
But neither was he smiling. It was a look of appraisal
in his eyes.

Pulling the counterpane up to her throat, Honore said, "Can you not leave a prisoner in peace?"

Abdee raised his eyebrows, as if to deny that she was a prisoner. But he did not speak. He lifted back the netting.

Honore pulled away from him as he moved to sit next to her on the bed. He reached for her hair now. He sat feeling the long, soft ringlets against her nightgown.

Looking from his hand, up to his face, Honore was speechless. She wondered what he was going to do. Was he going to pull her hair? Had he come here to beat her? She would not be surprised. She knew his taste for violence in love-making had only increased. She could hear.

Raising his head, Abdee stood and walked to the door. He closed and locked it. Then, he strode back to the bed. Pulling up the curtaining, he sat down again.

"Richard?" she repeated nervously.

He shook his head. But it was not an imperative movement, more a movement of loss.

"Richard?" she repeated. Her voice was less frightened. More puzzled. He did not have that beating look to him. She felt safer.

But, still, he did not answer her. He sat quietly on the edge of the bed. He looked almost helpless.

She asked the third time, "Richard?"

Silence.

So, gathering courage, Honore lifted herself up from her pillows on the other side of the bed and reached to feel his forehead. It was her nature to help others, even enemies.

And, at that moment, he took her hand and held it.

Honore felt her heart beginning to pound and she cursed herself. But how long had it been since she had felt any tenderness, a touch, this soft silence from anyone? How long had it been since anyone had held her hand?

Next, Abdee lay down—but outside the covers—beside her on the bed.

"Richard, are you ill?"

He shut his eyes, still holding her hand.

So, with her other hand, Honore reached again to touch his cheeks for a fever, pressing the back of her palm against his dark, sun-tanned face.

But, before she removed that hand, Abdee grasped it, too, and he held it with her other hand. He was encasing them both in his, and held them against his chest. His shirt was half-opened. Her skin touched his.

"Richard?" she asked softly. She would have given her life to say "my love."

Next, he moved both of her hands to his mouth.

And as he gently began kissing her hands, she fell back on her pillow. Their heads were not touching but they shared the same pillow. And he was kissing her hands.

But, despite the stillness of her body, Honore's mind was racing. Her memory. What he had done to her in the past. What was happening now. What could it mean?

Next, Abdee removed one hand from hers and lifted the counterpane from her body. He began to trace the line of her shoulder, arm, thighs.

Honore's body lay rigid—tense with fear—until Abdee reluctantly moved his hand away. It was as if he sensed her resistance. He lay his head back down on the pillow and did not take her other hand back to his chest. But he did do one thing new, though. He did speak. He did say, "Honore?"

The passion which she had always felt for him—multiplied by the frustration of these last long years—tumbled out in a mad rush at the sound of her name. She took control of the situation now. She executed the undressing. The throwing down of sheets. She guided him inwards.

His body had not changed at all. His thighs were still lean and hard, brushed with that soft, yellow down.

His stomach was muscled exactly how she had remembered it, like a pattern of iron within his smooth but tough skin.

His buttocks, pale, curvaceous, squeezing as he sank into her.

But of all her memories, all her dreams, the one that *had* changed substance was the object of her nightmares: the phallus.

That demonic shape which had previously pierced her brain now was undergoing a metamorphosis from evil to pure goodness in Honore's mind.

As Honore felt her husband deep inside her—and deep he could only go, too, because God had endowed him to match the greatness of his passion—she knew for the first time that only goodness could emerge from this act tonight.

And, for the first time, too, Honore felt herself expand and contract, actually accepting that area of masculinity which had only represented sin to her up to now.

Her soul was alive; her senses quivering at the slightest touch, both inside and out. And as she was abandoned in the delirium of this unexpected union, she did not realize how strongly his great, wide hands were holding her breasts—pummelling the softness of the skin, pressing her nipples—until she felt a great explosion within her. But all pain was washed over by a flood, an overflow not only from herself but from him. And, as she lurched up toward the hardness of his jerking body, he drove her back down to the bed. And she accepted it. Even when, slowly, he inched his way out from her hold.

Her breasts. Her body. Her soul. Everything was still alive, but smouldering like a hearth at the end of day.

She had a flicker of life.

But she had more than just her life.

She knew that inside her, Abdee had planted his seed.

Limp, she lay on her pillows, her slim arms dropped helplessly to the sides of her head. Her naked body still quivered from the encounter.

Even when she became vaguely aware that Abdee

was standing beside the bed, gathering his clothes, she did not stir.

Nor did she move when she heard the door to her bedroom open, then close.

He was gone.

But she had his seed.

She was slightly conscious of the door opening again. And then felt the coolness of a sheet being placed over her body. It was Ta-Ta. But Honore did not even murmur. By now, she was deep in a dream-free sleep.

The silvery crescent of the moon reigned in a clear sky tonight, the lesser magnificence of the stars twinkling in silent attendance. And the entire North end of the island languished in a cool, peaceful stillness.

But the country roads to the south were alive with coaches carrying the plantation aristocracy to the Lord Governor's palace.

The streets of Basseterre were also crowded with the townspeople hoping to catch a glimpse of European finery.

Gowns of pale gossamer. Tiaras which twinkled with garnets, emeralds, and sapphires. Brocade frockcoats. White silken hose clocked with silver. Jewel-headed canes. And spreading fans made from the tail-feathers of albino peacocks. The opulence of the St. Kitts hierarchy exploded on Basseterre tonight like the glitter of Chinese fireworks, the warm night lighting up as each carriage door was opened by a Negro footman, wearing a scarlet turban topped with black egrettes.

But all the activities were not centred at the palace this evening. Apart from the private receptions at various townhouses, there was another fete being planned in Basseterre.

Chez Naomi shone especially bright, too. Or, would be gleaming later when the white gentlemen unattached themselves from their separate parties and stealthily found their ways to Barracks Lane.

Naomi was planning a special presentation for this

evening, another one of her theatrical *pièces de résistance*. And, in keeping with the occasion, she had titled it: THE LORD GOVERNOR'S BALL.

But she still had three hours, though, before her customers began to arrive.

Now, in her bedroom, Naomi lay on her plum-coloured chaise longue and talked to Calabar. He would be playing the "Lord Governor" in tonight's cellar drama. He sat on a chair across from her.

Having only arrived moments ago from his hard ride from the north, Calabar's clothes were still dust-covered, his tribal-marked face still tight from the wind.

But Naomi was completely relaxed. Time had been good to her. She looked like a girl of eighteen or nineteen. But, as she was twenty-six years old now, she still did not have to worry about the ravages of age. Or those small dark spots—skin blotches which looked not unlike freckles, or liver marks—which occur on the faces of even the darkest African woman. Naomi's complexion was still smooth and satiny, the colour of a prune . . . but soft and without lines.

Because of the prosperity which her business enjoyed, Naomi was dressing more exquisitely than ever before. Now, she wore a dressing-robe of luxurious white satin trimmed with ecru-tinted marabou. The heels of her satin slippers—in keeping with the tradition of European courtesans—were red. The slippers were white this evening but, always, the heels: scarlet red.

She asked Calabar now, "How does a man as clever as Richard Abdee still not know that you come here? You've been stripping down here for six years and he still has not said a thing to you?"

Calabar shook his head. No, Abdee had not.

"But he's no dummy! Either he knows and he's not letting on or . . . he doesn't care what you do! You still have the Jubiot pass to travel so Abdee lets you use it, probably glad to get you out of his way." Naomi threw back her head and laughed.

Calabar realized that that might be true, too.

Heaving her breast now, Naomi said, "Richard Abdee is the only whitie I've ever taken to."

Calabar spoke now in his dry, even voice. "I hate Richard Abdee."

Naomi frowned. If Calabar did not possess such extraordinary personal equipment she doubted if she would continue to use him for these theatrical evenings. But there was no other man as generously endowed on St. Kitts. The young boy, Nero, had been blessed, too. But, regardless how much Naomi still coached Nero, he still had a block about making a show of himself. Nero was too earthy. He did not even respond to Naomi's harangues about hatred for the whites. Nero liked everybody.

But Calabar was an ideal performer for *Chez Naomi*. Not only was he an exhibitionist, but he had that something to exhibit. Also, Calabar had a great contempt for the whites. He liked to make them squirm, to make them crawl for him. But then he did not like the blacks very much, either.

Calabar was a special kind of Negro, Naomi realized. He was from the Fanti tribe. Naomi was a Fanti, too. But Calabar still practised their ancient religions, a sacred animal cult.

Now, he was beginning to tell Naomi about the other Fantis on Dragonard. Their progress since their arrival on the island. Which ones had become his acquaintances. Their mutual interests.

But, as always, Naomi held up both slim arms and pleaded, "Spare me that nigger talk! I don't want to hear about niggers. I'm black but I'm a female first. The whites say we blackies aren't human. Fine! I'm not even going to argue about that. But female animals have tastes to satisfy, too, and mine is money. And the freedom that comes with it. Why in hell do you think I get on so well with that white 'master' of yours? Richard Abdee thinks the same way as me! Call us both ruthless. Call us savage. Call us cold and inhuman. Say that we'll do anything to get what we want. And you say all those things and they're true. Richard Abdee is going his way and I'm going mine. People might say that we're both headed for hell but we keep on going, don't we? Look at him! Why, he's one of the finest specimens of a white man I've ever seen. He was a bit more cocky when I first met him. Anxious. Eager. Greedy to make his own way and not caring how he did it. And now that he's doing it, he's taking his work seriously. He's living and breathing that plantation. And if I know that Richard Abdee, too, he'll do anything—*anything*—to hold on to it. And so he should. But that doesn't mean I have to sit listening about it, does it? I've got my own life here and so that's what little Naomi thinks about. Not Dragonard. Not niggers. But what happens to little Naomi."

Calabar stared at her, amazed at her articulate philosophy.

"Listen," Naomi said, rising from the chaise longue, scooping the silky white train of her robe in her right hand, "your white 'master' and I have met off and on since he's been married. Only a few times. But we know that each other's out there someplace. And I'm sure we'll see more of each other again. But until then I don't want to hear about him. Got that straight? I've got my money to make, too. My life to lead. Just like him. We understand each other."

Then, reaching down toward Calabar's breeches, Naomi poked her long, slim forefinger down into his crotch and said, "If that white 'master' of yours *does* come back to stay for any length of time, you better watch out, brother! You might be out of a little job here. He's got the mate to this greasy, old doodad, you know, honey!"

Standing up, she quickly told Calabar to take a bath now and get himself in a more public mood.

Then, pouring herself a glass of champagne, Naomi opened the door of her bedroom and began to make last minute checks around the house. Although she still had to get dressed herself, she was not worried. Naomi was not in a hurry for anything.

Singing to herself in French, Naomi slowly descended the stairs, her marabou-trimmed robe dragging over the Oriental carpets.

14

Bamboche

A man's taste for entertainment changes as he grows older. He has less time—or desire—to exert himself in finding pleasures.

But when a man enters full maturity, he also discovers that the variations on the sexual act become less necessary, or as frequently as when he was young and eager to assert himself.

Abdee was not becoming unskilled, losing his taste for venery practices other than the moment of penetration. But the taste for those diversions of his early days on St. Kitts, those nights spent on Barracks Lane at *Chez Naomi* now seemed to have diminished. At least, becoming less self-conscious. Much of Abdee's energy, too, had been going into his work.

In the past five years Abdee had ridden to Basseterre no more than once every two months. His presence was too necessary on Dragonard. And only on a few of those rare visits to the capital city had he been to Barracks Lane to see that Negress who had lied herself into his life as "Lucretia Borgia."

But Abdee knew that Naomi was prospering. Her reputation was growing, not only on St. Kitts, and neighbouring Nevis, but to all the Leeward Islands. And, for his part, Abdee also honoured that pact made long ago—that they would remain constant in their friendship regardless of the amount of time which spread between their meetings.

He secretly suspected that Naomi, too, had less time to spend bending the wills of others. Even when it's a bordello which a person is running, he—or she—can not conduct his, or her, business successfully if they think solely about sex. The dominating role.

The dominating role. Now that Abdee had slaves to punish—black Africans whose faults or misdemeanors often demanded strenuous correction—did he still feel so aggressive toward the female sex? Was running Dragonard a sexual outlet to him? Yes, Abdee knew that many people asked that question, or these things about him. But those curious people did not know that sex to Abdee—the experience of his animal instincts— was different from his other desires, that self-bestowed vocation to make a plantation work.

Regardless of what many people still believed, Abdee did not punish the slaves for the mere act of punishment. In fact, he whipped them very infrequently. Whipping only weakened their working capacities. But when a slave did step out of line, did stray from his field of duty, then Abdee had no other choice. He would do the same with a white man. A worker must work. The boss must rule.

He also knew that flagellation was by no means the worst sentence which could be placed upon a disobedient slave. Abdee, too, heard the stories about punishments far worse than the bite of black leather. It was true that one or both ears of an African was often severed in conjunction with a whipping. But many local planters often slit a Negro's mouth from ear to ear if the slave told a lie, spoke irreverently to his master, or failed to address a white person with proper respect.

If a Negro buck raped a white woman—or mated with a Negress of his own choosing, as was more commonplace—the condemnation then was for the buck to be "nutted"—a mild overture compared to the death which often followed.

If a Negro ran, tried to escape, it was not unknown to cut off a leg, or to slice away part of a foot if the slave disobediently failed to show at a designated place.

And, then, too, there were those punishments which explained no crime, symbolized nothing but the subservience of the African in many white men's eyes. One such inexplicable sentence was to nail a Negro to the ground and tie dried twigs to his legs, midsections, and arms. Then he—or she—was set afire. So, in comparison to these other punishments, the cat or the bull whip seemed to be the least harmful. At least, to Abdee.

He also found that the Africans were generally a fearful race. They respected authority and fitted into the actual work pattern of a plantation much easier than many white workers would do—with wages paid!

Rumours of revolt, plans of Negroes rebelling *en masse* still plagued the island. But, then, all the people of the West Indies lived in daily fear of a slave revolution. From the Bahamas to Trinidad, all white communities were predicting trouble. Already in Barbados revolutions were said to occur monthly. From Antigua came regular reports of fires started by Negroes. In Tobago, entire crops had been put to the torch. And the vast American estates were all resting on quicksand, the European colonials trembling at the impending threat of faceless, discontent black hordes.

Abdee, though, found that if he slowly encouraged the slaves to participate in the running of Dragonard, their eyes seemed to lose some of that look of revenge. And he had indirectly realized that trick—that solution—from Naomi. She was a Negro but she also was a very clever person. Naomi was the first African who had truly impressed upon Abdee that Negroes were people like anybody else.

But, in the passing years, Abdee had met no African—male or female—who possessed the guile of Naomi. Her business acumen and the ability to gauge appetites ranked even higher than any white person whom Abdee had met.

There was only one black person, though, whom Abdee had come to respect, if not as much as Naomi, and not for similar reasons, then at least someone whom he could place above the other Africans who peopled his small, insular sphere of activities these days.

That person was Manroot, the tall leader of the Fantis, the towering black man who looked like a roughly-hewn sculpture of a fertility god.

Abdee had come to notice that many of the Dragonard blacks still worked, and lived, in a somnambular state. It was as if they had forfeited their spirit to their new roles as slaves. They did not show any interest in the plantation, and Abdee could understand that, too. But the only time they seemed to come to life was at the recently organized *bamboche* parties. But, even then, their brains seemed to fly from their heads. None of them were as self-possessed as Manroot.

But it was because of one of those Saturday night gatherings, the *bamboche*, that Manroot solved the problem of the Lord Governor's supplementary tax for excessive produce. Or, at least, Manroot had come closer to a solution than anyone else had done so far, black man or white.

Manroot had noticed that the uneaten sugar cane from the *bamboche*, when buried in the ground after the feast, came to fertilize the earth. And he had suggested to Abdee to try it in the field. He said that by burying sugar, there would be no waste.

Abdee consented, and, so far, it seemed to be working.

He admired Manroot for seizing upon a piece of information learned at a party. He respected him for keeping his brain working at all times.

And so that came to be another reason why Abdee mixed more and more with the blacks. He, too, indulged in this one bit of play on Dragonard, the *bamboche*, which had been instigated by Captain Geoff Shanks.

Shanks, in the meantime, was becoming a bigger problem for Abdee than any of the Negroes. But Abdee was slowly formulating a plan to solve the problem of Shanks, too. And perhaps that other worry which had been pressing him, the next taxation. Yes, Manroot's idea for burying sugar could very well work but Abdee was beginning to suspect that he might not have reason to use it.

But, true to his tradition of taking the best from everybody, Abdee allowed his plot for Shanks to ferment—and how to deal with the new Lord Governor, too—and he quite readily accepted the Shanks-inspired occasion, the *bamboche* . . .

Tonight's party looked as if it was going to be ideal. It was eight o'clock now, the work was done for the day, and the weather had been cooled by a refreshing wind from the Northeast.

The sky was reddening with the setting sun and the hour for the *bamboche* grew nearer. The slaves scampered happily between their wattle huts, trading pieces of bright calico at the last minute, or borrowing shell necklaces, strands of painted beads, bright collars made from parrot feathers. Their usual drab, oat-meal coloured clothing had been cast off for tonight and out came their cherished lengths of vividly dyed cottons, gaily embroidered shifts made from flour sacks, or tunics torn from strips of sheeting. Everything that was gay and exotic, bespoke of joy and happiness, was sported to the *bamboche*.

All the Dragonard slaves co-operated for these evenings, too. These weekly festivities were even responsible for some of the homogeny slowly being created between the Fantis and other blacks. It was true that certain factions, or ethnic groups, had emerged at the *bamboche*. The most significant to date was the Voodoo ritual dancers. But Abdee had given Shanks orders to squelch those tall, black men from the Ashanti tribe who danced until they fell to the ground in a trance. He realized the powers of religion and magic.

As usual, the *bamboche* was being held tonight in the valley behind the main house, down in the flat area which lay in front of the white, pitch-roofed shed known as "the laundry house." It had come to be the customary spot for the *bamboche* because of the hill which gently sloped down to the drying area, forming a natural amphitheatre of the hillside.

At the moment, four Negresses, who were still dressed in their osnaburgh shifts from the fields, were quickly pulling back the clothes line to make room for the dancing area. The *bamboche* was basically an evening of dancing, the word brought here from France, meaning a wild spree or country fling. But those blacks who wanted to sit, lie back, and relax, could enjoy the merriment as they peacefully ate the specially prepared food on the hillside.

In a deep pit, a fire already blazed and the long iron spits waited in piles. Nearby, another group of black women squatted around wicker cages of cackling hens. One woman would pull a fowl from the portable coop, stretching its feathered neck between her hands. Then, after she quickly bit the veins in the chicken's neck, she would toss it—bleeding and flopping—to the next Negress who then began to pluck the feathers, preparing the hen for roasting.

At the same time, children carried large platters of sliced oranges, coconuts, mangoes, bananas, and sugar cane from the Cook House and sat them on long tables covered with white cloths.

Also, the first set of musicians was beginning to bring their instruments to the dirt-floored amphitheatre. They carried drums, coloured gourds, and any other home-made instrument which they had made from bits and pieces found around the plantation—barrels, horses' jaws, hammerheads, bottles. The Negroes' music always began with no rhythm but, as the players continued and the enthusiasm spread, the tinny but melodic African beat soon engulfed the whole valley with abandoned happiness.

Tonight, Abdee did not join the *bamboche* until the sky was already dark, and only the fire lit the faces of the jigging, chanting, shaking, twisting dancers.

Standing against the wall of the laundry house, Abdee solemnly watched the half-naked, perspiration-covered bodies as they moved hypnotically to their home-made sounds.

And, among the dancers, he saw Sabine. She was

corpulent now, with pendulous breasts. A succession of childbearing had changed the body of that girl whom Abdee had first seen through the willows as she sat singing Papist hymns. At last count, Sabine had given birth to fourteen piccaninnies, all who had been—or were still being—raised down in "the Pen." But from the way in which Sabine was bending herself toward a tall, lanky black boy now, Abdee wondered if her total would soon swell to fifteen.

Catching Shanks's attention, Abdee beckoned him over to the laundry house. He asked, "Are you keeping a check on our stud list?"

Already thick-tongued from *taffa,* Shanks slurred, "Grandma Goat keeps total."

Abdee knew that. He had given the parsimonious old Negress the special task of which stud should mate with which dam. Grandma Goat—who was tiny, with more hairs on her sharp chin than on her small skull—doled out the men's seed to the wenches as if each spurt were a penny of a household's kitchen money.

"I don't want Ta-Ta having any more," Abdee said to Shanks now.

But, holding up his bottle, Shanks bellowed, "More what?"

Abdee shot him a cold glance. He was getting tired of Shanks's perpetual drunkenness. He was getting tired of Shanks. His pox-marked face. His *taffa.* Those ambitions for a chunk of Dragonard lurking in the back of his mind. But he was being patient for the moment.

He slurred to Abdee now, "Time you start mating up your Manroot."

"He's doing fine," Abdee answered coldly.

"I mean mating him with something else than those Fanti wenches. Let some of the other ripe bellies have a shot of that hot, royal juice."

"Manroot has more to do than sow kids."

"He's pretty good at the sugar cane, too, I hear," Shanks said, swaying like a dead tree in the wind.

"Better than you and I have been doing," Abdee answered honestly.

Hoisting his bottle again, Shanks called, "To nigger brains! And may they never get as big as their peckers or we'll all be found dead in our sleep!"

"Get a hold of yourself."

Shanks belched.

Suddenly, something in the crowd caught Abdee's eye. It was a specific group of dancers. And somehow they reminded Abdee of the Ashanti Voodoo men. He asked Shanks, "What is that?"

"What's who?"

"There," Abdee said, pointing toward the small and isolated group of men. The other dancers were making room for this new group—even pulling back. And, as the crowd cleared, Abdee saw Calabar among the dancers. Their number was made up entirely of men. Their black faces were gashed with white paint. Their chests were bare. But they were all skirted in dried palm leaves. Abdee noticed, too, that the brittle leaves had been dabbed with oil, making spots on the skirts like markings on an animal's skin.

"Just some of your niggers," Shanks said, looking toward them with blurred eyes, "Niggers dressing up. Having a good time."

"That's more than for a good time," Abdee said, looking now at the strands of teeth hanging around all their necks. "It means something. Those outfits are all uniform!"

But now, though, Shanks had slumped against the wall. He was beyond any condition to see dancers or anything.

So, moving forward to find out more about this new group of dancers for himself, Abdee suddenly noticed Manroot approaching them, too. Abdee watched the tall, black man begin to argue with the dancers. Then Manroot grabbed one of the blacks by the neck.

Next, Abdee watched as the male dancers slowly moved away, their dried skirts crackling as they retreated from Manroot's anger.

Pushing a path through the crowd, Abdee put his hand on Manroot's arm. He asked, "What was the trouble?"

But Manroot shook his head.

Abdee carefully studied Manroot's face, that skin which looked like polished walnut. The eyes spaced wide apart. His enormous round nostrils. The massive, square jaw. Manroot's looks were always brutal. But now there was a sharpness in his eyes which Abdee had never seen before. A determination.

Abdee asked him, "Aren't you going to tell me what the trouble is?" He knew there was trouble. He knew that there were warring factions within the Fantis. All this time he had left the problems to Manroot, though. They had not interfered with the running of Dragonard.

Manroot lowered his head now, the straight line of black wool across his forehead bent in deference to Abdee. Or was it a plea for consideration? A request for privacy?

Abdee asked, "Is it some problem you're having with your people?"

Manroot looked at Abdee. His eyes were beginning to soften. And, at the very moment that Abdee thought that Manroot was going to confide in him, share his secret, his broad face instead widened into a grin. And, with a sudden flicker of benevolence in his eyes, he looked over Abdee's shoulder and said, "Other Fantis. Women from the mill."

Abdee turned to see what he meant.

Then he, too, saw the reason for Manroot's change of temperament. And he also forgot about the spotted frond dangers.

Eight black females, ranging from a nubile eighteen-year-old to a fulsome forty were beginning to dance in a line on the far side of the blazing bonfire.

But it was more than the widths of the colourful cloths wrapped around their gyrating bodies which made these women into a team. Although it was night, and clear-skied, each Negress held an umbrella. They had obviously found these old umbrellas discarded in a dump heap—tattered and ripped. But now each triangular section of each umbrella was covered with a different pattern of bright colours: Red chequered. Pink floral. Yellow and orange striped. Some of the sections were even bordered with fringe.

And, as the women moved their shiny, bare shoulders and twisted their sheathed hips to the tinny music of the plantation band, they also hoisted the multi-patterned umbrellas over their heads in unison, or twirled them to make a dizzy design like cartwheels.

Slowly, the other slaves began clapping their hands in accompaniment to this unexpected display.

And Manroot bragged proudly to Abdee, "We good people, too, Master Sir."

For the first time since Abdee had known Manroot, had come to respect him, he put his arm around his broad shoulder. It was almost a fraternal squeeze. An acknowledgement that—although this was slavery—it was still life. They were all here together.

Then, turning from the music Abdee left the Africans to enjoy the raucous joy of their *bamboche*.

But a young Negress who had also been watching the dancers now slipped into the shadows of the laundry house, too.

Abdee was walking ahead of her, and by this time he was half-way up the hill toward the rear darkness of the main house.

He paused on the footpath, though, thinking that he heard a noise behind him.

Turning, he saw the slim outline of a figure standing between him and the crowd gathered around the fire below. Then, he saw it was a young Negress.

"Why aren't you dancing?" he called.

Silently, the girl moved up the hill toward him.

"What's your name?" he asked.

"Dido," she murmured, reaching with trembling

hands toward his breeches now, as if she were cautiously trying to pet a dangerous animal.

Abdee asked calmly, "Don't you know you aren't supposed to make approaches toward your master like this?"

The girl quickly withdrew her hand from him.

But Abdee moved down to her now and, reaching into her blue tunic, he felt the softness of warm flesh. He said, "You aren't very old, are you?"

"Fourteen," she said softly.

Feeling the fresh, new proportions of her breasts, he asked, "Wouldn't you rather be dancing?"

Reaching for his trousers again, she said, "I wants a gold sovereign."

"I only give sovereigns to a wench who gives me a sucker."

She nodded.

"Have you been to see Grandma Goat?" he asked.

The girl shook her head.

Abdee could feel that she had the excitement of an adult, though, pounding inside her chest. He said, "Well, Dido, we have a regular pattern for mating wenches. But I might give you a sovereign for something else."

Her large eyes lit up.

So, taking her by the small hand, he led her toward a small clump of nasberry. And, lying down on the grass, Abdee lowered his trousers to his boots and gave the young Negress her first lesson on how to satisfy her master in another way. He coached her how not to hold her mouth, warned her of sharpness, and told her that she had big lips so use them, too. Abdee swelled even more as he watched young Dido responding to the briskness in which he moved her head, shoving her mouth toward him deeper, even giving her a few hard, slaps on her tender buttocks.

No, indeed, there was no reason for him to go to Basseterre any more. He had all the delights which a man could want right here on Dragonard. He must not lose it.

Below them, the *bamboche* still shook with excitement, the steely rhythms continuing to rise in the night with the sparks from the fire.

15

An Intrigue

"Honore, you must be joking!"

If Arabella Warburton had not been such a good friend, Honore would have taken offence at the remark. Instead, she stared sweetly at the slim English woman sitting next to her on the divan and shook her head.

"But you are no young girl."

Honore shrugged. "That is why I am so glad. I never thought it would happen to me. Not now."

"Yes, I can see. I can certainly see." But, still not satisfied, Arabella snapped her fan shut and asked, "What about complications?"

Honore's answer was honest, "I would rather die like this than to die . . ."

"Oh, now don't be silly! Stop talking about dying! You are not going to die. But . . . I'm just flabbergasted. I mean, I thought you and Richard never . . . I mean. I mean everything would be perfectly all right if you two saw one another . . . but, then you two obviously *do* see one another if you . . . Honore, are you certain that you are going to have a *baby*?"

"Yes."

Arabella quickly reached for the glass of wine setting on the draped table. Taking three large swallows, she set down the glass and said, once for each gulp, "Indeed! Indeed! Indeed!"

"And are you happy for me?"

"Happy? Why, I'm, I'm . . . I'm thrilled for you, my dear. Absolutely overcome. You see how I'm reacting. But I want to congratulate Richard, too. Why, it's al-

most like you getting MARRIED, married all over
again, isn't it? Of course, no one was allowed in on
that! But, then," she said, lowering her head, "before we
knew what was happening, everything seemed to be
over between you and Richard. And, when I come to
see you, it's just *you* I see. Lately, I understood that
the two of you weren't speaking. And, well, I'm just
flabbergasted. That's all I can say, flabbergasted that
it's happened!"

"But about the baby? Isn't that wonderful?"

"Of course it's wonderful. What do you think I've
been talking about?" Turning quickly away from Honore, Arabella said, "I wish that if Richard were joining
us for dinner that he would hurry. It has been so long
since I've seen him. In fact, it's been so long since I've
been invited to ... to ... Dragonard for dinner! You
and I have our little get-togethers but I never seem to
see Richard! It's not like Randolph who is always away
in Basseterre at the courts. You have Richard right
here! But I never seem to see him when I come. Not
how I thought I would." Arabella seemed to be flus-
tered now, grasping for words. She was trying to control her over-patient desires for Abdee. She still took
her respites from the musty blacks of Warburton Field
to visit the young man, Nero, at *Chez Naomi*. But Arabella was bored with his lack of true authority. Nero
had a magnificent body, with male proportions which

. . .

She needed Abdee. A white brute.

Suddenly turning to Honore, she said, "Forgive me,
my dear, but with all this good news, may I tell you
something?"

"Please do."

"I am really quite famished. Can't you call Richard
now?"

"He said that if he was not here by eight o'clock to
eat without him."

"We could never do that!"

"Somehow I think he would want it that way, Arabella."

She frowned. "If you insist. But he will know where we are, won't he?" She wondered if Honore suspected her feelings for Abdee. Was intentionally keeping him from her.

"We will only be in eating," Honore said.

But Arabella was out on the porch now, looking down the drive for any sign of a rider. Turning back in, she said to Honore, "Dear friend, do you think that he has come back and perhaps we did not hear him?"

"Arabella, please! Forget about Richard!"

"Oh, I didn't mean about him especially. It's just . . ." She thought quickly. "You know the stories of all those slaves missing recently. Do you ever worry about Richard being alone?"

"No."

"Or aren't you ever frightened about . . . Negro men? That they might attack you? And you will be helpless? And they will take advantage of your weak femininity? Throw you on the floor and . . ."

"No, Arabella. Not with Richard around."

"Is he that brave?" she asked intrigued. "Strong enough to over-power a black man?"

"They're all terrified of Richard, Arabella. Everybody is."

Arabella stared at Honore.

But it wasn't difficult for Arabella to visualize Abdee dominating this weak French mouse! Honore was no challenge for him at all! And Arabella thought how tedious it must be for such a strong man to try to satisfy himself with such overt weakness! Yes, he needed a stronger woman, a person who would struggle in her submission, have the courage to ask for his magnificence. Yes, Arabella clearly knew now that Abdee needed her as much as she needed him.

The problem, though, still remained the same: How to let him know that she was available.

Now, together, the two women went into the centre garden to begin dinner without him.

With only half her powers of concentration, Arabella

answered Honore's questions about swaddling, wet-nursing, and cribs.

Abdee was taking his forthcoming issue more personally than Honore. An heir meant freedom for him, an escape from the new inheritance rule which would pass a plantation to the government if no English member of the family succeeded. Abdee's heir would be a tool against such legislation, but more so, against Shanks, the one man who had his eye on a partnership in Dragonard. Abdee knew that, if a solution against the government such as a partnership were taken, Shanks would not hesitate at murdering him for sole possession. So, with that knowledge, Abdee had decided to retaliate further. Like the ties of lianas which grew beyond the iron fences of Dragonard, so did Abdee's mind move in a twisting, diverting, clinging fashion. And this evening he had decided to begin his plot to secure what was his, whatever the outcome of a family might be.

The two ladies finally began their supper, not waiting for the expectant father. Proud of her maternity, Honore had decided not to confide in Arabella that her husband never told her what he was doing, where he was, or why.

But Abdee was only two floors above the centre garden. He was ostensibly trying to settle Manroot in the big house.

Abdee, too, was taking every precaution with the giant-like Fanti. He had never mistreated him. And, even now, he was not treating him overly kindly. Manroot was bright, a born leader of men. He knew when not to trust other men. Abdee was moving slowly with his plan.

But Manroot was a slave, too, a foreigner brought to a white man's land to serve and obey. Abdee had told himself that he must also be conscious of that fact when dealing with Manroot—and how it must gnaw at the very core of his soul.

Manroot stood uneasy in the bare room, moved in it

as if the room were only an ante-chamber to something bigger, a scale more fitting his size. And Abdee planned to give him much bigger things, too, if he proved himself capable here. And not only with the house. Abdee was testing for his plan to save Dragonard. Its perjury justified the end result.

But Manroot was reluctant to sit down on the bed, even to stay here. He said, "This is the first time I am away from my people."

"Go ahead. Try a European bed. It's not going to fly you away. We both know there's no such thing as magic." He remembered the stories of the slaves, their interpretations of the slavers.

Something troubled Manroot.

But Abdee assured him, "Your people are safe. Haven't I always provided well for them?"

"They have new problems with each other. Old but new again."

Abdee argued, "Your people have problems with others, too. What others want to do with them. But there's nothing that even *you* can do to solve those problems."

Manroot looked quizzically at Abdee. He did not understand this argument. He asked, "You know something?"

Abdee began his lie calmly. "I know something. But not enough." He studied the objects in the small room as he planted this seed in Manroot's head. He looked from the cracked cistern, the bowl, the table. The wooden bed which would obviously have to be replaced with a pallet for Manroot—if Manroot co-operated with him, believed what he was telling him, offered to help. Abdee would put many things at Manroot's disposal if he agreed to his plan. But knowing that Manroot was a shrewd man—and what the universal law, black or white, called a man of integrity—Abdee knew that he had to present his plan to Manroot in the most cunning way. At moments such as this, Abdee wished that the Africans were the dumb people which Europeans made them out to be. Base animals. With such a creature, Abdee could simply order him to "kill."

"You tell me when my people are in danger?" Manroot asked with deep concern in his mahogany-rich voice.

Abdee prevaricated for the sake of his Dragonard. He said, "It is not just your people, the Fantis, but all the blacks here. Perhaps even more. The whole island. All the West Indies."

"Something is going to happen?"

"It has been happening since the beginning of time. It is called 'greed.' White men. Black men. Red men. Even men whose skins have grown so crusty with disease and covered with sores that you can not see their colour, those men plot for greed, too."

"Shanks?"

Good. We are moving, Abdee thought. So, he asked, "You have known Shanks for a long time, haven't you?"

"Shanks came to Africa."

"But do you think you know him well enough to say that he is a greedy man?"

Manroot was silent.

"And do you think you have seen enough of him to say that he would betray the person closest to him?"

Manroot's face tightened. Abdee knew that honour was one of the Fantis's most cherished virtues. He also knew that he had won Manroot's respect long ago.

He continued more easily, "You heard that there is a new leader on St. Kitts. A man King George has sent to govern us."

Manroot nodded.

"This new governor is an Abolitionist. Do you know what that means?"

His silence confirmed that he did.

"But he is an English politician, first. Do you know the word 'politician'?"

Manroot nodded.

"The new governor is a 'political Abolitionist'."

"And Shanks?" Manroot asked.

"Shanks?" Abdee repeated, staring Manroot straight in the eyes. "Shanks is nothing but greedy. He is anything that suits him for the moment. Even an Abolitionist. But whatever he is, I do know that Shanks has been meeting with the Governor and I know that with Shanks's help, the Governor means to start with Dragonard." He motioned to the windows, the darkness beyond.

"Start?"

"To start to decontrol the plantations. That is their term for it. The Political Abolitionists. But to me it means to take away. Steal. And, to you, it means to be sent to the Louisiana markets."

"America?"

"Yes. The American colonies. That is what kind of Abolitionist the new governor is. An Abolitionist for English politics. The English have lost the American colonies now. And any fool can see that slavery will continue in America. Their whole economy is built on it. Even their king—their president—has slaves. His home, Mount Vernon, has been built and run by African sweat. So when the African people go from here, they are not to be set free. They will be shackled and broken into lots—friends broken, families severed, tribes parted—and then shackled on to ships and sold to America."

"This is soon?" Manroot asked. In front of him stood the man who gave his people good food to eat. Listened to his words about plantation soil. Treated him like a man. This man who had not pressed him about his troubles. Abdee had allowed Manroot the honour of dealing with his people's problems in private. Had come to him now with news of greater dangers. Yes, Manroot respected Abdee.

Abdee continued, "Shanks is going to see Lord Rothwell tomorrow night. That is how soon it is. And I want you to go with him. He is taking a note to Lord Rothwell about a slave rebellion."

"Here?"

Abdee shrugged. "Who knows?"

"But slaves will not rebel here. Things will only get worse for them. We only want to be better. Revolt will not achieve that."

"Neither will being shipped to America do you any good."

"Shanks goes tomorrow night?"

"Yes. And, Manroot, I want you to go with him. I want you to make certain that, if Shanks does get through to the Governor, he does not come back alive. Do not worry. I will arrange so he is not suspicious of you coming along. He is expecting Paw-Paw to go with him anyway. But I can trust you better. Paw-Paw is too young. Also, I do not know if Paw-Paw understands honour and the importance of his people." Then, looking at Manroot, Abdee said, "But I know that for your people you will do anything."

Manroot agreed to help ... if Shanks would go to meet the Governor, as Abdee had said.

Leaving Manroot's room, Abdee quietly but quickly crept down the stairs. He smiled to himself as he thought of his plan. Or was he smiling because he was seeing Dragonard secure once more in his grasp? He had worked to make Dragonard into one of the finest plantations on the island. And, now that it was, he did not intend to let it slip easily away from him.

Maggots.

He remembered those people who used to climb, craw, wiggle toward him.

This time they wanted Dragonard.

So Abdee would squash not one maggot but two. And Lord Rothwell would be the first. Curse him and his profit-devouring tax!

Now, Abdee was on his way to pay a personal call on the second maggot. Shanks. And he was planning on Manroot's big, black finger to come down hard on that particular vermin.

Reaching the foot of the stairs, he heard Arabella's voice trilling out from the centre garden. She and Honore were still at the table. Abdee could hear Arabella talking about the fleet of ships leaving for France on the day after tomorrow.

Good, Abdee thought. I hope Arabella goes with them. Then he crept out the front door.

Even from the outside of Shanks's small cabin, Abdee could hear him snoring. Good! Shanks is alone, Abdee thought. But before he entered the cabin, he looked around him, even up to the big house, to make certain that no one saw him enter.

"Shanks!" he whispered, shaking his bulky body. "Wake up, Shanks."

Fumbling, jerking for the wad of his coat which doubled as his pillow, Shanks grabbed for his dagger.

But clasping his hand, Abdee said, "It's only me. Abdee. Wake up."

"Ah, you. Hmmmmm," Shanks snorted, smacking his lips in half-sleep. "Dozed off I did. Sun tired me out too much today."

But Abdee could smell from Shanks's foul breath what had really tired him out. *Taffa*!

Towering over Shanks's cot, Abdee said, "Let me come back. It's important. But I will save what I have to say till you're awake. Nothing is important enough to ruin a man's sleep."

Chomping his peeling lips, wiping his mouth on the sleeve of his shirt, Shanks said, "No, if it's important, tell me now. I'm awake as I'll ever be." He brushed at scabs which had rubbed off onto his sleeve.

Abdee protested. "No. I'll come back. I insist. It's only a confirmation I've had on Rothwell. But it can keep till morning. Get your sleep."

"Rothwell? Lord Rothwell? Lord Governor?"

"Yes. But we'll talk in the morning."

Shanks was thoroughly whetted now. He would not let Abdee leave even if he had to detain him physically.

So, sitting beside Shanks on the cot, Abdee explained the insight he supposedly had received on Rothwell's brand of Abolitionists—a story not too dissimilar from the tale he had planted minutes before in Manroot's brain. But there were slight alterations for Shanks.

Listening to Abdee's story, Shanks patted his face and said, "It figures. It figures. Everything is political anyway. But I don't see what good Rothwell will do by selling off the slaves to America. Who are they expecting to run the plantations here anyway? The monkeys?"

"Ever hear of immigrants?"

Shanks's sudden loud laughter shook the small cabin. "Immigrants! Working these scorching fields? They'd die. In the old days, they tried working the indentured whites here after they worked the indians to death. What did that get them? Nothing. Whites can't work this land."

"You go to Parliament and tell them that there."

Sobering, Shanks asked, "It's got that far, has it? Parliament?"

Shrugging, Abdee said, "Even a little farther than that. The Tory Abolitionists are now already proposing what they are to do with slave runners."

Shanks bit the bait. "And what do they plan to do with the slave runners?"

"One Tory speaker is gaining support for execution by accusation alone. Which means . . ."

"Execution? Of slave runners? By 'accusation alone?' Why, those are jungle laws! That's not England you're telling me about. That's jungle law. What's happening to that country?"

Abdee did not argue. It was all working too smoothly now with Shanks carrying it by himself.

Shanks spluttered, "Execution by accusation. That's mutiny. That's unlawful. That's . . . that's . . ." Pausing, he asked, "And who could do the accusing? Who could point the finger and say, aye, he, Captain Geoff Shanks, he was a captain on the *Alexandria*? And that was a slaver?"

"Most anybody I suspect. As long as it was someone in a respected position."

Turning to Abdee, Shanks asked, "But you would never do that?"

Slapping Shanks on the back, Abdee said, "Do you

think that Rothwell would listen to me even if I would do that. No, Shanks, relax. You're safe while you're here."

Slowly pounding his fists together, Shanks growled, "Ah, he's the rascal then, isn't he? He's the one causing the trouble. Rothwell. Political Abolitionist. Come here to make a political name for himself. I spit on him, that's what I do!" The floor was nearer.

Abdee soberly asked, as if this were the time for business, "But how can we stop him? Stop all our problems? Get on with our work?"

The questions took Shanks by surprise. Abdee could see it had suddenly become a bit too involved for his *taffa*-sore, slow-moving brain. Shanks was an animal, a big bear with a fair knowledge of survival. But he was no match for any member of the cat family.

And, feline-like, Abdee repeated, "Do you think two men like you and myself could stop a man as big as that?" The word *big* was what counted.

"Course we could!"

Abdee warned, "He's powerful. More than the last one. Better protected, too. Guarded like George himself."

But Shanks would not accept that. "You could get him right in his bed if you wanted!"

Abdee slapped Shanks on the shoulder again and said, "Why, that's even better than I thought, you old fox. And Manroot could go with me. I could take a note to get in. And Manroot would go along like a witness for what the note warned about happening."

Scratching his head, rubbing his face, Shanks said, "Slow down a minute. I know I said something. But I know I didn't say all that."

"But you tied it together, Shanks. You tied it together. See, I had planned on going to see Rothwell—" Abdee paused for Shanks to catch up with him.

Shanks, taking the slack, said, "But you would never get into Rothwell. Not you, tax-missing Richard Abdee." Shanks loved to lord it over Abdee when he could.

So, Abdee privately thanked Shanks for his secret ambitions. He said aloud, "No, I suppose he wouldn't. You're right, you know. But I was thinking that *I* could go—"

"*I* will go," Shanks boomed.

Abdee paused and looked at him suspiciously.

"Me!" Shanks said.

Abdee narrowed his eyes. He knew that that look made Shanks testy.

"Don't see no reason why I can't. Tomorrow night. Same as planned. But me."

"In his bedchambers?"

"Catch him in his nightshirt. Any man will listen then!"

Abdee paused. This was dangerous now. "Do you think that you really have much to talk to Lord Rothwell about? Much that he will listen to? You know, Shanks, he might not take kindly to your, ah, station—past or present."

"He'll take kindly to *this*!" Shanks shouted, reaching for his dagger.

"Shanks, I haven't seen you like this in—how long?"

"What are you talking about now?"

"You! Captain Geoff Shanks! The adventurer."

Shanks grumbled, still fierce for killing, proving his worth.

But Abdee was relaxing. "Yes, I'm glad that I stayed when I found you sleeping. I found the man who first came here."

Not actually certain what Abdee meant—or willing to admit that he had changed, found a niche for himself at Dragonard—he growled, "No one ever sneaked up on me in my sleep."

So, grabbing Shanks around the shoulder, Abdee said, "I would like to try some of your *taffa* now—if you have any left for a white man . . . now that *most* of our problems are done, we can share a little drink."

" 'Most of the problems'? What's left?"

"Only the point of getting Manroot in with you. Course, I suppose that won't be as big a problem now

as it was when I was going. You got it up on me with
that one, too."

"Manroot?"

Abdee nodded.

"I don't need no nigger to help me."

Abdee shook his head. "Ah, but that was my fine
point. See, if I was to take a note to Rothwell, as I had
planned—a letter which would need immediate attention, a note which tells about a slave revolt—what suspicions would there be when I had a nigger to uphold
the story? Or, as you suggested, *you*?"

"No white man needed the word of a nigger before.
Or even believed it once he heard it."

"But, ah! Don't forget that we are dealing with an
Abolitionist! And a Political Abolitionist."

"I see your point," Shanks said, screwing the dried
corners of his mouth. "But why him? Can't it be another? You've got six, seven hundred to choose from."

"But not any that we can trust like Manroot."

"I'd still prefer another," Shanks said hesitantly. "I
wouldn't want to walk in there with no Fanti in chains.
And, like you say, Rothwell being an Abolitionist and
all, he would naturally wonder why the nigger was
chained. Or me with a whip."

Now Abdee was lost. "But why would you have a
whip? Or he be in chains?"

Shanks began to speak. But he stopped. Shaking his
head, he said, "No, choose another nigger. That's all.
Any nigger but him. Or any other Fanti. No Fantis
alone or otherwise."

"But he's not going to come to any harm."

Shanks blared, "It's not him that I'm worried about."

"What do you mean?"

Turning away from Abdee, Shanks said, "Figures
you might have solved it for yourself by now. But,
seems that you haven't, I suppose I could tell you."

"Tell me what?"

Shanks fidgetted. His fingers looked like breaded
garden slugs.

"Go ahead. Tell me."

Dragonard

"It would come easier with a swig."

"TELL ME, SHANKS!"

Dropping his head, Shanks confessed, "Them Fantis are flesh-eaters."

"Cannibals? The Fantis?"

Nodding slowly, Shanks said, "That's the reason for the niggers disappearing in the neighbourhood."

"Why haven't you told me this before?"

"No need to."

"But there was no need *not* to tell me."

"No, I guess not. But ... I just can't take Manroot with me, that's all." Shanks was standing now, his back was to Abdee. With his head still lowered, he said, "How do you think we kept alive at sea after the corn mash and horse beans disappeared? The Fantis fed themselves on the others."

"But you weren't frightened then."

"Aye. But they were in chains."

"You mean you *fed* them the other blacks?"

"They kept dying, didn't they? Had to do something with them, didn't we? Throw them overboard or. . . No, Abdee, I'll not take Manroot with me."

Abdee's mind was working fast now. He was busily taking in these new facts. Quickly trying to keep his own scheme afloat. He argued now, "But you told me yourself that Manroot was different from the rest of them. That they had their quarrels. This is probably one of their quarrels."

"When a Fanti is hungry, he doesn't quarrel."

"I do not believe that Manroot is a flesh-eater."

"Then how did he keep alive?" Shanks asked.

"He's a giant! He's a horse! But one thing he is not is . . . a *cannibal*!"

Softly, Shanks said, "You never knew about it till now, did you?"

"No. And do you think I would move him into my house if I knew he was—" No, Abdee did *not* believe it! "—a man eater." But this knowledge did not alter the fact that Manroot still had to accompany Shanks to Basseterre. Manroot *was* a killer.

224

Sitting back down on the cot, Shanks said, "Yo, you're probably right. Manroot does not practise flesh-eating. But I've seen Fantis do funny things. I know how they felt back then. I told you stories about Fa-Da-Lono. They always looked at me, you know—just looked at me."

Abdee jumped up in front of him. Excitedly, he said, "There! That proves it! You told me yourself that Manroot started that lie about syphilis, too. He is obviously not one of them."

"That's true, too," Shanks said, brushing the scabby roughness of his eyebrows. "He was not one back then. He was the best."

"And he still is. He is the best man to take. And Rothwell would be impressed with him. He is an Abolitionist's dream of the noble African."

Neither could Shanks find fault with that.

But to make certain that he would take Manroot, Abdee said, "But if you are still frightened, we can return to our original plan! *I* will go."

"You go to hell!" Shanks roared, reaching under the bed for his bottle. "*I* go the Lord Fancy-Ass palace."

So, like old times, the bargain was sealed with some *taffa*.

At the same moment, Manroot enjoyed not the liquor nor the mental ease which Abdee and Shanks were sharing. Manroot was thinking about Abdee's request. And his own people.

Manroot was a serious person. And, although he was not familiar with the ways of white men—people like the Abolitionists—he knew that he must help Abdee because Abdee was in a position to help the blacks.

The basis of Manroot's problems was the tribesmen whom Abdee had seen at the *bamboche,* those black dancers who filed their teeth to sharp points and dressed themselves in the dried palm leaves splattered with black dots.

But palm leaves were not the usual outfits for those certain tribesmen. Those makeshift costumes were meant to simulate the skin of a sacred animal. The leopard. Yes, those certain tribesmen within the Fantis were called the Leopardmen.

Manroot lay thinking now on the hard floor of the small, humid bedroom. Above him, the window was open and he looked blankly out at the twinkling stars. He thought of peace. He speculated about a harmony in the future.

His world had suddenly become so new, the ocean had seemed to devour him and his people, taking them into a hell beyond the African shore. Now, apart from coping with old problems, Manroot was also faced with new ones.

He saw no choice but to trust Abdee. To kill was not new for Manroot. He had fought bravely in battles before. And he must help Abdee to kill this evil Englishman who wanted to sell his people to America. He must work against Shanks, too. It was Shanks who had brought them here in the slave ship. True, it was Abdee who worked them, but he worked them with consideration. They were better treated here at Dragonard than they would be at other plantations.

Manroot's mind, though, kept moving back from the problems of this new world to the ageless vices of the old. The bad ways brought from Africa.

The Leopardmen.

It was one thing to kill an enemy in battle. But it was completely against a warrior's honour to devour the enemy, to consume the conquered body with his mouth.

Manroot had seen this phenomenon with his own eyes. The worst was when the Leopardmen ate their victims alive, rending the flesh from the bones with their jagged teeth, tearing the skin with their fingers.

And Manroot had seen, too, that when one man eats another, his organ for procreation becomes erect. Cannibalism excites a man sexually. Manroot was even ashamed that he possessed merely the knowledge of it. But without the knowledge of a vice, how can you conquer it?

And yet, Manroot had hoped that once his people had come from Africa they might begin to make a headway, to infuse themselves into the pattern of other African nations who were already enslaved in the West Indies. Manroot knew that from evilness, goodness often springs. The secret was patience.

The voyage from Africa had been anguishing for Manroot. But it was not the chains that tortured him. It was his people's loss of dignity. They had run out of food. Manroot tried to set an example for his people by not eating. But his followers soon weakened and began to consume the bodies of those dying around them. The Bantu. The Ashanti. The Hausa. And even in their state of near malnutrition, the Fantis became overcome with the excitement of eating the sweetness of human flesh. Although chained in the most ghastly conditions, they reached a sexual hysteria and tried to perform lurid acts with one another, often not able to accomplish anything but the basest of animal depravity. It shattered Manroot's soul to watch his people excitedly consume one another's excrement, languishing their faces in urine. It was no wonder that such sadness led to further disease. And added to the horrors of the slave ship.

But Manroot was a man of hope. His people were gaining respect again on Dragonard. And, as he had prayed on the ship, they had come to a land where fruit and game were plentiful.

On this land, though, was a certain African who had come here earlier, a black who had been waiting like a demon on St. Kitts. There was another Fanti on Dragonard. And Manroot had a deep sinking of the heart when he learned of that Leopard highpriest. He was Calabar.

At first, the evil Calabar kept his distance from the Fantis. But when he discovered that there were tribesmen among them with similar beliefs, he soon began to make friends, to lure certain Fantis away from the control of Manroot.

Manroot hated Calabar with a bottomless passion. Calabar was a fanatic. He was a destructive man who stopped at nothing to satisfy the dictates of his animal religion. The more poisonous the human skin, the more delicious it tasted to Calabar's perverse appetites. And he was teaching all this to Manroot's people.

Manroot wondered now if he should inform Abdee about Calabar going to Basseterre? That was another heinous side of the man. He visited a Fanti woman who ran a house of sin for white men in Basseterre. Manroot had learned from his people that Calabar made frequent visits to that house on a pass he had received from his former master. Manroot did not know if that Fanti woman in Basseterre was a high priestess of the ancient animal cult. All he knew was that she—her name was Naomi—ran a house of unworthy sex.

Manroot did not believe in sexual blasphemies. The body was noble, meant to improve the beauty of the world. And when an African misuses his natural magnificence to titillate the curiosities of the white people, then he does himself more harm than them.

Tonight, Manroot did not get any sleep. He lay staring out at the infinity of the stars, wondering how he could make a union of all black people. He wondered what good he could do being locked up here inside the fineness of this white man's palace? It was for the refinements of the soul which Manroot longed. And his people.

He thought, too, of sharing his life, and troubles. He dreamed of a nice African woman, a good wife who would give him children. He hoped someday not to plant his seed by command, but to do it for a family.

There was much work for Manroot to do.

In the meantime, he must ignore those other longings. Try not to pine for a wife. A wife was a luxury now and he must not even dare think about making a family, to become attached to one person—a wife—or hope for children. As the black peoples' world stood now, his wife and children would only be sold like animals. Perhaps even to America.

Manroot thanked his gods for giving him the dignity of the stars. The heavens were a glimmering goal for Manroot. He must try to work side by side with the white men. Be their beast of burden. Help them solve the soil problems when he was able. If burying sugar cane did not work, he would try to find new methods to help them. Manroot knew that it was through planting, through harvesting, through the work of the soil, that he would help his people regain their dignity.

For the time, Dragonard was their world. They all must work—and even kill—for its safety.

16

Scapegoat

Dating back to the sixteenth century subjugation of the Caribbe Indians, the Lord Governor's palace in Basseterre was Spanish-built and stood behind Pall Mall. The huge, white walls were covered with bougainvillea, jasmine, and the bright red blossoms of the tropical camellias. In the full moonlight, the broad porches shone like milk glass, here and there a window lit behind their curved darkness.

The night was heavy, the hour late. And the two horses moved slowly through the cobbled streets, the echoes of their hooves carried by the humid air.

Abdee's written note got Shanks past the sentry house at the wrought-iron gates. Then, as he clattered across the courtyard, Manroot followed closely behind. Yes, for a Negro to be out at this late hour—even with a white man—the news must be urgent.

But the reception inside was not as trustworthy as Shanks and Manroot had received at the gates. The Palace Night Steward discredited the note and, when Shanks said, "Mutiny," the steward told him to go to the guards and not come here to the Governor. He asked Shanks, "What is His Lordship to do? Rush out of bed and fight the niggers himself?"

Shanks was quick to dishearten. But, as he turned to leave, Manroot stepped forward. He spoke to the steward. "We have been to the guard house . . . Master Sir."

The steward snapped, "Then, if they kicked you out, why should we let you in here?"

Manroot answered, "They did not 'kick us out'."

The steward stared at the black giant, waiting for a further explanation. And Shanks stood frozen, waiting to hear the rest of this unrehearsed lie.

Manroot said, "Their throats. All cut. Field machetes."

Drawing in his breath, the steward said, "If that is true, why haven't . . ." But then he stopped. He said to himself, "No! If their throats were cut, I suppose they couldn't inform us. Wait here," he said, turning toward a large, carved door.

In two minutes' time, Shanks and Manroot were both ushered into the Lord Governor's sitting-room. Lord Rothwell himself was just coming through the door on the other side. Tying the robe to his gown, he said, "Now what is this about an uprising and slit throats?" He was a tall man with an aquiline nose. His head was bald except for a wreath of white hair which stopped short of his large, red ears. When he saw Manroot, he paused and fumbled for the peering-glass hanging around his neck on a black cord. He studied Manroot as if he had never seen a Negro before. At least, a Negro as fine as this one! He exclaimed, "William Shakespeare must have been thinking of you when he wrote Othello!"

The comment fell on ignorant ears.

So, dropping his peering-glass, Rothwell motioned to two divans. Seeing Manroot hesitate at taking a seat, Rothwell asked, "Is there some problem?"

It was Shanks, then, wondering how to get rid of the guards, who seized upon this situation. Stepping gallantly forward, he said, "What this . . . man has to tell you, Your Lordship, he—" Shanks motioned to the guards. "It is natural, Your Lordship, that he does not trust *all* white men. It took me all my effort to get him to come even to you!"

"But I was told it was—that it was you who had some kind of note for me to see."

"Yes, Your Lordship. But this is the witness. He will be far more explicit than ten of me. And he speaks English!" This enthusiasm for a "nigger" did not come easy.

"Very well! Very well!" Rothwell said, waving the guards out to the ante-room. Then, as the doors shut, he said, "Actually, you will probably find it rather strange when I tell you that I welcome no one more than you people." Rothwell stopped and looked at Shanks. "You did say he speaks English?"

Manroot answered for himself. "Yes, Your Lordship."

"Good! And before I hear what you have to tell me, I want to make you most comfortable by saying how honoured I am that you chose to come to see me! I know how difficult it must be for you people, but I want you to understand that there are men in the world who are trying to help you. People in high places. Both here and in England." Rothwell was addressing all this to Manroot, who was now seated across from him on the edge of a brocade divan.

But, as yet, Shanks had not taken a seat. Lord Rothwell, though, did not seem to be interested in Shanks. He was intent on making his point with the Negro.

He continued, "Having arrived not long ago on St. Kitts in my new position as Lord Governor, you can imagine how much work I have to accomplish. But with all the points pressed upon me, there is no problem which weighs more heavily, or keeps me more awake at night, than the problem of the exploitation of the African—how it is up to England to stop making money and lead the way to some enlightenment."

Shanks stood beside Rothwell's divan, unable to believe the garbage he heard tumbling from that white man's mouth. But quickly, his astonishment turned to anger and that anger soon reminded him of his mission.

Rothwell spoke on, "Everyone speaks about Abolition these days but no one does anything about it. And I secretly doubt if America will ever let the shackles drop from your people. They are too dependent on your commercial value. You keep their country throbbing. With currency!"

The hypocrite, Shanks thought, remembering Abdee's words. The Tory hypocrite is double-dealing America, too!

"But the Parliamentary law in our country, being as it is, can muster political ammunition to bring issues such as this to bear."

Shanks fumed. So the swine even admits to being an Abolitionist. A Political Abolitionist. And explaining it to a nigger as if a nigger could understand!

Next, he heard Rothwell ask Manroot, "What plantation did you say you were from?"

That was the cue.

"DRAGONARD!" Shanks bellowed, rushing toward him with his dagger, and repeated the name with each thrust of the blade into the emerald night-gown. "Dragonard, Dragonard, Dragonard."

The struggle, the gasping, the muffled shouts for help brought the guards rushing in from the next chamber. But too late.

Shanks was standing back from the corpse, pointing at Manroot. The dagger lay at Manroot's bare feet.

"You dirty nigger," Shanks screamed at him. "You tricked me! You dirty nigger! That good man could have helped you! Could have saved you!"

Manroot's rough trousers were splotched with blood.

And Shanks rushed for Manroot to revenge the supposed murder.

But before he could grab him, the guards had seized Manroot. And they dragged him from the sitting-room as Shanks repeated to them exactly how he had seen him attack the Lord Governor—whose green robe was splotched with scarlet, the same colour red as the camellias at the gate.

The Negro had killed Lord Rothwell.

Soon all the bells of Basseterre rang the tragedy.

A Negro had killed the Lord Governor.

There was a white man as witness.

17

A Freeing of Slaves

The next morning, Honore woke early. She could not sleep. The golden dawn found the cracks between her curtains and sent exploding shafts of light into her dark bedroom. First, she tossed on her bed for a while, restless from all the sleep one body could stand. True, the doctor had told her that she must eat and rest for two people now.

But Honore was not able to resist the compulsion to rise, to dress herself, explore the house. Why, she had not even decided on which room she was going to turn into the nursery!

In one corner, Ta-Ta stirred on her pallet. When she saw Honore dressing through her heavy eyes, she bolted up from the floor. But Honore waved her back to sleep assuring her that there was nothing to become alarmed about, that she could cope quite well by herself.

In the kitchen, Sugar Loaf already had a large pot of coffee brewing on the stove. Beside it, a tin kettle sang with water for tea. But, shocked at seeing her mistress up at such an early hour—and double-shocked to see her in the kitchen—Sugar Loaf said, "Mistress, can't you sleep with your morning sick-feeling?"

"I slept fine, Sugar Loaf," Honore answered, stopping by the stove to kiss Sugar Loaf on the lovely, soft cheek. Then she continued with a vase toward the barrel of water in the corner. She called, "Do you mind if I take some of this water, Sugar Loaf? Or, were you saving it for something special?"

Sugar Loaf stood stunned, holding the pink tips of

her brown fingers to the spot where Honore had just kissed her. "No, Mistress! You use all you want, Mistress. Water there for you to use. But, you parched, let me give you some already poured into nice, clean pitcher."

"No, it is not for me. It is for some flowers," Honore said. Next she quickly disappeared out the door with a large knife she had taken from the rack. Returning in a few minutes, she carried six stems of white lilies. Holding them out to Sugar Loaf, she said, "Smell! Aren't they lovely?"

Sugar Loaf took a sniff from the soft folds of white and her breasts swelled under her apron. Closing her eyes, she sighed, "Smelling those Calla lilies, Mistress, just smelling them reminds me when we used to load up the pony trap and take flowers down to Père Brett. Remember those days, Mistress?"

"I certainly do. And *you* used to drive."

Sugar Loaf said, "I sure likes to drives the pony trap. Just about holds me and that all. But sure likes to drive that pony. Makes him go, too!"

"And I have the feeling that we will be making those little trips very soon, Sugar Loaf."

"But Père Brett dead, Mistress."

"I am sure we will get a new priest."

Studying Honore more suspiciously, Sugar Loaf asked, "You sure the doctor says it all right, Mistress, for you to be up and around this early? Cutting flowers? Drawing water? Making plans?"

"The plans I have always had. Sometimes they were hidden, but they were still there. And the flowers? Well, if I want fresh flowers, who else is there to get them for me? You have your hands full in here. Sabine used to do it but she can hardly move from the Wash House now. And Ambrosia is always busy in the Sewing House. And Ta-Ta, you know how Ta-Ta sneezes when she goes into the garden. And I certainly can not depend on that Paw-Paw for flowers, can I?"

"No, Mistress. That Paw-Paw not much good for anything not to do with Master. Besides, I think Paw-

Paw, he getting the boot back outside. I sees Master brings in that big Manroot. Figures he might be new head-nigger now. You sees how big he is! And better than most Fantis, too. Anyway, ones I see. Still don't trust him, though. But Master, he brings him in."

"Oh, that *is* true, isn't it?" Honore said, studying her vase. Then, she picked it up and moved toward the door.

But Sugar Loaf protested. "Mistress! What you carrying that heavy vase for? Not in your condition!"

"I am in very good condition," Honore said, moving past her. "I'm in the best condition in the whole world. Now, if you will kindly open the door to the hall for me, I will let you get back to your own work."

Opening the door, Sugar Loaf screamed, "Ta-Ta! Ta-Ta, come down here right now and helps your mistress! You forgetting you the nigger! Thinks Mistress do your work?"

"Leave her alone, Sugar Loaf. I am the only one up. And you. Even Mister Abdee is in bed." Then Honore slowly moved down the servants hall and out through the doorway under the stairs, and into the main foyer. She thought for a moment that she heard a horse galloping outside the house. But thinking that it was probably only one of the drivers, she continued toward the door of her husband's library. These flowers were for his table!

But a loud pounding began on the front doors. The bell clanged. So, stopping, Honore set down the vase on a hall table and quickly moved to see who could be banging on the front doors at this early hour.

When she opened the door, she saw an old, hard-faced man, wearing dust-covered clothes. He quickly doffed his tricorn hat and said, "Monsieur Abdee? May I see him please?"

"Who are you?"

"Gerrard Delon."

Honore remembered the name, and, even if she could tell by his accent that he was one of her countrymen, she did not take kindly to him. But a bit tipsy from all her early morning efficiency, and the envigorating effect of the Calla lilies, she said, "Perhaps *I* can help you!"

"It is very important."

"Too important to tell his wife?" she asked. But then, by the look on his face, she saw that, yes, the news was too important to tell to a mere wife. "Wait here," she said, beckoning him into the hallway and closed the door behind him. Then, she walked quickly up the stairs. And, as Honore moved up, up, up, holding onto the banister, she felt how badly it needed refinishing. She noticed, too, that the floors were buckling in the corners from the moisture. She thought how remarkably fast a house can deteriorate. Then, next, she realized how long it had been since she had noticed the house, its condition of disrepair. And so she thought that it was remarkable, too, that after five years that she could still resurrect herself. But it would be corrected soon. She did not want to raise a child in a surrounding like this! There was much work to do. And she would not be stopped this time. She was two!

Crooking her forefinger, she rapped firmly on the bedroom door. "Richard!"

"Who is it?"

"Honore. There is a man to see you."

"What does he want?"

"He won't tell me. It's a man from Basseterre. Monsieur Delon. Gerrard Delon."

There was a silence in the room now. Then she heard, "Tell him I will be right down ... and Honore?"

"Yes?"

"You haven't seen Shanks this morning, have you?"

"No."

"Is Manroot around?"

"I am the only one up," she answered and moved quickly away from the door, quickly blocking out the sound she had just heard from within the room, the sound of another person: the bare feet of whatever black wench he was sleeping with now. But Honore did not care about that any more. She had what she wanted.

At the foot of the stairs, Honore said to Delon, "Mister Abdee will be down soon. Would you like some coffee?"

Honore could see that the idea of coffee appealed to Monsieur Delon. But she could also see that he was too nervous to say "yes." Or was it because he thought that he might have to leave the coffee for whatever his important business might be? So quickly deciding not to worry about him, or his news, Honore turned to the table on which she had left her vase of lilies.

And she had been right! Monsieur Delon did forget his coffee. Before Honore had even picked up the vase of long stems, Delon was already rushing across the floor to the staircase. Abdee had appeared at the top and Delon was suddenly blurting to him, "Monsieur Abdee! There is terrible trouble. I get here as fast as I can. I know that your Captain Shanks is not back. But I doubt if the government men have left yet themselves to tell you the bad news. I am the first."

"What bad news?"

"The Lord Governor! He has been assassinated. Stabbed. Killed."

Abdee's voice lowered. "But why come here, my friend?"

"It was one of your *Nègres* who did it! A slave called 'Manroot.' "

Then Abdee was surprised. "Manroot? I do not believe it." He moved down the stairs.

"It is true. They have him in gaol. I suppose he will wait there until your arrival. He is your property, *non*?"

"Then where is Shanks?"

"I saw him in a tavern. Yes, *The Good Prince*."

"Was he drunk? Was he talking?"

"Not at all, Monsieur. Not at all. I do not even think that he would have told me what had happened if I did not recognize him." Tapping his head, Delon said, "I know much, Monsieur. He must tell!"

"You've done very well to come here. We will get you a fresh horse and you can ride back into town with me."

Abdee continued down the stairs with more haste.

Honore, who had been standing, listening to all this, did not speak until Abdee was by the door. Only then did she say, "Richard, should you not eat?"

He did not answer her. His mind was busily working. Only half his plot had worked. Shanks was still . . .

"Richard, if you are to ride into Basseterre, you must eat."

Turning from the door, he irritably said, "Didn't you just hear?"

"But if you are riding to Basseterre . . ." she pleaded, standing in the half-open door of his library.

Abdee looked at the vase she held. "Where are you going with those flowers?"

"I am going to put them on your table."

"To hell with my table! To hell with those flowers. You keep out of that room, understand?" Then he turned.

But he could not talk to Honore that way. Not this morning. Not now. Hurling the vase to the floor, she screamed, "Why don't you say to hell with me, too?"

"To hell with you," he said and then rushed across the porch and down the steps to the drive.

Running to the door, Honore called, "Richard?"

But he did not answer. He had enough confusion about a horse for Delon.

"Richard?" she called.

He did look up once. But seeing it was still her, he quickly looked away.

"RICHARD?"

But, by then, he and Delon had mounted and were on their way down the wobbly avenue of palm-fronds. Then, under the iron gates of Dragonard. And out.

Honore's anger knew no precedent. Never before in

her entire life had she been so outraged, so humiliated and now so furious about being sluffed-off, ignored in such a heartless way. She understood a little why he was going. But it was not about the Lord Governor. It was for his slave! That Manroot. A Fanti. Honore's anger swelled, hating her husband beyond the last boundaries which her religion allowed. She wished him dead. In hell. Worse. She grew more irate when she thought about their child. No! He would not sacrifice the child, too, tear it apart for one of his slaves. Or spurn it for the life of that syphilitic Captain Shanks. If God had not delivered her from these sins, then, at least, he would take mercy on the child.

So, it was for the child that Honore made the decision to leave and, once the decision exploded in full certainty through her brain, her following movements were quick. For the first time in years, perhaps her whole life, Honore felt capable and responsible. She knew what she had to do for her child but she did not know exactly how she was going to go about it, proceed in what manner. But she began.

She did know, though, where the deeds were kept, the receipts from the *vendue* for the slaves. So, grabbing the pile of documents from the bottom drawer of a cabinet in Abdee's library, she began to wonder how she was going to do this—how she was to give these poor people their freedom before she left . . . DRAGONARD!

Damn Dragonard! Damn Dragonard! Oh, God! Damn, damn, DAMN DRAGONARD!

Bursting into the kitchen, Honore did not see Sugar Loaf. But there was Calabar. And, at his side, Monkey.

To the child, she said, "Go upstairs to my room. Tell your mother to wait there for me."

The child looked dumbly at her. He was eating part of a banana. Calabar had the other half.

So, to make the child precisely understand her, Honore said, "Ta-Ta! Go tell Ta-Ta to wait in my room with you. I will be up immediately."

As the child reluctantly left the kitchen, Honore said to Calabar, "I remember that day I went to Mt. Misery. And to make me get over my squeamishness, Pierre made me *buy* you. In person. Myself."

Calabar nodded at her suspiciously, his tribal marks narrowing.

Jabbing a sheet of paper into his stomach, Honore said, "Here! This is your freedom. Take it! But get out of here. Never come back."

Looking at the paper being thrust at him, Calabar cautiously asked, "Abdee?"

"You were not bought by him, you fool. You were bought by me! It says so here. Now go." Honore dropped the paper to his lap and rushed to the kitchen door. But her head suddenly started to spin with the complexity of running through the fields, the enormity of such a task, distributing bits of paper to the Africans who might not even understand them. She realized that that was impossible. Even absurd. Turning she asked, "Where's Sugar Loaf?" But she saw that Calabar had already gone. He had understood what the paper meant. His freedom. And even the door from the kitchen into the hallway was still open.

So rushing through that door herself, Honore decided that, for the moment, it would be wisest to have Ta-Ta start the packing. They would not need much. She would take mostly valuables. Jewels. Some enamelled boxes. Silver. Gold. Her mind made a quick inventory of negotiable possessions as she ran up the steps. She remembered, too, the money she still had in a Paris bank. And remembering Paris, she recalled the French convoy. And the ship, the *Thérèse*. The ship which Arabella had told her about at dinner. It sailed tomorrow.

Quickly crossing herself, Honore said, "Thank you, Holy Mother. Thank you. It was a difficult battle but you are showing me the way. You have given me the first sign of my flight."

Honore rushed down the hall.

"Ta-Ta," she said, bursting into her bedroom. "Ta-Ta, pack clothes for me, yourself, and Monkey. The three of us are sailing tomorrow for France!"

"Mistress!" Ta-Ta gasped, grabbing the child to her skirt. The idea terrified her.

Honore glared at her. "No, I refuse to stay in this house one more day with that man. I refuse to have my child born under this unholy roof. I have too much love for you, too, to leave you behind, Ta-Ta. But to be perfectly honest with you, I need you. I do not know if I could attempt such a voyage alone." Staring at her, Honore asked, "Will you come with me to France, or will you stay here at . . . Dragonard?"

"Mistress," Ta-Ta said, seeing by Honore's face that she was serious. "I come with you, Mistress." She fell to the floor in front of Honore, holding the hem of her skirt in fear.

"There is no time for any of that! We must start packing. And Monkey, you go get Paw-Paw. Tell him to bring three large trunks down from the attic. And Ta-Ta, you pack the dresses with the softest, the fullest skirts. I want to pack them with silver and jewels." She remembered an icon. She remembered a pearl box. The Buhl caskets. The snuff boxes. The spoons. The *faïence*. So, dropping the slaves's deeds onto the unmade bed, Honore said, "I shall start gathering the valuables now."

"But what about these, Mistress?" Ta-Ta asked confused, pointing at the deeds lying on the white sheets.

"Those are pieces of paper I will have to deal with later. Now we must hurry with other things." Then, stopping again, Honore spun and ran to the door to call to Monkey; she hollered for him to tell Sugar Loaf to be ready in two hours. She wanted Sugar Loaf to drive them in the pony trap to Basseterre.

Then, turning back to the bedroom—her mind whirling with a thousand things to be done—she thought, *Helas*! Arabella! Of course. I can trust Arabella. I can leave the deeds with Arabella on our way to Basseterre.

She is strong and will understand. She will negotiate on my behalf. Also, her husband is an attorney-at-law. Of course! I *know* I can depend on dear Arabella.

With a freer mind, Honore began to gather, select, choose, but mostly discard, eliminate, leave behind for the mildew and rot.

The packing took less time than Honore had imagined. But it would have even gone faster if Ta-Ta would have allowed her to help with more of the work. But Honore still managed to achieve quite a deal by herself. Then, as she sat watching the three wooden trunks being buckled and padlocked shut—three trunks of possession from this enormous plantation and house which once all belonged to her—she still felt that she was doing the right thing. It was her only choice.

Ta-Ta moved swiftly, asking few questions, questioning not a single decision once it had been made by her mistress. But with the swift assurance with which Ta-Ta moved, Honore could tell that she, too, was also glad to be escaping from this festering den.

It was Sugar Loaf who was the most hesitant about the impromptu departure. But, as Honore had ordered, the pony trap stood waiting in front of the house. And, as neither Paw-Paw nor the groom, or any male slaves from the stables were around when the women and child rushed out onto the porch, Honore began lifting the trunks to the back of the small trap by herself. But Ta-Ta and Sugar Loaf quickly took charge.

Then, climbing into the trap beside Honore, Sugar Loaf asked, "Is there more you wants to say goodbye to, Mistress?" Sugar Loaf still wore her apron, her intricately twisted head-piece. But around her shoulders was a red shawl.

Honore tied the blue ribbons of her straw bonnet and answered bitterly, "I said good-bye to it a long time ago. Sabine has let herself go so much I do not recognize her. Ambrosia is always drunk from the *bamboche*! No, it is only you and Ta-Ta and Monkey who are dear to me. But I have all you with me."

Sugar Loaf's eyes widened. "But you not makings me go on that big ship across the ocean with you, Mistress?"

"No, Sugar Loaf," Honore assured her. "As much as I would like to take you with me to France, and have you near when my child is born, I am not taking you with me. I am not making you do a thing. In fact, Sugar Loaf," Honore said, firmly holding the sheaf of papers in her lap, "if you hurry now and take me to Warburton Field, I will leave these with dear Arabella. Then, if all goes well, no one will ever make you do anything again, Sugar Loaf. Now, hurry."

So, with a neat crack of the whip, Sugar Loaf shouted at the small brown pony and the trap rumbled down the drive. Honore and Sugar Loaf sat in front while, behind the trunks, Ta-Ta sat with her slim arm wrapped around Monkey, their bare feet hanging over the back. They were only beginning to learn how to act—to live—as mother and child. As the trap passed under the wrought-iron gates, Honore held her head high, closing her eyes. She always hoped to remember this place as "Petit Jour." Twilight. Not the darkness it had become for her as Dragonard.

But the time now was midday. Already the sun scorched hot from the sky. And clouds of grey dust followed the trap as the odd-looking travellers made their way south to Basseterre.

Reaching the forks in the road which led to Warburton Field, Honore told Sugar Loaf to draw the reins just inside the stone pillars. Then, hopping down from the trap, Honore ordered Ta-Ta and Monkey to wait by the cart. She wanted to see Arabella alone.

Warburton Field was a smaller house than Dragonard, not a plantation but more of a minute country estate. The neat, white-gabled house would have looked more suitable in some European countryside than on an opening in a West Indian island. Rather than bananas and mangoes, Warburton Field needed hedgerows and blackberries.

Letting her shawl slip to her skirt, Honore banged loudly on the oak door, thinking for the first time about her appearance. The straw bonnet. The same blue dress she had put on at dawn. Blue, light-soled shoes. Hardly the outfit for travelling. But, once they were at an inn tonight, she would organize her clothing for tomorrow.

A white-haired Negro finally answered the door. He said slowly that Mistress Arabella was not at home.

Honore asked anxiously, "When does she come back?"

The Negro answered slowly, "Don't rightly knows, Mistress."

"Where did she go?"

"Mistress not say."

"Did she go to Basseterre?"

"Ain't able to tell you that, Mistress, either."

Honore's thoughts suddenly became muddled. She had not planned on this, Arabella not being at home. But she must think fast! Yes, she decided quickly, it would be pointless for her to take the deeds into Basseterre herself. *He* would most certainly hear about it. Or, perhaps, if there was trouble about Manroot at Government House, they might seize them. But Honore hated to think about trouble. But she hoped that it was the worst. All she wanted to do, though, was to get her unborn child out of this island and never come back. She saw then that her only choice was to leave an imploring letter for Arabella, throwing herself at her mercy, confiding in her trust. Honore told the Negro that she would come in. She also told him to go quickly and find quill and paper. The note she wrote was brief. She explained that, due to circumstances which will soon become apparent, she had decided to leave for France. And enclosed with this note, Honore wrote, Arabella would find the deeds to Honore's slaves. Please take these deeds to Government House and have them send a military escort to Petit Jour—for legality's sake, Honore added "Dragonard"—and to post on the gates there which slaves were to be freed.

Sealing the note, Honore rushed quickly down the drive to the pony trap. She felt much lighter now. She felt that she was doing not only the right thing for herself but for everybody. She crossed herself again.

And, as Honore had not looked back at Dragonard, neither did she glance around at Warburton Field. There were no memories of St. Kitts which she wished to take with her.

But Arabella Warburton stood at a window, watching the loaded trap move back toward the forks in the road. She was seeing the whole exodus. She was smiling. She could make her availability known to Abdee at last.

To Arabella, the dust from Honore's pony trap disappeared into the air like a tedious, long-suffered cloud.

When a rider's dust rose ahead of them on the road, Sugar Loaf suggested that they should draw in by a naseberry patch until the rider rode past. But Honore refused to waste any time. She would not hide.

Sugar Loaf said, "But, Mistress! Might be some of our folk. Master Abdee. Or Captain Master Shanks. Or . . ."

Snatching the whip from Sugar Loaf, Honore said, "Keep moving. And let whoever it is try to stop us!"

The rider *was* someone headed for Dragonard. It was Captain Shanks. And when he saw the women, he drew his reins.

But Honore stood bravely next to Sugar Loaf, facing him defiantly. She whispered, "Keep moving, Sugar Loaf."

Snapping the reins, Sugar Loaf called, "Get up, you lazy pony. Get up, you!"

The trap clattered by as Honore balanced herself on the rough board edge, the other holding the whip.

Shanks remained mounted, doffing his hat.

But Honore stood motionless, even when the dust had finally obscured him from her sight.

So, on they continued to Basseterre.

Then to . . . France?

Like money and property, Honore did not know about politics, either—what was happening at this moment in her homeland, the executions close at hand.

18

The Leopardmen

Captain Shanks found Dragonard deserted—the big house. The front doors were open and, as he cautiously entered the hall—the mahogany panelling gleaming with sunshine—he looked into Abdee's library on the right. On the dark green carpet, he saw a mess of papers, books and documents. On the hallway floor in front of him, he now saw bits of the broken vase. A puddle of water. The six stalks of lilies. To him, the house looked ransacked.

Dragonard was quiet, as still as a tomb.

Shanks dragged his heels on the runner-carpet as he moved toward the door under the stairs. Slowly turning the crystal handle, he looked into the servants' hall. Then, the kitchen.

But the kitchen was deserted, too. And the back door was open. So, moving stealthily to the back door, Shanks stood on the top step and looked outside down toward the huts.

Everything seemed normal out back, though. Negresses moved slowly in and out of the Wash House. He saw linen flapping on the clothes lines. Smoke curled from the stone chimney of the Cookhouse. He saw a gaggle of piccaninnies chasing a yellow dog. Nothing had changed outside.

Then, turning back into the kitchen, the tops of his boots slapped against one another as he moved to the black iron cookstove. He felt the top. It was cold. No mid-day meal had been cooked on that stove. He decided to look upstairs.

And, as he had expected, Honore's room was a mess. It smelled of lavender and clove sachets. But drawers lay upturned everywhere. The four-poster bed was un-made. The mosquito netting hanging like torn shreds of spider-webbing. And Shanks thought: *The fly has escaped. Honore has finally left that cold-hearted bastard. She and that damned, bloody heir of his!*

Slowly walking down the carpeted steps, Shanks walked across the hall toward the porch and decided to wait. He had sat waiting for eight years in Africa so lolling a few hours around Dragonard was not going to matter. Not with Abdee's heir gone now.

The burnt-orange sun was dropping behind the western tangle of the forest when Shanks heard the distant sound of a rider. Then listening to the galloping, he heard more than one rider. He shielded his eyes from the sunset and looked down toward the gates. Finally, he saw them. There were two men on horseback. One was Abdee. The other, a Negro. Then, as the two horses galloped up the drive, Shanks saw that the Negro was not Manroot as he had feared but merely Calabar. He breathed easier.

Remaining seated on the bottom step of the porch, Shanks called to Abdee, "Where's Manroot?" He then cursed himself for bringing up the name. He had planned to let Abdee bring up the debacle.

Although Abdee's face was covered by dust, Shanks could see his firmly set jaw. Abdee had not answered him.

But Shanks tried to keep himself under control. He called, "It's too bad. He *was* a good nigger. You *were* right about him."

Abdee was brief. "He will get out."

"You saw him?"

"He's mine, isn't he?"

"So they let you talk to him?"

"I *went* to talk to him," Abdee said.

"And he . . . talked?"

"You know Manroot never talks much." And neither was Abdee.

"But they will let you have him back?"

"He's my property, isn't he?"

"Then that means they will let *you* deal with him?"

"Ummmmmm."

Shanks then thought it was time to tell Abdee the news. He began. "Your cook, Sugar Loaf, is gone!"

Abdee asked quickly, "And Honore?"

"She's gone, too. I saw them in the trap with Ta-Ta and that yellow kid."

"Where were they going?"

"I passed them on the south road. They seemed to be headed down toward Basseterre. I was coming back here."

Abdee looked quickly at Calabar who was still standing by his horse. Abdee asked him, "I wonder how many more she got to?"

Shanks called, "The missus do something?"

Turning toward the house, Abdee casually explained, "I ran into Calabar in town by accident. He told me that my *spouse* had just given him his freedom!"

Shanks struggled to his feet and, following Abdee across the porch, he said, "That explains the confusion in your library then."

"What confusion?"

"Go look!"

"Have *you* been in there?"

Shanks defensively answered, "I wasn't the first. The blimey place is a mess in there. But if you say your wife has freed the niggers, it must have been the deeds she was looking for. But she couldn't have got many. There are still a lot of niggers out back."

Abdee let out a big sigh. "Well, I can see to all that later. In fact, Shanks, I would not mind if she *did* weed out a few of the lame ones, to be quite honest. I was thinking about selling off some myself." Then, looking at Shanks more closely—a softer look—Abdee said, "You know what I could use, don't you?"

Shanks's eyes brightened. He did know. And he

quickly offered, "Got me some out back in my shack. Got me five jugs all ready and waiting for the right occasion."

"Then get it! We might as well turn this into a celebration . . . for both of us!"

"Celebration?"

Abdee shrugged. "It's clear what *I* am celebrating, isn't it? You say you saw Honore running off to Basseterre. That means one thing."

"But she can't run far."

"Shanks, that bitch can run as far as she wants!"

"But what about . . ." Shanks did not want to finish. He even wondered if he had said too much. He had learned that it was never wise to rush business with Abdee.

He was not rushing it, though. Abdee said, "That's why you and I are going to celebrate. We being partners."

Like an ice glacier cracking, a big grin spread across Shanks's pusky face. He gratefully grabbed for Abdee's hand.

But, sluffing it off, Abdee said, "Go on. Get that damned *taffa*. And now that Calabar is a free man, we will see if it's changed his cooking."

Shanks was much more relaxed now and, walking into the house arm-in-arm with Abdee, he asked, "Where did you run into that sour, black geezer?"

Abdee explained, "Calabar and I seem to have a friend in common. A fancy on Barracks Lane. He was headed to her when I saw him."

Shanks leered at Abdee, asking, "And you were headed for Barracks Lane, too?" It was exactly like the old days. The *taffa*. The sprees. The whore-talking. Dragonard was like home again!

"No, I said *he* was headed there. But when I saw him and called out to him and asked him where in hell he thought he was going, he told me. And I laughed and asked him what good it was being free if you don't have no money? See, my good-willed *spouse* didn't

think of things like that when she set about handing
out freedoms."

"So you offered him a job."

"Just a small job. Not long."

Slapping Abdee on the back, Shanks bellowed,
"You! You can talk a man into anything. You can talk
a slave back into shackles, you can!"

"That's right, you old pirate. And just to show you
how smooth I can be, you and I are going to open the
big dining-room for our celebration. That's my welcome to you!"

"You mean the one with the long table and that
crystal chandelier?"

"None other."

"Only for you and me?"

"Nobody but you and me. And all the niggers we
want to wait on us."

Hurrying toward the front door, Shanks said, "I better nip down and get that *taffa* right now."

And Abdee gladly let him go for a while. He wanted
to see Calabar and learn how many Fantis had agreed
to join in on the procedures—the plan which Abdee
and Calabar had been discussing on their ride back from
Basseterre. Calabar's first job as a freed Negro. Then
he could go back to Naomi or wherever he wanted to
go. Abdee would have no more use for him.

The dining-room blazed.

In the dazzling chandelier hanging from the frescoed
ceiling and standing in the crystal sconces on all four
walls, a myriad of beeswax candles gave a brilliant
glow to the splendid, long room. On the mahogany table itself, two towering, silver candelabra reflected their
flames in the mirror-like finish. All thirty-four chairs
stood at the table but only in front of each chair at either end of the table—the two arm-chairs—had plates
and cutlery been arranged. Three forks, four spoons
and, although there was an absence of knives, the space
was amply filled with a salt cellar, vinaigrettes, and an

incongruous level of matched Bavarian crystal. It was a
setting for a small but auspicious occasion.

Shanks had been well primed with *taffa* by the time
Abdee led him into the dining-room and he stared in
awe at the grandeur of the rich surroundings. He
stopped in the double doorways and, blinded by the candles, the crystal, the silver, the tapestries and brocades,
he muttered, "God Blimey! Never in all my days."

Leading him immediately—but not too rushed—to
the far end of the table, Abdee said, "I asked myself—why in the hell not start out my partnership with
the best foot forward?" He then held back the chair for
Shanks. And as the gawking Captain finally lowered
himself onto the tapestry-upholstered chair, Abdee
looked quickly toward the six-sectioned screen.

And from behind that screen—at the far end of the
dining-room—Calabar nodded to Abdee. Yes, soon it
would commence.

But Shanks was oblivious to Calabar's nearness. He
was too concerned with the table. And, pointing to the
collection of plates and glasses at the far end, he asked,
"Is that where you will be sitting? Way down there? I
will hardly see you, let alone talk."

Abdee was being most gracious. "Then we will move
some of these candles," he said, bending to slide back,
first, one candelabra. And, then, the second. Now, turning to Shanks, he asked, "How's that?"

"I can see. But what about hearing?"

"When you *see* what's to come from the kitchen, you
won't want to talk!"

"I'm *starved*!" Shanks bellowed, thumping his head
against the tall-backed chair. "I haven't had a decent
bite since we set out last night for Basseterre . . ."
Shanks stopped. He quickly remembered that he had
made up his mind not to mention last night. Manroot.
The Lord Governor's Palace.

But Abdee paid no notice. He pulled out a chair on
Shanks's left and sat down. Just like a friend. Partners.

Shanks motioned to where Abdee sat now—to his

left—and asked, "Can't you stay there? It would be easier for talking."

But Abdee's ear was distracted by a movement behind the tall screen, the rustle of dried palm leaves and the sound of bare feet padding on carpet. Quickly looking back to Shanks, he answered, "Perhaps I will stay here—at least until we get started."

Shoving a plate toward Abdee, Shanks growled, "There's plenty enough equipment down here for all of us." Next, he pushed a goblet. But the thin vessel fell crashing against the table.

"Ah! I broke it! I didn't mean to do that! And bet it was an expensive one, too. Come a long ways."

Abdee's voice betrayed his impatience now. "Yes. And out here we must take care of our possessions, Shanks."

And detecting that note of seriousness, Shanks quickly added, "But it was only a damned goblet!"

Behind Shanks, Abdee saw Calabar now. He was in full view. He was fully nude, except for the stark gash of white paint across each black cheek, over his tribal markings. Between his fists, he held a short rope.

Looking back to Shanks, Abdee said, "Until we start, then, my friend, perhaps you'd better put your hands to your side. Keep you from causing more trouble till you get accustomed to your new role."

Shanks muttered, "No, you should have listened to *me*! I am too clumsy to be in a house. You and me. We should have eaten in *my* shack."

But Abdee was not listening to him again. From the corner of his eye, he now saw the spots, the animal markings painted on to the palms which covered the Fantis. He saw three, six, and then ten Fantis—the Leopardmen—creeping from behind the screen, following Calabar.

Slowly rising, Abdee looked down at Shanks slumped in the chair.

Stirring, Shanks noticed that Abdee had moved. So, raising his head, he asked, "Where are you going? I thought you were going to sit there." He jabbed at the place to his left with his peeling finger.

Abdee answered, "Hands down. Don't knock over anything else."

Shanks grunted but obediently lowered his arms. But, raising his dewy eyes to Abdee, he saw the expression on his face. That relaxed conviviality of a friend had transformed into the face of a different man. And Shanks knew this new look, too. It was the expression which he had been fearing all day. Shanks, filled with panic, moved to sit up in his chair.

But Calabar had already thrown the rope around the back of the chair and circled Shanks's throat.

Shanks gagged, gripping for the rope, but the Fantis sprang swiftly for his hands and legs.

Abdee stepped back as the rest of the Fantis streamed from behind the screen. No longer did they move cautiously. The dried leaves of their ritual costumes rustled and cracked as they sprung at Shanks like voracious leopards.

Shanks's bloodshot eyes widened with terror when he saw the Negroes surrounding him. From their painted faces and pointed teeth, he looked at their costume. Back to their teeth.

Calabar saw, though, that his men had a firm grasp on their victim. So, as he let the rope slacken from Shanks's neck, the loud shout which had been trapped in his throat now burst out and shattered the stillness of the finely-lit room.

"AWWRRRGH!"

Shanks lunged forward.

Goblets, plates, cellars, and cutlery flew from the table. But the Leopardmen held Shanks, turning his body over on the gleaming mahogany table, holding him down on his back. Their black hands feverishly began to rend his clothing from his body, as if it were the sacred skin itself.

But Abdee did not stay long. Only until he saw Calabar lift the machete high above Shanks's chest. In a moment of fleeting envy, though, Abdee wished that he had the honour of sinking that first wound. But as this was a Fanti ritual—from the rending of the heart, the sharing of the liver, to the scaling of the skin—there was no place for Abdee. So, he turned to leave them. He grabbed a goblet and a carafe of wine from the far end of the table and locked the doors behind him.

With determination, Abdee had so far achieved many of his ambitions. And, after locking the dining-room doors, he slowly made his way across the dark hall and quietly mounted the stairs. He was going up to envision his future.

Gently opening the door to Honore's bedroom, he remembered the feeling of visiting his old nursery at Thornhurst. Except for repainting his toy soldiers—putting them in the black and yellow uniforms of his own imaginary army—Abdee had hated his childhood. Children were always set upon by adults. And husbands were often similar targets for wives. Any member of the family. Even heirs.

Abdee smiled at the room's emptiness.

And with only the luminescent moonlight pouring through the voile panels on Honore's windows, Abdee looked around at the dishevelled state in which she had left her home—Petit Jour. It warmed him, made him feel victorious to think about the terror, the anger, the frustrations she must have felt in this room. And he smiled, too, when he imagined how she must have also felt a certain surge of power here this morning—being decisive after such a long period of inertness. He grew angry, though, when he thought about the slaves. The act of freeing them was one thing he would have to try to correct later. But he became frustrated thinking how stupid she had been to think that freedom meant *freedom*. Had she lived in the West Indies in blindness? Had she not even taken a good look at the world? But, more specifically, had she not once seen the state of poverty into which most Negroes declined after they received their freedom? He loathed that brand of humanitarianism. It was narrow-minded, incomplete, imbued with destructive religiosity, he felt. But it was also so Honore—impulsive charity.

Yes, he was glad she was gone. Such so-called "goodness" can be more harmful than an infection of what she termed *evil*.

Abdee turned to her tall, netted bed, the bed on which he had conceived his heir. The pillows on which he had deceptively fondled her. The sheets which she herself had torn back and greedily took what she had craved, cried, waited for in vain through most of her married life. But that had been only one isolated, almost meaningless moment of victory for Abdee, a small token of proof that singularity wins out in the end. And to uphold that conviction, he thought now how he could continue without that wife, disregard his heir, eliminate his so-called "partner," and stand taller in his world. He was stripping himself down to nothing but the essentials of one man, what truly mattered. And he *was* still standing tall. And all around him the others grovelled in prostration. Yes, this was the most free that he had ever felt. Up to now. Without dependants, there would be no concessions. And without concessions, he would achieve more. Acquire more. Build. The world lay outside for his moulding. Or, as he had said to himself a long time ago: his beguiling. But now he had no need to beguile. He could concentrate on his grasp. The take. And hold.

Reviewing his achievements thus far, the long and singular battle which had brought him to this hilltop fortress, Richard Abdee stood in front of Honore's window—the carafe of wine in one hand, a goblet half filled in the other.

Like his repainted childhood soldiers, the people whom he had met on St. Kitts marched through his mind, high-stepping to his tune:

Secretary Cranwell. He was gone. Replaced by a Welshman at Government House whom Abdee had seen today and would see again tomorrow. Early in the morning.

Gerrard Delon, a colleague who needed little retouching from Abdee's black and yellow paint-pot. But better than a compatriot in subjection, he was an accomplice. An acolyte. The second.

Franklin Topper. He was in England. But in Plymouth? Alive? Still the new Lord Wycliffe? A cohort of Wilberforce? Or had he really gone to America by now?

But, ah, Lucretia Borgia! The prostitute, Naomi. Abdee smiled and slotted her into tomorrow, too. But tomorrow afternoon. After The Circus. He enjoyed how history repeated itself. With a little push.

Then he thought of the other woman in his life: Honore Jubiot. Gone. And hopefully never to be seen again.

And Pierre Jubiot. Dead.

Sabine, Ambrosia, Ta-Ta, those three tasty Negresses in pink, yellow, and lavender gingham? Fat. Drunk. Gone.

Captain Geoff Shanks? Abdee remembered Paw-Paw describing his teeth as chicken bones and he wondered what bones he looked like at this very moment.

The Fantis? Calabar? Manroot? Tomorrow was for Manroot—Abdee would not kill him, only deepen the usual bite—and the entire future for his pet Fantis.

And it was not until the carriage was directly under the porch that Abdee noticed that someone had arrived at Dragonard. But when the clattering drew to a halt in front of the house, he broke from the parade of faces passing in review.

He suddenly thought: Honore! No! It could not be Honore! She would not have the courage to return after what she had done. But then he remembered her willingness for punishment—that willingness she fought—and he wondered if the carriage was bringing her back to Dragonard. Turning from the window, Abdee thought, if she left once, I can make her leave again.

He walked quickly down the hallway, the steps, taking two at a time but not running. Instead, he moved with the long languid steps of a cat and he was actually hoping now that it was Honore. And the heir in her belly. He planned what he could do to her. Them.

But, opening the door, he saw the face of a woman he had forgotten to include in his memories. She wore a claret-coloured cape and a hood. And inside the dark folds of the hood, he saw the eager, angular face of Arabella Warburton.

She was breathless, excited, as if she had at last stumbled onto some key. And holding out a sheaf of papers to Abdee—as if they might constitute that key—she said, "I have brought them back to you ... Richard!"

Abdee looked down at the papers she was thrusting at him. He was not drunk. Not with wine.

Arabella explained, "Honore brought them to me. There is a note to explain, too. A note she left for me before she left to board the *Thérèse*. She came to me for help. But I thought this would not help her. And I saw she was leaving. I knew that even I could not stop her. I knew that she did not *want* to be stopped. I knew that she must go. For you, too, she had to leave!"

Abdee lifted his eyes to Arabella's face. Instead of focusing on her, he thought of the *Thérèse*. It was travelling with the French convoy. Honore was sailing on the *Thérèse*. For France! Honore was leaving and she would never come back.

"Richard?"

Looking at Arabella now—still thinking that her eyes were placed too close together—he glanced down at the bundle of papers. Putting the carafe and goblet in one hand, he reached for them.

She stepped closer. "Tell me that I did the right thing, Richard. Tell me!"

He stared at the papers and, then dropping them to the floor, he looked up at her.

Arabella gaped at the deeds scattering to the floor of the dark hallway. She gasped, "Doesn't this mean a thing?"

Abdee asked, "Was that all, Mrs. Warburton?"

Her face froze. But she was determined. "Can not *I* at least come in?"

As his answer, Abdee looked down at the goblet and carafe in his one hand.

"Do I have to explain what really brought me to you?"

Grinning boyishly, he shook his head.

And, taking that as her answer, the invitation for which she had been waiting, Arabella rushed forward and, throwing her arms around Abdee, she said, "Randolph does not suspect a thing. No one knows how I feel. No one."

But in her anxious rush forward, Arabella knocked the goblet, the carafe, from Abdee's hands.

He froze.

She clung to him, whispering, "But here we are at last. Finally."

Abdee grabbed for her shoulders and he held her back from him.

Staring up at his lean, sunburnt face, Arabella quickly lunged her lips toward him.

He let her continue briefly. He let her throw her body against him, rub her small frame on his, endured her lips as she grasped his chest, his stomach, his thighs, clutching in desperation at the groin of his breeches. He let Arabella fully express that she had come here to Dragonard as a passive object before— Abdee bit down hard on her cloying lips.

Pulling back, Arabella held her mouth, screaming, "You bastard!" It was not the treatment she had anticipated at all.

Abdee smirked.

And as Arabella held her hand to her mouth, blood began trickling from her lips.

"YOU BASTARD!"

Then, she also was going. Gone. Arabella Warburton, too.

And he was left thinking:

The *Thérèse*. Tomorrow. Honore is going on the

Thérése tomorrow. Even by the time I get to Basseterre, she will be gone.

And thinking of going to Basseterre, this was the first time in months—years—that he made the immediate association of going to Barracks Lane.

Climbing the stairs that night, he enjoyed a renewed feeling of freedom. He realized that by leaving him Dragonard, Honore had also given him his whole, true self. This was his second re-birth.

19

Lesser Evils

It was the next morning, another day smelling of lemons and fresh dung.

Abdee arrived in Basseterre just before noon to keep his appointment. He went directly to Government House.

And when he saw how Lionel Cranwell's successor looked today, he thought, Pull up your boot-straps, Lad, if you want to survive in the cradle of the Caribbean. That was another name for the island of St. Christopher now, too.

The young, barrel-chested Welshman had not as yet made the necessary adjustments to this tropical climate. His broad forehead was peeling from sunburn, his cheeks and throat badly nicked from tender shavings, but despite his general appearance of slovenliness, the stout young man still struggled to exert his petty authority. Abdee was the first white planter with whom he had to deal. Since the thirty-six-hour-old assassination, authority was being dolled out with no heed to capability or position. That was yet another weakness of far-flung colonization.

Fine, Abdee thought, we will make it a baptism by fire for you, Mister Spinnell. You will see that laws are made by the man. Not by the land.

Spinnell had objected to Abdee using the whip. A firing line or hanging would be more in order.

Abdee shouted, "Are you telling me how to deal with my own property? This is not a case for the King, you know. It's private treaty."

Young Spinnell found this thick air difficult to inhale. He was trying not to gasp. "You are dealing with the man who assassinated the Lord Governor, Mister Abdee." He mopped his brow. He was on the brink of the same mess as Government House was teetering. Authority was near crumbling.

Abdee answered the unarguable truth. "I am dealing with a NEGRO! An African. My property."

Spinnell was trying. "We have a witness." But he was trying with the laws from back home, jurisprudence not applicable in the peculiarities of Negroes. It was as if a dog had attacked the mayor and the owner now called in to take the cur back to its kennel.

And Abdee capitalized on his countryman's lagging esteem of the Negro. To the Crown—officially—the Africans were still cattle. He asked Spinnell, "Do you want to hold my slave, then? Be responsible for one valuable worker until you find your witness? Oh yes, Mister Spinnell, I can wait patiently for a colonial trial, if that's what you want. And I will gladly wait three, four, even the five years it takes for the Lord Justice to arrive from London to preside over a case such as this. A case that will be ultimately dismissed because the accused is a . . . *nigger!*" He was using their words. He remembered how Cranwell had spoken to him about Africans in this very room. When? Six years ago?

Like Cranwell, Master Spinnell was nervous, too. But for different reasons. He saw himself losing his newly-bestowed authority.

Abdee continued. "But in the meantime, Mister Spinnell, let me remind you of the value of that slave at the moment of custody. And, also, the expectant value I have on his life in the next five years. *My* investment!"

This humidity. The newness of these extemporaneous laws. Men talking about other men in terms of work expectancies. Spinnell felt his ground slipping. But, again, he tried. "Perhaps, Mister Abdee, we should wait until at least the Consul General arrives from Jamaica."

"Why? To deal with what the Consul General will see as one nigger mutiny. A mutineer whom you would not surrender to the rightful owner? Do you know what happened in Jamaica just five weeks ago?"

Spinnell waited.

"An English woman. A mother. A mother and her three children were killed by a coachman from a neighbouring estate. A *nigger* coachman. And do you know why she was killed? And how? She and those children?"

He shook his head.

"By accident, the coachman had trundled over her husband. The authorities there, they seized him—like you think you are going to seize my nigger—and they thought they would just that once try to execute a nigger by *human* laws. Well, Mister Spinnell, they tried. But the nigger escaped and he returned to that neighbouring plantation and he killed the widow and drank the blood of the three fatherless children. And do you know how they finally caught that nigger?"

Spinnell was finding the story most uncomfortable. And Abdee's piercing blue eyes and that shock of straw-blonde hair thrown back from Abdee's hard, lined face.

"That nigger ran back to his master. The rightful master. That's where he knew he belonged and if the Consul General's *secretary* would have realized that fact sooner, that woman and those three children would still be alive."

Loosening the stock around his neck, Spinnell glanced to the table and said, "You did sign the regulation form, assuming responsibility."

Abdee pounded the table, the sheet of paper lying on top of it. "Damned right I signed it. And if you don't believe in these forms why waste the time printing them?"

Spinnell could not argue with that, either. But he did say, "The only further thing we could possibly do is to re-examine the witness."

"The witness you keep mentioning."

Gaining courage from what he interpreted as weariness, Spinnell said, "Yes. Captain Shanks!"

"Captain who?"

Again, it was too ludicrous for Spinnell. "But Captain Shanks is fixed at your address, Mister Abdee. At Dragonard."

"My address?" Abdee asked, looking puzzled. "There is no man called Shanks at Dragonard! Ah! Perhaps, though, Mister Spinnell, you would like to check with the French on that account? A Frenchman called Jubiot used to live there before me. Perhaps he had a . . . *Shanks*? Yes, perhaps you would like to tell Consul General to wait a few more years while you check out that!"

The table seemed to hold the only answer. And looking back at the signed document, Spinnell said, "As you say, Mister Abdee. You have signed here. And this is the form for the release of all Negroes to their owners. You agree to accept responsibility."

"God-damned right I agree. You witnessed!"

Raising his head, Spinnell looked toward the fantopped window. "And you have definitely decided on whipping."

"While you still argue for execution."

Spinnell tried to smile. Or tried not to smile. The only thing that he could say was: "It will take some time to bring the prisoner from the guardhouse."

"Dammit, Lad! Do not call a nigger a prisoner! He is my slave. Mine! Call *me* a prisoner. Call *yourself* a prisoner. But do not call a nigger a prisoner. He is my property."

Spinnell said softly, "I do understand that."

Turning from the table then, Abdee said, "Good! So see that my nigger is out there and manacled *now*!"

Abdee left Spinnell standing in the cavernous white room.

And outside, Abdee saw Gerrard Delon waiting for him at the foot of the raised platform in the middle of The Circus. It was just after one o'clock now and all the surrounding jalousies were shut. There were no signs of people. They were eating or drinking, or both, or sleeping it off.

Around The Circus, the Banyan trees looked as old and their roots as octopus-like as they had when Abdee first arrived in Basseterre. They were older.

So was Delon, who walked toward Abdee now. He was carrying a long, slim parcel which was wrapped in black velvet and tied with a scarlet silk cord.

Delon was excited with the good news he had to tell Abdee. He began, calling, "Madame has left, Monsieur!"

Abdee frowned. He thought how age had not lessened Delon's excitement for trivia.

But that was not the good news. Delon continued, "In her haste she forgot to give her cook—the fat woman who brought her down to Basseterre—your wife forgot to give her the pass to travel back North. I see this fat black one. I know how they must have the pass. I tell you that she will be in much trouble if she travels alone. *Helas!* So we have the driver and the trap to take your Manroot home to Dragonard! We sling him in the back."

"Don't talk as if he's going to be a corpse."

"Ah, *non*, Monsieur! You have the touch! I was thinking more about you being free to go to Chez Naomi."

"Naomi is coming to Dragonard, too!"

"*Oui*, Monsieur. But do not forget. She is waiting for you on Barracks Lane. You leave from there. So I think—ah—this Sugar Loaf, she takes back ..." He motioned toward the raised platform. And, doing so, he saw the two Footguards dragging Manroot toward them.

"As usual, you have done good work, my friend."

Handing Abdee the black velvet parcel tied in red cording, Delon said, "But wait till you see this."

Abdee took the soft parcel, felt the slippery contents.

And behind him he heard the dragging of chains, the foot soldiers leading Manroot up the narrow steps. Abdee did not look toward them. And, knowing Manroot, Abdee suspected that he was not looking at him.

Abdee asked Delon, "You say the trap is waiting to take him back to Dragonard? Sugar Loaf in it?"

He nodded enthusiastically. "I left her in Market Street. I took the liberty of marking her pass myself."

But that was unimportant. Abdee told Delon, "I will come back into Basseterre at the end of the week. I do not know how long Naomi will stay at Dragonard. I may bring her back or we may come to town to collect all her belongings. On any account, I will see you then."

"Do not worry, Monsieur. I am always at your service."

Abdee put one hand on his shoulder. "You are a good friend."

Behind them, then, on the raised platform, Abdee heard the echo of the manacles snapping shut, the iron pins being pounded into the fetters.

Delon said, "You do not look so happy, Monsieur."

"I am not happy. This is a duty I must perform. And I hate to be made to do things."

"But you are saving a good man."

"Yes. He is a very good man. That is why I am going to make him my overseer. I am going to have the only African overseer on St. Kitts. But first . . ." Abdee lowered his head and opened the black velvet parcel. From its red-lining, he withdrew a black leather whip. And glancing at the perforated tip, he saw that the leather was splayed like the tongue of a snake. Or a dragon.

"A beauty?" Delon asked anxiously.

But Abdee was gone. His mind was elsewhere. And now he was slowly mounting the narrow, wooden steps, the shiny blackness coiled in his hand.

Alone, he was carrying the tradition forward . . .

And, in the African tradition, Manroot was silent.

But for the first time, Abdee said—shouted to Manroot—"I'M SORRY . . . MY FRIEND."

Manroot remained silent, not flinching, not acknowledging any bond—spoken or merely understood.

Then once, twice, for the third time, the length of black leather sang through the still afternoon, gathering a coagulation of black skin and blood as the strokes continued to fly. For the first time this was more of a punishment for Abdee than the victim. But his original plot had gone wrong. Now a lashing was the least harmful, least deadly way out of the situation.

He hoped that Manroot understood. Abdee credited him with that faculty, too.

20

Friends

By night fall, Dragonard was ablaze.

Lights filled every window, spilling over the porches and out on to the lawn around the house.

But close to the sides of the house there was enough room—darkness—to move undetected.

So, first, keeping to the shadows of the west porch, Sugar Loaf slowly moved with Manroot's arm over her shoulder. She had brought him back from Basseterre in the pony trap. Abdee had given her orders to take him to Shanks's cabin. But now she was slowly walking him down the slope behind the main house, carefully guiding the big Fanti—weak from the lashes—to a place where he would be more comfortable.

At the foot of the hill, they rested against the tubs of the Laundry House until Sugar Loaf felt Manroot lift his body against hers. It was a sign to begin moving once more.

Struggling under his great weight, Sugar Loaf paced forward in the darkness, muttering, "Ain't leaving no one in that bug nest. Good enough for that Captain Shanks, mayhap, but that's about all. Happier to sleeps on the floor in a hog barn than to sleeps on that bug roll back there. I cleans it up and *then* Master Abdee moves you there. And I going to tell him so, too!"

Manroot remained silent, allowing Sugar Loaf to mark the pace.

They approached the long line of the slaves' quarters now. And, at the first shack on the end, Manroot dragged his bare foot in the dirt as a signal for Sugar Loaf to stop again.

"Another rest?" she asked.

But Manroot did not answer.

He looked.

These were the wattle huts of his people. At this late hour, though, the low doors were all locked. The people inside sleeping on their mats. Dawn was not far away. And work.

Much work, Manroot thought.

Then, looking at the shacks, he suddenly saw the additions to the bone decorations over the door of one cabin. Even in the moonlight, he could see the extension of white bones which had been wired to one, two, four, at least six of the huts in his short absence from Dragonard. They were all new bones, too. Fresh. Larger than the others. And he knew their significance. From what specie they had come. And he knew then how much work he himself had to do to pay for those scant adornments. They were the bones from a human being.

Hoisting Manroot to her shoulder again, Sugar Loaf said, "You sees your people when you gets better. Now we goes to an empty shack I knows down yonder."

Manroot let her continue.

And, as she sweated under his weight again, Sugar Loaf said, "We gets there and washes those welts on you. Then we puts some pimentade on you. Know what that is? Pimentade?"

Manroot did not answer.

But Sugar Loaf kept talking, talking about anything, because she knew that words often made a sick person feel better, too. Sometimes even better than medicines. She said, "Pimentade's a mixture of some salt and cayenne pepper and a bit of lemon. Makes the skin grows back without leaving hardly no marks at all. Pimentade stings but there's nothing better. I learns all about it at The Star Plantation in Louisiana. It's a French idea but I learns it from the best nigger woman in the whole world. Her name is Old Mama Gomorrah and she teaches me everything. Ever hears about her? Old Mama Gomorrah?"

Manroot shook his head now. Although he did not feel like talking, he recognized what Sugar Loaf was trying to do. And he appreciated her doing it.

Sugar Loaf walked Manroot slowly, saying as she watched her feet, "Yes, Sir! Mama Gomorrah is the most famous nigger lady in the whole wide world. At least in Louisiana she is. Folks there, you knows, talks a lot about sin. Sins from their holy book, the Bible. And they especially talks a lot about two famous cities. One city is called Sodom and the other city was called Gomorrah. Those places are in their Bible and they be very, very wicked places. The white peoples says that everybody knows what sins went on in Sodom. But some says in Gomorrah it was a different sin. A sin so much wickeder that no one talks about it. Or, for that matter, knows what really happened in Gomorrah. That is, no one knows what sins were there except Old Mama Gomorrah. She knows the truth because an angel comes from the white man's heaven and he tells her. Tells her to watch for that sin on the Star Plantation and when she sees it happening she must strikes the persons dead. I sees her strikes down three' "

But then Sugar Loaf suddenly stopped. They had reached the vegetable patch. And there in the middle of the leafy sea, she spotted a figure.

She called out into the night, "Who's that in my vegetable patch?"

The figure quickly turned to look at her.

Sugar Loaf saw that it was a tall man, a Negro. But he was dressed in the shiny white satin breeches of a city nigger. He was a fancy. And he glittered in the moonlight.

She called irritably, "What you doing in my garden, nigger boy? Wheres you comes from?"

A friendly voice answered, "I ain't stealing nothing."

"Then what you doing there trampling all my vegetables with your big feets?" Sugar Loaf called, her tall head-piece bobbing in the darkness as she spoke.

Being extra careful where he stepped now, the Negro stranger came toward Sugar Loaf. And as he drew closer, she could see that he was young. And, although he was big, he looked harmless. Gentle.

Sugar Loaf demanded, "What's a city nigger like you coming out heres for?"

He answered proudly, "I comes up with Mistress Naomi and Master Abdee. I works for Mistress Naomi in Basseterre. My name's Nero!"

Sugar Loaf looked quickly up at the main house behind them.

But, preferring not to talk about Abdee and the Negro wench he had brought from Basseterre—or to waste her time talking to fancy Negroes—she quickly resumed moving Manroot down the dirt path.

But Nero said, "I'd much rather works for you in your garden, though, if I had a choice."

Sugar Loaf snorted. "Just because your mistress comes here don't mean all you fancy niggers is taking us over." She stubbornly continued with Manroot.

But Nero still followed, trailing them like a large, eager puppy. "I ain't really no fancy nigger. I used to work in the fields. My insides raised on the outdoors."

Straining under the load of Manroot, Sugar Loaf said crossly, "Well, you so anxious to help, grabs hold of the other side of this man here. Can't you sees it's rough going for two of us alone."

Scrambling quickly to help Sugar Loaf, Nero put Manroot's other arm around his sturdy shoulder. And, as he fell into pace, he said, "You knows how long my Mistress goings to stay here?"

"Don't knows nothing," Sugar Loaf grumbled. But she had to admit to herself that this fancy nigger boy was indeed strong. He had eased her load considerably. She was also thinking that he was a pretty buck, too. One of the prettiest and creamiest skinned bucks she had ever seen.

Nero asked now, "You reckon if Mistress Naomi stays here long that I can helps in the gardens?"

"Any more than garden work would probably kills you."

Nero stopped dead in his tracks. He objected. "I'm strong. You see I'm strong."

"But you ain't seeing that this big man ain't feeling so strong! Now grab holds of him again."

Moving again, Nero asked softly, as if Manroot might be too sick to hear a whisper, "He's the one who gets whipped, ain't he? The one who the whities says kills the governor?"

"Just keeps your mouth shut and help lift."

Then, as they moved on, Sugar Loaf turned to look at Manroot's face, to see if he was in bad pain.

But instead she saw him smiling.

"What's you can grin for?" she said.

Manroot's large eyes twinkled now under the straight line of black wool across his forehead. Nodding toward Nero, he said in a weak voice, "He's a good boy, Sugar Loaf. He's how our people gets stronger. Try to keep him here, Sugar Loaf."

"Course he's good boy," she grumbled. "All nigger boys are good boys. But he be a lot better out of them clothes. And get some of my cooking in his belly. Maybe work up enough spunk to sow a few suckers, too."

And Nero, who had been listening to this discussion about him, smiled as he helped to inch Manroot toward the cabin.

Yes, this was the kind of life he wanted. With these kind of people. He was thinking: If I'm a nigger, then I might as well be a farming nigger. Gets close to the earth so I can smell the sweet smells of the real life.

The trio moved on. It was slow going. But they were making it.

And, inside the house, Abdee and Naomi were discussing a few future possibilities for themselves.

They were in the dining-room.

Abdee sat at his end of the long table.

But Naomi stood. She was wearing a slim-fitting scarlet silk gown, which rose high under her bosom. And holding out one long, bare arm—its blackness glittering with diamond bracelets—she said, "I'll try one of the girls running the house for a while. My customers expect to find a female in charge."

"But Calabar will live there?" Abdee asked, his boots up on the table.

"For the time being. Now that he has his freedom, he doesn't want to be around here any more than you want him."

Abdee asked her, "But you will stay here for a while?"

Naomi looked around at the panelled room. "Imagine! My 'Master Sir' landing himself this! And for over five years you've been lording it up here. Living like a real gentleman."

"You didn't answer my question."

She turned to him now, the paint on her eyelids looking like a yellow sunset. She asked flatly, "Your wife isn't coming back?"

"I doubt it."

"You don't worry that people will see a black whore living here and—" But then she stopped. And said, "Of course you don't. I didn't have to ask that, did I?" Then, spinning around in the middle of the room she said, "Oh, what will I do here, though? I'm used to working. I've got to keep busy! There's nothing for me to do on a . . . sugar plantation!"

"I don't exactly expect you to turn it into a brothel," Abdee said, smiling.

Arching an eyebrow, all of her diamond bracelets tinkled as she threw up both arms and said, "No! But it is a big temptation for me."

"Why don't you just try sleeping in until noon for a while. It's been a long time since I had good company . . . until noon."

Turning to him, she said seriously, "I'm going to ask you a question."

He nodded.

"Aren't you scared of me? A lot of people are."

"Are *you* frightened of *me*?"

Naomi threw back her head and laughed.

And watching Naomi's sleek body, swathed in red silk, Abdee thought: Black. Why is it so damned attractive?

Now, she was sitting on his lap. With her back to the table she said, "Imagine a white man letting—Calabar do that!"

Abdee asked, toying with one of her diamond and gold pendant earrings, "The Leopardmen?"

"Yes. How did you know about them?"

Raising his eyes, he said, "Am I asking you how Calabar has been coming to you all these years?"

She pulled back in mock indignation. "And you better not ask! You had the chance to perform in his place. Remember! So don't complain."

Beginning to unfasten one of her earrings now, he said, "You're a Fanti, too." He then threw it behind her on the empty table.

Beginning to unclasp the other earring herself, she said, "You English?"

He understood.

Then, tossing the second earring over her shoulder—to the table, too—she ran both hands up through her pile of shiny black ringlets and said, "There's one thing you and I don't have to worry about."

Abdee nodded. He knew. "Getting married."

Again she laughed. "But what about babies? You won't ever want any of them, will you?" She wrinkled her pert nose.

Abdee reminded her, "There's a good market for yellow suckers." He reminded her from long ago.

And, remembering, too, Naomi instantly held up seven long fingers and mimicked, *"I has this many suckers, Master Sir!"*

Watching her laugh again, Abdee realized that it was him who had come a long way. Born from a death.

Worked toward blackness. Gashed with red. Strengthened by leather. The Dragonard was no longer a public executioner:

He was Dragonard.

ABOUT THE AUTHOR

The author was born on the Leeward Island of Nevis. The seventh generation of an English colonial family, he was the first to break away from plantation life. After attending preparatory school in Rhode Island, he studied on the Continent. Then, traveling extensively in Africa and the Far East, he returned home when he first came up with the idea for *The Dragonard Trilogy,* which was published under his pseudonym, Rupert Gilchrist. He now lives in Montserrat in a 17th-century captain's house, which he has faithfully restored himself. His hobbies include horses, skin-diving, collecting African artifacts and tuning the engine of his Lamborghini. He has also written under his real name.